LIVING GRY

MARLEY

DLP Publishing

100 Andover West, Suite 150 #164

Tukwila, WA 98188

www.dlp-pub.com

Ordering Information:

Quantity sales. Special discounts are available on quantity purchases by corporations, associations, and others. For details, contact the publisher at the address above.

Orders by U.S. trade bookstores and wholesalers. Please contact DLP Publishing: Tel: (312) 767-8293; or visit www.dlp-pub.com.

Printed in the United States of America

ISBN 978-0-9995957-0-1

First Edition

PREFACE
GLASS CASES

This world doesn't know freedom,
only compartmentalization.
Can't let anything exist without frame.
Won't let anything be without characterization.
Boxes are prerequisites for acceptance.
You do not get to live outside them
without appraisal and condemnation.
You have to be inside them
to receive praise or understanding.
All around us are glass blowers and carpenters.
Pious crafters who believe that they know.
Who won't be told otherwise.
Perception becomes the components of glass cases
covering us in judgement.

When your purpose and destiny,
worth and wisdom,
aptitude and ability,
wants and desires,
strengths and weaknesses

are on display
you learn what a fetishizing gaze
feels like.
You learn that gawking
is a seductive
dance with voyeurs whose
admiration is a selfish satisfaction.
Whose appraisal is a callous
attempt to situate themselves as better.
You learn that sometimes
presence isn't possibility,
it's just momentary possession.
We
the victims of glass blowers
and carpenters.
We are here.
Trapped
in glass cases
for all the world to see.
-Dasan Ahanu

TABLE OF CONTENT

LIVING GRY

1

There was no line-up at the curbside check-in station this afternoon and Glen found himself remembering the morning rush fondly. At the time, he couldn't wait for it to end. Doing nothing was only appealing for so long. He straightened his uniform and tried to catch the eye of some of the prettier female travelers hurrying by, but none of them seemed interested in his services.

Sarge wandered over, adjusting the cap over his graying head with a weary sigh. "Not exactly raking in the tips today, are we?"

"I did pretty well this morning and the day's not over yet," Glen tossed him an encouraging smile.

Sarge sighed again and looked toward the bustling terminal. "Any big plans for your day off tomorrow?"

"Well, that hot drug rep from San Diego, Elena, is going to be in town. Actually, her flight is landing in less than an hour. Maybe she'll stop by and say hi. We're supposed to have dinner later tonight."

Before Sarge could reply, a family of five with a dog in a crate tumbled out of a car, the harried parents each wearing a baby carrier and herding a toddler between them. Despite the dark circles under her eyes and her messy ponytail, Glen could see the mom was pretty. With a practiced motion, the couple leaned in for a kiss, angling their bodies slightly to avoid rapping their infants' heads together.

Smiling, Glen stepped forward and started to help them sort out their paperwork while Sarge went to grab them a luggage cart. The wife handed Glen a crumpled pile of printouts from Expedia and it took him a few minutes to even figure out where they were going.

"What's taking you folks to Portland, if you don't mind my asking?" He asked as he sorted their papers into a more useful order and entered their details into the computer.

"Visiting my parents," said the woman. "We want them to see the babies, but my mom can't travel."

The man rolled his eyes. Clearly there was more to the story, so Glen tactfully changed the subject, complimenting thebabies on their thick caps of curly blonde hair. Sarge and Glen loaded up the cart, taking extra care with the whining German Shepherd in the crate. When they were done, the man took back all their paperwork and handed Glen a five. Glen thanked him, pocketed the cash and watched them trail behind Sarge as he wheeled their cart into the terminal.

He pulled his phone out of his pocket and checked the time. Less than an hour to the end of his shift. He'd drive home for a quick shower and change before heading out to meet Elena. He had a good feeling about tonight. At the very least, he was in for an excellent meal.

When he looked up, a smiling woman stood directly in front of him. She looked young, no more than twenty, her nostril pierced and bright blue hair shaved nearly down to her scalp on one side. She carried only a battered Herschel canvas backpack, stuffed to bursting, and a small cross-body bag. Her hands were shoved into the pockets of her jean miniskirt. Glen didn't let his eyes linger on her cleavage—or the intriguing hint of a tattoo peeking out from under the hem of her skirt.

"What can I do for you, ma'am?" he said, answering her smile with a grin of his own?

"Can you point me to international departures?"

6

"Of course. Right over that way. When you get to the kiosk covered in balloons, make a right." Eyeing her dimples and full lips, Glen decided to extend the conversation a bit. "Where are you headed? Do you need to check in for your flight now?"

"London is my first stop," she said. "I'm taking a semester off school to spend a month exploring Europe. Cliché, I know...but it should be fun." She scuffed one of her Converse sneakers on the floor and shrugged. "I'm actually not sure if I need to check in now. My flight's not for like five hours. I'm a bit paranoid about missing it. And I may or may not just have been dumped by my boyfriend."

She took her hands out of her pockets and shrugged. Glen let his eyes fall and admired the way her breasts rose and fell with the motion. A strand of her blue hair fell in front of her eye and she pushed it away with an abrupt motion.

"Oh, that sucks. Was he insecure about your trip?"

"Yeah, that pretty much sums it up. I mean, it's not like I'm traveling alone. My best friend Briana's meeting up with me in a couple hours. But apparently Josh thought we were just going to fuck our way through of Europe. Well, joke's on him, because now I can."

She shrugged again and heaved a sigh. The top button of her skinny flannel seemed to be hanging on by a thread and Glen doubted it could survive another shrug.

"Young guys are like that sometimes. Very fragile egos. Maybe he'll come around and realize he's being an ass."

She gave a bitter laugh. "I doubt it. He was always an ass. Not much of a loss, really. Besides, he had a tiny dick and sucked in bed." She laughed again and a tongue stud glinted in her mouth.

"I have the feeling you're going to be fine. Josh doesn't sound like he deserved you."

The girl looked up sharply at Glen, seeming to really notice him for the first time. She was only about five feet tall and had to tilt her head back to see his dark olive face fully. She blushed. "Wow, you're really tall!"

"Six-foot-six and totally proportional," said Glen, his grin bold.

She blushed even deeper. It suited her. She had eyes nearly as blue as her hair, and they shone with unshed tears over Josh, Glen thought.

"Since you already know so many intimate details about my life, I guess I should tell you that I'm Amy." Her blush emphasized a cluster of freckles across her nose and cheeks. Glen guessed that she probably had red hair under the blue dye.

He stuck out a hand. "Glen. Pleased to meet you, Amy."

She took his hand and gulped when her own small hand was engulfed in his. "Big hands..." she said.

"Like I said:,proportional," he laughed.

Amy licked her lips, her tongue stud winking into view. She adjusted the straps of her bag on her shoulders and looked around.

"Is there anywhere I can get a drink? Get my mind off things, you know?"

"Sure," answered Glen. "There's a place called Panopolis in Terminal 2, just before you go through security. You can get a beer and a sandwich or something, if you want."

"Thanks," she said. She seemed about to say more but closed her mouth with a snap. She looked down and scuffed her shoes again.

Feeling brave, Glen took a chance and leaned in. Hey, listen. I get off in - he looked at his phone - about half an hour. Go grab a drink and I'll come meet you and you can keep telling me what a small-dicked "fuckboy" Josh is until your friend shows up. How does that sound?"

She nodded and smiled, although Glen thought she looked a little nervous. She thanked him again and headed off toward Terminal 2. Glen watched her ass under her skirt as she walked and wondered if it felt as firm and plump as it looked. He imagined gripping it tightly and lifting her tiny frame off the ground as she wrapped her legs around him.

"I thought you had a date with Elena tonight?"

Glen looked over to find Sarge standing next to him, also watching Amy.

"Well, yeah...But this girl's flying out soon and I'm not meeting Elena until later."

"You should leave some for the rest of us, kid," said Sarge, shaking his head at Amy's retreating figure.

"I'm young, Sarge. Gotta sow my wild oats, as they say."

"Thirty ain't that young. Don't you ever think of settling down?

Fathering some NBA-bound babies?"

Glen was saved from answering by the arrival of a small group of Japanese tourists. Twenty minutes later, Glen and Sarge sent the group on their way, boarding passes in hand. Sarge caught Glen eyeing one of the younger women in the group and rolled his eyes dramatically.

"Seriously...Give it a rest. I think you've got enough on your plate as it is."

"I was only looking. Can't a guy appreciate the view?"

While Glen looked after the tourists, a tall, slim woman emerged from the crowd and made her way toward him. She was dressed in a prim, navy blue business suit. Her long, dark hair was pulled back in a severe ponytail. She wore very little makeup, just enough to highlight her dark eyes. Her heels clicked sharply as she strode across the pavement. She carried a small bag over her shoulder and pulled a wheeled sample case behind her.

"Elena," said Glen, when he spotted her. "You had a good flight, I hope."

She stopped and smiled at him, her face losing all its seriousness. She reached one hand back to massage her neck.

"Good enough. Flying's never much fun. Or comfortable. But I do have tonight to look forward to."

Glen pitched his voice low so only Elena could hear him. "I bet I can help you out with that neck rub. But I can't promise you won't be sore elsewhere when we're done."

Elena's cheeks flushed. "I'm staying at the Hilton by Duke University Hospital. Meet me in the lobby at eight sharp. I'll be starving by then, I'm sure."

"Starving, huh?" said Glen with a wink.

She bit her bottom lip. "See you at eight, Glen. Don't be late." She adjusted her shoulder bag and walked off as briskly as she'd arrived. Glen watched her step into a cab without a backward glance. He looked forward to seeing her with her hair down in a few hours.

He pulled out his phone again. Just a few more minutes and he'd be able to go meet up with Amy. He wasn't sure where that was going, but he definitely wanted to find out. He idled at the computer, impatient for Rashid to come and relieve him.

Within a few minutes, Rashid arrived, still tying his tie, vest awry, like he'd just pulled it over his head. He tugged at his shirt and pinned on his security badge.

"I'm here, bro. You are free to go. Judging by the look on your face, I'd say you're ready and raring."

"He's got a date with Elena tonight. And he's meeting a half-naked little girl at Panopolis in a few minutes," said Sarge.

Rashid laughed. "Two on the hook at once. You lucky bastard. I expect some good stories next shift." He thrust his hips suggestively, eliciting a scowl from Sarge.

Glen raised his eyebrows at the obscene gesture, thinking Rashid had been a little off over the last few weeks. The image of Amy waiting for him pushed further thought about Rashid out of his mind. "Do I ever disappoint?" Glen said, grabbing his bag from behind the counter. "I'm off, guys. See you later."

He made his way to one of the staff washrooms and quickly swapped out his uniform for jeans and a tee. His t-shirt showed off his pecs and biceps. He stopped briefly to inspect himself in the mirror and to loosen his hair from his man-bun and artfully muss his dark waves, brushing over his 5 o'clock shadow with his hand. He stuffed his security badge into his jeans pocket and grinned. It was going to be a full night.

He spotted Amy sitting alone, chin in her hand, staring at her phone and looking bored. The table was littered with crumpled napkins, an empty glass, beer froth still clinging to its sides, and a half-eaten bag of chocolate covered pretzels. He slipped into the booth across from her.

"Hey, how's it going? Not texting Josh, I hope." Amy brightened and set her phone down.

"No, no. Just my friend. She's running late, like always. I'm glad to see you. Airports are boring as fuck."

He laughed. "Imagine working here every day. Actually, though, airports are kind of interesting. I get to meet new people constantly, from all over the world. Of course, I definitely see pissed off, tired people all the time, but I also see happy, excited people. People going on adventures. People coming home and reuniting with their families."

"I never thought of that," said Amy. She picked up a pretzel. When she brought it to her lips her tongue darted out briefly to lick the chocolate. Glen saw her tongue stud flash again and wondered what it would feel like on his cock. Without asking, he took a pretzel of his own. It tasted faintly dusty, like it might have been sitting in that bag for a few years.

"The food's pretty terrible here," he observed after a moment. "Do you want to get another drink?"

"I'm good," said Amy. "I don't like to day drink—gives me a headache. I prefer weed."

Glen watched her as they ate pretzels in silence. Every time their eyes met, she blushed and looked away. He noticed that the piercing in her nose was set with a bright blue stone that matched her hair. She seemed like the type of girl who might have some more piercings hidden under her clothing and Glen was eager to find out where.

"Do you want to get out of here?" she asked. "Maybe you can show me some more interesting parts of the airport."

"Sure, whatever you want. I can think of a few places. And a few funny stories I can tell you." He gathered up their bags and led her out of the restaurant.

Without going through security, there really wasn't that much to see, but Glen gave her the grand tour, sharing little snippets of events he'd witnessed. It didn't take very long and they wound up sitting on a bench watching the empty baggage carousels.

Amy scooted down the bench, pressing her hip against his. She looked up and slid a tentative hand high on his thigh. Her fingertips almost brushed his cock and he felt the first flush of arousal surge through him.

"You are much better-looking than Josh," she said.

"Am I?" he asked. Before she could answer, he bent his head and kissed her. She opened her mouth eagerly and he let his tongue play over her tongue stud. He cupped the back of her head and drew her firmly into the kiss, pressing their lips together hard enough to bruise. He felt her quiver, her hand tightening on his thigh briefly before relaxing again.

When they parted she was breathless and flushed, her lips reddened and glistening. She brought a hand up, and trailed a finger along her lower lip. "And a much better kisser," she said.

"I'm sure I'm better at a lot of things. I've got experience on my side," he said, grabbing her waist and pulling her close. "I've got another place I'd like to show you. It doesn't look like much, but I think you'll enjoy it."

She kissed him again, wrapping her arms around his neck. Her breasts were a yielding softness against his chest and he felt his cock twitch and start to press uncomfortably against his boxer briefs beneath his jeans.

"Let's go," she whispered when their lips parted.

Holding her hand, and looking around carefully, he drew her to the staff washroom where he'd changed earlier. He was reasonably confident they wouldn't be interrupted. She quirked an eyebrow at him when she saw where they were, but didn't say anything. He dropped their bags on the floor and pulled her into the handicapped stall.

As soon as the door was closed, he kissed her again, pressing her back against the door. She was so tiny that she had to strain up, standing on the tips of her toes, to reach him. She bit at his bottom lip hungrily and her hands were already pushing up the bottom of his t-shirt. Her fingers brushed over his abs and chest and he felt the hot breath of her moan in his mouth.

He stood back and started carefully undoing the buttons of her shirt. He was pleased to find she was wearing a front-clasp bra and he undid it quickly. Her breasts sprang free, creamy white with a light dusting of freckles. Her nipples, pink and hard, were pierced with captive bead rings. She shivered as the cool air touched her, but she made no move to cover herself.

"Gorgeous," he said. "Those are some of the most perfect tits I've ever seen." He reached for her, cupping her breast and running a thumb over her erect nipple. He tugged gently on the ring, eliciting another moan that made his cock twitch again.

Her small hands worked swiftly to undo his jeans and lower his zipper. She ran one hand up the length of his cock, her eyes widening. She freed it from his underwear and gasped.

"Damn. Much bigger than Josh, too. You weren't lying about being proportional." She stroked him a few times, enjoying the feeling of him growing fully hard in her hand.

She dropped to a crouch and, still holding his cock firmly in one hand, she slowly licked the tip, drawing the ball of her stud over the most sensitive parts of him. Her other hand reached up and cupped his balls.

He gasped and suppressed an urge to thrust his hips forward. The stud felt incredible, and he wondered how he'd gone so many years without finding that out. She continued to lick and suck on the tip of his cock, never quite daring to go farther. Many women were intimidated by his size. He was used to it and stayed still, letting her gradually grow more comfortable.

He held her head with both his hands, wanting desperately to fuck her throat, but holding back. As he'd known she would, she eventually started taking in more and more of him, as much as she could. The hand wrapped around him stroked in time with her bobbing head. She was doing her best, but less than half of his massive cock was receiving attention. He needed more.

Letting go of her head he stepped back. His cock popped out of her mouth and she looked up and him, inquiring.

"Stand up," he said. She obeyed. Glen took note of the flush spreading across her chest and the way her breasts heaved with every breath. "Take off your skirt."

She unbuttoned it and dropped it unceremoniously around her ankles. She stepped out of it, kicking it to one side. Her panties were pink cotton, with a pattern of red flowers. They made her look innocent and young, an interesting contrast to her pierced nipples. He could finally make out the tattoo on her upper thigh. It was a complex floral design that crept upwards almost to her hip.

"Take off your underwear," he said.

Again, she didn't hesitate. Her panties soon joined her skirt on the floor. She'd had a wax recently and the neat little strip of hair that remained was red, confirming Glen's earlier suspicions. He caught a flash of something sparkling in her folds.

"Touch yourself."

This time she paused before obeying him, her gaze a little surprised and uncertain. She slipped a hand between her legs, her fingers moving slowly at first, but soon with more urgency.

She closed her eyes and brought her free hand up to one of her nipples. She leaned back against the wall for support, spreading her legs a little to give herself better access.

She looked incredible, her reactions so raw. She was completely lost in the moment, utterly unselfconscious. Glen watched her, saying nothing, enjoying the little faces she was making and the way

she'd plunged her fingers inside herself. She was moaning and her breathing had turned almost to panting. He knew was going to cum soon.

"Stop," he said in a low voice. She seemed not to hear him at first, but managed to pull her fingers away from her now soaking wet pussy before she reached orgasm.

She opened her eyes and stared. "Why?" she asked, a desperate note creeping into her voice.

"Lick your fingers. I want you to taste yourself."

She did as she was told. She let her gaze linger on his still rock- hard cock and then looked into his eyes, her pierced tongue licking every one of her wet fingers in turn. When she was done, she dropped her hand to her side, awaiting further instructions.

"Touch yourself again, but keep your eyes open. I want you to look at me. And don't you dare cum."

They were only a few feet apart. He could have reached out and touched her, but he wanted her needy and begging for his cock, and she wasn't quite there yet. She resumed stroking her clit, though only softly, mindful of his wishes, trying to stay in control of herself. She watched as Glen wrapped one of his hands around his cock and started stroking himself slowly. A drop of precum glistened on the head of his cock and she licked her lips as she watched.

Despite her attempts at self-control, she soon found it difficult to keep her eyes open. Her knees were shaking and Glen could see she was fighting the urge to plunge her fingers into her pussy again and make herself cum. She trembled and moaned and finally spoke.

"Please fuck me."

"What did you say, Amy?" he asked softly. "Please fuck me. Please," she said again, pleading. "Come here."

She obeyed instantly, nearly throwing herself into his arms. He lifted her easily, her ass just as round and firm as he'd imagined it. He braced his back against the wall and she wrapped her legs around him, locking her ankles together at the small of his back. Her pussy was hot and wet. She was a girl ready to be fucked.

He eased her up just a little higher and pressed the tip of his cock right at her entrance. She moaned and squirmed, trying to push herself down, but he held her firmly and kept her in place.

"You're such a little girl, are you sure you can take such a huge cock?" he asked, lowering her just slightly so that the first inch of him was inside her.

She gasped. "Oh, yes, yes. I want it so badly."

When he couldn't wait any longer, he pulled her down, impaling her on his cock. She made a sound like a wild animal, part pleasure, and part pain. She wrapped her arms around his neck and leveraged herself up for a moment before lowering herself again, engulfing the entirety of his ten inch cock.

"Fuck, so big," she moaned.

Her pussy was almost too tight. He groaned as he slid into her. He was glad she'd gotten herself almost to the edge, because he wasn't sure how long he could last. Her perfect tits bounced as he started to fuck her, her pierced nipples grazing his chest. He could feel the piercing between her legs, too, the jewelry adding a friction to each thrust.

She reached between them with one hand and touched herself, rubbing her clit in slow circular motions. She brought her wet fingers back up and Glen thought she might lick them again, but instead she offered them to him. He tasted her and immediately longed to bury his head between her legs and fuck her with his tongue. Maybe next time, he thought hopefully.

She moaned and panted in his arms, her body growing slick with sweat. Suddenly, she arched her back and dug her fingers into his shoulders. He hissed at the pain, fairly certain that she'd drawn blood.

"I'm going to cum," she cried. Her whole body stiffened and she shuddered violently. As her orgasm washed over her, her pussy clenched rhythmically around Glen's cock. He pulled her now limp body closer to him and buried his face in her shoulder to muffle his grunts.

He kept thrusting in to her for a few moments as she squirmed and moaned in his arms. His knees were shaking, as hers had earlier. He looked down at her flushed and heaving breasts, her parted red lips, and knew he couldn't hold back any longer.

In one smooth motion, he lifted her up and pulled himself out of her. He lowered her again, trapping his cock between them. She took one hand from his neck and grabbed him, stroking him once, twice, then making a pleased sound when he groaned and shot a stream of cum so high it landed on her chin and breasts. She continued moving her hand up and down slowly, drawing more moans and several more spurts of cum.

She laughed, happy with her accomplishment. "You made a pretty big mess," she said, admiringly.

He put her down carefully, still not quite trusting his knees. She stood quietly, making no move to clean herself off as he buttoned and zipped up his jeans. She considered him for a moment but didn't speak. She bent and retrieved her panties and skirt, putting them on quickly.

She exited the stall, bare breasts on full display and went to the sink to clean herself. When she returned, Glen was still catching his breath.

"That was pretty amazing," she said. "I don't think I'm going to miss Josh very much at all, after a fuck as incredible as that."

She closed her bra and buttoned her shirt before reaching for her phone to check the time.

"Oh, shit. I've got to run. Briana's meeting me back at that restaurant in ten minutes."

They retrieved their bags and exited the washroom, faces still flushed. They crossed paths with a pretty blonde flight attendant. Glen gave her a sheepish little shrug as she raised a sardonic eyebrow at him.

Glen walked Amy back to Panopolis, sharing another amusing airport anecdote on the way and asking her about her plans after London.

"Paris, Rome, I guess. Or maybe we'll visit some less obvious places. I want to make the most of this, experience new things." She looked at him and winked. "Maybe get laid."

Briana was waiting impatiently outside the restaurant. Amy made quick introductions, but the girls had to make a quick exit and Glen didn't have time for more than a polite greeting before they were gone. Briana's cute, thought Glen, with her halo of dark curls and her lip piercings. She was a bit plumper than Amy, but equally as appealing. He wondered if they'd stop by on their return trip in a month.

Feeling satisfied and like a nap might be in order, Glen headed home. The drive was uneventful and he didn't hit any traffic. It afforded him plenty of time to daydream about the more mature pleasures his evening with Elena might hold.

Once home, he eyed his bed longingly, but decided he didn't have the time. He showered and shaved and chose his most flattering suit from his closet. It looked deadly good on him, though he didn't wear it often. He picked out a dark red tie and laid it over the charcoal gray jacket. Before getting dressed, he looked at the tiny, bloody crescents that Amy's fingernails had left in his shoulders. They looked like they would heal within a few days, but they were unmistakably fingernail marks. He shrugged and pulled on his shirt. Satisfied, he was done with his dressing a few minutes later. He looked impeccable and ready to visit whatever upscale restaurant Elena might choose tonight.

It was 7:55 when he stepped into the Hilton lobby. He asked the desk clerk to call up to Elena Martinez's room and let her know he was here. He wandered around the lobby, looking at the bright decor and helping himself to a glass of water with a slice of lime and a few slivers of ice floating in it.

As he sat sipping his water, he pulled out his phone and checked his messages. Every time he heard the elevator doors open, he looked up, but Elena appeared to be running late.

Just as he was about to ask the desk clerk to call her room again, the elevator doors opened and she appeared. Glen's irritation and impatience vanished immediately. He'd never seen her hair loose before. It fell down her back in one long, sleek curtain of almost pure black. Her olive skin glowed under her forest green cocktail dress. It hugged her curves without being too revealing, but plunged daringly in the back, showing off her flawless skin.

"You look absolutely stunning, Elena," he said, taking her hand and pulling her close. He kissed her slowly, parting her lips with his tongue and running a finger up her spine, making her shiver. "Why don't we skip dinner and head straight up to your room?"

She laughed and swatted at him with her clutch. "You're terrible. But I really am hungry. I promised you dinner and we're going to have dinner. We'll see about dessert after."

He kissed her again, more chastely. "Your wish is my command.

Follow me. My car is right outside."

LIVING GRY

2

Rebecca stood outside the washrooms, gnawing a fingernail. She'd seen the off-duty skycap and the blue-haired girl go in there just a few moments before. They'd been obvious enough, making out on a bench near the baggage carousels. Rebecca hadn't been able to resist following them.

Now she couldn't decide what to do. Call security? Barge in and make a scene? She knew she should do something responsible, but what she really wanted was to sneak in and spy on them. The skycap had been hot in that arrogant way and the girl with him looked like she was up for a good time.

Rebecca shifted her weight from one foot to the other, pulled out her phone and glanced at it without really seeing it. Her imagination raced. What were they doing in there? More making out? Something more? She had a brief mental flash of the girl on her knees, sucking his cock enthusiastically as her bare breasts bobbed in time with her head. Rebecca blushed furiously and turned to walk away. She almost ran into another flight attendant and tripped over her own small, wheeled bag as she tried to move out of the way.

"Out of order," she muttered. "What?"

"Out of order. It's out of order. The washroom, I mean," said Rebecca, averting her eyes.

"Oh," said the other woman, disdain clear. Without a second glance, she turned on her heel and walked away.

Exhaling slowly, Rebecca leaned against the wall, wondering why she'd done it. It would have served that lecherous skycap right to get surprised by someone. It wasn't a favor she'd ever be likely to see repaid. She couldn't imagine ever trying to explain to him, or anyone, why she'd been standing outside the washroom like co- conspirator. She pushed away from the wall, squared her shoulders and grabbed her bag. As she straightened her blazer and prepared to walk away from it all, the washroom door banged open.

She did her best to maintain a blank, neutral expression as the sweat-sheened duo walked past her, but when the skycap gave her a cocky grin, she raised an eyebrow at him. Once they were around the corner, she slumped again and congratulated herself on her composure.

She wheeled her bag through the airport, quick and focused. She headed directly to the cab stand and was relieved not to find a queue. Sitting in the back of the taxi, she rubbed the back of her neck and sighed. She removed several well-hidden bobby pins from her hair and untied the rather severe bun at the nape of her neck. Her honey blond hair tumbled down her back, uncurling from its long confinement.

She stared out the window, beyond the landscape racing past. Her thoughts returned to the skycap and his pliable-looking companion. Rebecca found herself wondering what it might have been like to be in her place. She'd never done anything like that, so risky and daring. She didn't think of herself as a prude, but she was forced to admit that her sex life had always been fairly conventional. She shook her head, dismissing the thoughts threatening to grow into fantasies.

She wasn't scheduled to be back at the airport for over forty-eight hours, so she pulled out her phone, deciding she wanted some company that night. She checked her inbox on the dating website she'd been using, mostly unsuccessfully, for the last few months. She had over fifty messages, but more than half of them were lewd propositions, many including unsolicited pictures of male genitalia. She sighed, deleting them without responding. Did any woman ever respond to such advances?

She read through the non-pornographic messages quickly, creeping the profiles of the guys who sounded normal. When she was done, she was left with five promising candidates. She sent each of them friendly replies, letting them know she was in town for the next couple of days. With any luck, she'd have a nice dinner and an interesting conversation tonight. Some sexual chemistry would be nice, too, but she wouldn't hold her breath.

Finally home, she glanced around her studio apartment. She spent so little time here, it barely felt like anything more than another hotel room. An outsider would have had trouble guessing that anyone lived here at all. It was neat, almost empty. The closet held more uniforms than street clothes. Her jewelry rack was bare except for a row of conservative stud earrings. A book lay on her bedside table, a fine layer of dust on the cover.

She kicked off her shoes, picked them up and placed them on the rack in the closet. Her uniform jacket followed, hung carefully on it's awaiting hanger. The rest of her clothing went directly into the hamper, including her sensible white cotton bikini underwear. She lay on the coverlet, naked, curling and uncurling her aching toes. It felt good to finally be off duty and relax. to finally be off duty. She stretched luxuriously, taking up the whole queen bed, easing the built-up tension in her body.

Sensing that sleep was an imminent threat, she stood up and reluctantly made her way into the bathroom for a shower. The hot water chased away the last of her aches and the pervasive grimy feeling she always had from being stuck in an airplane cabin. She stayed under the water longer than necessary, enjoying its steamy embrace.

A few minutes later, while standing at the sink applying moisturizer, one towel wrapped around her chest and another around her hair, her phone pinged. She darted out of the bathroom, leaving a trail of wet footprints, and snatched up the phone. One of her potential suitors had written back.

Hi, MileHighBecky.

I was really happy to get your message. It must be difficult to have such a crazy schedule. Owing to the fact that I'm such an exciting guy, I'm completely free tonight and would be more than happy to take you to dinner or a drink.

He'd included his phone number and signed his message "BoringUsername34 a.k.a. Mike."

Elated at her success, Rebecca forgave the typo(?), texting to propose meeting at a cute little Thai place close to her apartment. The food was to die for and the cocktails weren't half bad either. She felt like a few strong drinks with little umbrellas in them would be the perfect start to her days off. While she waited to hear back, she poked through her meager wardrobe and supply of makeup, trying to find something appropriate for a casual date.

She eventually settled on a simple orange shift dress she hadn't worn in years. It was casual and bright, just the image she wanted to project. Twirling in front of the mirror, she admired the way it showed off her legs. She applied her makeup to match, with a hint of bright yellow eyeshadow and a pink lipstick that hinted of orange. Her outfit was so unlike her usual day-to-day look that she barely recognized herself. It felt good to shed her flight attendant skin.

She surfed the dating site to kill time until her date with Mike. When she grew bored with the men's profiles, she switched to women, curious how she stacked up against them. She scrolled through women her own age, raising an eyebrow at all the duck faces and exposed cleavage. She followed her whims, clicking on a few profiles, never lingering long. Before she knew it, she was late.

In a panic, she stuffed her keys and wallet into the first purse she found and grabbed a cardigan that she set out on the couch. At the front door, she slipped her feet into a pair of ballerina flats without looking at them, and darted out of the apartment, slightly damp hair flying behind her.

The restaurant was bustling. Most of the other customers looked like couples on dates. The atmosphere wasn't exactly romantic, but it suited her mood. She spotted Mike immediately. He looked just like his photos: dark hair and eyes, and a smile she believed was completely genuine.

"I'm so sorry I'm late," she said after they'd exchanged a polite hug. "I lost track of time and had to run all the way here." Too late, she realized she'd just told Mike she lived nearby.

"It's no problem. You're barely more than five minutes late, anyway. And you look fantastic, so I forgive you."

Rebecca blushed at the compliment and opened her menu. She already knew what she wanted, but it gave her something to do with her hands. She hoped she was hiding her pleased embarrassment well enough.

"So, what's good here?" asked Mike.

"It's all good, but I always have the same thing: beef panang and sticky rice. And tonight, I'm definitely having a drink or three. I'm relieved to be off work." Wanting to believe in his smile, she ditched her usual reserve for honesty.

Mike eyed the menu dubiously.

"I wish I knew what any of this stuff was. I'm not a very adventurous eater, I guess."

"Maybe try the pad see ew, then," offered Rebecca, wincing a little in her head. "Noodles in soy sauce, with beef and Chinese broccoli. Nothing too crazy."

He looked at her gratefully and took her recommendation when the waiter appeared. He also ordered a beer, though he seemed slightly dismayed at the unfamiliar choices. Rebecca ordered her curry and rice and added some fish cakes, too. She requested the most flamboyantly decorated cocktail on the menu.

They chatted amiably until their drinks arrived. Rebecca was delighted with hers and smiled at the waiter when she saw he'd included extra cherries. It was nice to be recognized, even though she hadn't been here in months. She alternated between sipping her drink and nibbling on the maraschinos while Mike talked at length about his work. She tried to appear interested, but importing furniture was not a very exciting field.

Eventually, as they were tucking in to their main courses, the topic came around to Rebecca's work.

"It's really not that glamorous," she said. "It's stressful and demanding and it doesn't pay very well, but I do love visiting all sorts of interesting places. It's all about seniority, though, so I don't get to pick my routes. I've been doing a lot of boring domestic ones lately." She savored a bite of her curry slowly, her eyes closed. "I did get to do a few runs to Thailand last year and that's when I found out how much I love beef panang. Of course, it's better over there."

"I travel, too, for work," said Mike. "But I always just make a beeline for the closest McDonald's. Did you know they have Pizza Hut in the United Arab Emirates?"

She laughed. "No, I didn't."

"Pretty much the same menu as here, except no pork. It's a little weird to have a meat lover's pizza without bacon."

Less than rapt with the conversation, Rebecca signaled the waiter. When he leaned in to ask what she wanted, she ordered another drink. Pitching her voice low, she added: "And make it a double, please."

Seeing Mike was only picking at his noodles, she offered him some of her fish cakes, but he seemed put off after a bite, wrinkling his nose at the sweet sauce and the bright and crunchy diced cucumber garnishes. More for me, she thought, fishing a few slices of fresh chili pepper out of the dish and popping them into her mouth.

By the time their dishes were cleared, she was working on her third drink and Mike hard ordered his second beer. They'd both relaxed considerably and the atmosphere in the restaurant had grown quieter and more intimate.

"So, MileHighBecky, is your name a not-so-subtle hint that you've joined the Mile High Club?"

She laughed and blushed fiercely. "No, not at all. You're not the first to ask me, though. I wish I could change my username. It gives people the wrong idea."

"Would you, if the opportunity arose?" He quirked an eyebrow.

She laughed again, nervous. "No, I don't think so. It would get me fired before I could blink, if I was caught. And those bathrooms are honestly pretty cramped and nasty. They don't make me feel very sexy."

"You have a point about the bathrooms, but I guess I imagined flight attendants might have access to a super secret privacy area or something."

"Sadly, no. We're pretty busy, too. Not a lot of time for extracurricular activities during a flight." She sipped her drink and toyed with her little paper umbrella, opening and closing it. "What about you? Ever done anything illicit on a flight?"

It was Mike's turn to flush, and Rebecca suddenly found herself charmed. He reached for one of her abandoned paper umbrellas and imitated her nervous fiddling, spinning it on the table like a top.

"Well, no, not exactly. But one of my ex-girlfriends might have sort of given me a tiny little hand job once. My jacket was in my lap. I'm pretty sure we were undetected."

Rebecca hid a giggle behind her hand. "Maybe the other passengers were in the dark, but I bet your flight attendant knew what was up. We do let things like that slide, sometimes. It's better than making a scene."

An awkward silence settled between them. Finally, Rebecca up- ended and drained the last of her fruity cocktail.

"You know what I'd like?" she asked. "A nice walk, to clear my head after all this alcohol. Would you care to join me?"

Mike offered to pay for her meal, but she insisted on picking up her own tab. Ten minutes later, they were out on the sidewalk, staring up at the inky sky and debating which direction to go.

"There's a park over this way," said Rebecca, pointing in the general direction of her apartment. She slipped on her cardigan, grateful she'd remembered it.

They walked in silence for a few minutes, admiring the night and enjoying the fresh air. The breeze felt good on Rebecca's face. She wondered what her plan was. She was guiding Mike closer and closer to her apartment. There really was a park nearby, but her feet seemed headed to another destination. Part of her suspected she would sleep with Mike out of sheer boredom. It didn't seem like such a bad idea. Mike was nice enough and he was cute. She stole a small sideways glance at him, looking for details to admire. He had a friendly, open face. Square shoulders. Strong arms. She imagined briefly what it would be like to be held by him and pressed against his chest.

She was beginning to think she truly enjoyed the idea when she realized that the imaginary arms belonged not to Mike, but to the lecherous skycap she'd spied on. Chiding herself, she took a step towards Mike and threaded her arm through his. She gave a theatrical little shiver.

"Now that I'm out here," she said slowly, "it's a little chilly for my taste. My place is just a few blocks away, if you'd like to come in and warm up with a cup of coffee."

Mike seemed surprised at the invitation and hesitated before accepting. Still holding on to his arm, she drew him up a side street and towards her place.

Rebecca flicked on the light and watched Mike's face as he took in her sparse furnishings.

"It's a little... austere," he said.

"I'm not here much," said Rebecca as she walked to the kitchen. "There doesn't seem to be much point to spending money on stuff I'll hardly ever use."

Mike wandered around but there wasn't much to give him any hint of Rebecca's personality or interests. No DVD collection, only a handful of books on a small shelf. No magazines, no board games. No art on the walls. No pictures of friends or family. He finally noticed one small, framed picture beside the television. He picked it up and smiled ruefully when he found that the subject of the photograph was a bright-eyed tortoiseshell cat.

"Is this your cat?" he called to the kitchen, putting the picture back down and continuing his tour of the room.

"Yes. No. Well, she was my cat, but I had to get rid of her when I took the flight attendant job. I couldn't afford to pay someone to take care of her every time I was gone. Her name is Panopticon, Pan for short."

Rebecca reentered the living room carrying two steaming cups. "It's only instant. That's all I've got," she said apologetically,

handing Mike one of the cups. "I left it black, but there's sugar and

creamer in the kitchen, if you want them."

"Black's fine," said Mike, taking a sip. "Where's Pan now?" "With my mom, in Des Moines. I see them a couple of times a

year, I guess." She'd made her own coffee creamy and sweet and

after a few mouthfuls, it started to seem cloying. She set it down next to the picture of Pan and went to stand behind Mike, who was looking out her window and holding his coffee without drinking it.

She touched his elbow, her mind flashing again to the skycap. "Penny for your thoughts?" she said.

He turned to look at her and she saw that his brow was furrowed. When he saw her empty hands, he put his own cup down. "You're very beautiful," he said, smiling. "But I was thinking that I'm not quite sure how this date has been going, despite the fact that you invited me back to your place for coffee." He crooked his fingers in the air twice when he said 'coffee' and then gave a little laugh.

"To be honest, I really did invite you here for coffee and to get out of the cold." She looked down and bit her lip. "But I'm not against a little coffee, too," she added, making her own set of air quotes. She moved in closer, until their bodies were almost touching. She looked up at him, tossing her blond hair off her shoulder, and searched his face. She couldn't guess his thoughts.

He hesitated for a moment, then leaned forward and kissed her softly. She closed her eyes and saw the skycap again. She pushed him out of her mind, focusing on Mike, responding to his tentative kiss with a passion she didn't quite feel.

Mike wrapped his arms around her and pulled her against his chest. His arms were just as strong as she'd imagined, but she couldn't help thinking that the skycap's were probably even stronger. She wondered if he could have lifted her completely off the ground. She pictured him holding the tiny girl from the airport, both of them naked and sweaty.

"You seem distracted," said Mike. "Do you want to stop?"

Not trusting herself to speak, she shook her head no. Mike took this as an encouraging sign and pulled her even closer. They kissed again and Mike's hands started to explore her body, pushing her cardigan off her shoulders and caressing the revealed skin. He kissed along the curve of her jaw and down her neck. His lips were soft and his touch so gentle that it almost tickled. Rebecca shivered and closed her eyes tightly.

She felt her body responding to Mike, but only because she was imagining the skycap touching her, kissing her, slowly pushing the cardigan down her arms until it fell to the floor. She slipped her fingers under his shirt, enjoying the feel of his bare skin. He continued to kiss her, softly and gently, and she found herself wishing for something a little less soft, a little more demanding.

She curved her fingers and dragged her nails slowly across his abs. Not hard, but enough to catch his attention.

"Ouch," he whispered into her ear, moving back slightly. He took her hand and led her toward the couch. They sat and continued to kiss.

Mike pushed her dress off one shoulder and freed one of her breasts from her bra. He cupped it, dragging his thumb over her nipple until it grew hard. Rebecca shivered and pulled him closer. He lowered his head and took her nipple into his mouth, his tongue playing over it until she moaned. Almost involuntarily, she spread her legs and he pushed his hand under her skirt, brushing his fingers against her panties.

She relaxed against the couch, tilting her head back and letting her legs open even wider. Mike continued to suck on her nipple and tease her gently. She moaned louder and moved her hips. Her eyes were still tightly closed, allowing her to forget Mike almost entirely. Behind her eyelids, she envisioned the skycap and his diminutive companion. Had he sucked on her nipples? Had he teased her as Mike was doing, or had he fucked her hard?

Mike sat up and moved away from her. She made a small sound of protest, but still did not open her eyes. She heard him slide off the couch and onto his knees in front of her. He grabbed her hips and pulled her forward until her ass was on the edge of the couch. He spread her thighs and kissed them, going higher and higher until she could feel his warm breath on her pussy. She moaned and lifted her hips, trying to feel more than just his breath.

He took advantage of her writhing to hook his fingers into the waistband of her black lace panties and slowly pull them down. He dropped them on the floor and pushed her thighs apart again, leaning forward to taste her for the first time.

When his tongue touched her, she started to tremble. Gasping, she threaded her fingers through his hair, trying to ignore his curls and imagine instead the skycap's dark wavy hair. She bucked her hips again, pressing her whole pussy against his mouth. In her mind, it was the skycap's lips and tongue on her, his fingers pushed inside her and finding that perfect spot to press rhythmically.

She heard Mike fumbling with his belt and zipper. He groaned as he freed his cock. His attention on Rebecca never wavered, but he stroked himself as he continued to lick and finger her.

She kicked off her shoes and put her knees over his shoulders, crossing her ankles behind his back. As her excitement grew, she pulled him in more and more, burying his face between her legs. Her hands left his hair and instead cupped her breasts. She played with her nipples and moaned, moving her hips in a steady rhythm, grinding against Mike's mouth.

She wondered if the skycap's tongue would be as gentle and tentative as Mike's, or if he would fuck her with it, making her writhe and pant. She continued to imagine him in Mike's position, on his knees, pleasuring her and was surprised to find she was picturing the girl, too. It was the blue-haired girl's hands that were on her breasts, pinching and tweaking her nipples. Rebecca moaned and imagined kissing her. She'd never kissed a girl but the thought was suddenly, viscerally appealing.

Entirely consumed by thoughts of the couple she'd seen earlier in the day, Rebecca felt her orgasm approaching. She moaned and shuddered, her hands squeezing her breasts so tightly it almost hurt. Her thighs pressed hard against Mike's ears and she heard him groan desperately as he continued to stroke himself.

With a cry that was almost a scream, Rebecca came. Her hands fell away from her breasts and dug into the couch as waves of pleasure crashed over her. She dropped back, shuddering and gasping, little aftershocks still traveling through her body. When her thighs parted, Mike stood up.

She continued to shudder for a few moments, her breathing slowly returning to normal. Once the fog cleared from her brain, it occurred to her that she'd been extremely selfish. She cracked her eyes to find Mike still standing in front of her, one hand wrapped around his cock. She sat up and leaned forward, taking him into her mouth without hesitation. He gave a grunt of satisfaction and buried his hands in her hair, hips still as she sucked and licked him.

It took her less than two minutes to bring him to orgasm. He jerked once and gasped, "I'm going to cum" through gritted teeth. She moved her head back and angled his cock down so that his load shot all over her exposed and slightly bruised breasts.

He collapsed next to her and they panted together, gathering themselves. She collected her panties from the floor and used them to wipe off her breasts. She pulled her bra and dress back up, covering herself.

"That was unexpected, but nice," said Mike, as tucked himself away and buckled his belt. "I enjoyed it, but I have a feeling your mind was...elsewhere."

Rebecca fiddled awkwardly with her messy panties, unsure what to do with them. "I'm sorry. I guess you're right."

"Do you have a boyfriend or something? A recent breakup?" "No, no. It's nothing like that," she said quickly. "I enjoyed

myself, too. And you're a really nice guy, Mike, but..."

"I know. But I'm not what you're looking for. Or you're not ready for anything serious right now. No worries, MileHighBecky. I had a nice time, though I'm not sure I'll be eating Thai food any time again soon. I just hope you don't have any regrets."

Rebecca smiled at him and leaned forward to kiss him lightly on the cheek. "No regrets, but you're right. I guess I don't see this going anywhere. I'm sorry. I'm gone so often anyway. I don't really even know how to date like a normal person anymore."

Mike pulled her in to the crook of his arm and kissed the top of her head. She reflected on the fact that he really was a nice guy. But there was no spark. All her arousal had come from thinking of that rakish skycap. She tucked herself against Mike, content to stay like this for the moment, in the afterglow of their orgasms.

"Do you want to talk about what was on your mind all evening?" he asked.

She opened her mouth to say no, wanting to keep her strange and selfish fantasies private, but instead found herself telling him the whole story, including the awkward stalking episode at the airport. He nodded sympathetically the whole time, kissing her hair when she would get tongue-tied. She was glad her face was hidden from him because she could feel her cheeks flaming with embarrassment.

When she was done, he chuckled. "That's not so bad. So, you've got a little crush on this guy."

"I wouldn't call it a crush. And he's a pervert and a jerk. That girl must have been more than a decade younger than him! And he should probably be fired for seducing innocent young girls in public washrooms at work."

"I think it sounds like you might be a little envious of this pervert because of how free he is. And envious of that girl because she got to fuck the pervert." He pondered for a moment. "I do wonder what they did in that bathroom."

It was Rebecca's turn to laugh. "Believe me, I've been wondering that pretty much non-stop myself. What could you even do in a bathroom stall?"

"All sorts of things, I'm sure," said Mike, a little wistful.

They lapsed into silence, reflecting on the possibilities of furtive, lust-fueled sex in a public restroom.

Rebecca started to sag against Mike, her eyes growing heavier. Before she could decide if she wanted to kick him out or ask him to spend the night, her exhausting day and alcohol consumption caught up with her and she fell deeply asleep.

She awoke at dawn, hair a mess, tongue fuzzy. She glanced around her room for clues of the previous night. Memory came back slowly. She got up and padded around the apartment, but Mike wasn't hiding anywhere. He was gone.

Returning to the living room, she spotted a folded note tucked in to the corner of the frame that held the photo of Pan. Standing barefoot in the golden dawn light, she unfolded it.

"If you ever get sick of wishing for that pervert, give me a call," it read. She smiled, appreciating the sentiment, but she'd never see Mike again. Yawning and stripping her dress off over her head, she made her way to her bedroom and collapsed naked on top of the coverlet. She was asleep and dreaming of the dark-haired skycap within minutes.

3

As they walked across the parking lot, Elena eyed the sky. The last slanting rays of the day were golden and warm, the sky clear and blue directly above them.

"Let's walk," she said suddenly. "It's beautiful out. I spend so much time cooped up inside buildings and planes."

Glen offered his arm and told her to lead the way. She slipped her arm through his, but maintained a polite space between them. He hadn't won her over quite yet, but he knew the night was young.

She chatted casually about work and asked questions about his job as they made their way. By the time they reached the restaurant, dusk had settled. Elena looked even more stunning in the dim light, the shadows casting an air of mystery about her.

She'd chosen a small French bistro. Despite the relaxed ambiance, Elena knew from past experience that the food was excellent and the service discreet and impeccable. It was charming and intimate, sans extravagant romantic trappings.

They were seated in a small booth tucked away in a corner. Glen's tall frame was a cramped, but Elena only laughed at him and told him he was welcome to stretch out his legs on her side.

"I'll take you up on that. It'll give me lots of chances to not-so- accidentally brush up against those enticing legs of yours." Elena rolled her eyes when Glen gave her a grin to show that he was joking.

A waiter brought the menus and a wine list, she noticed Glen lingered over the menu. Glen enjoyed wine, but often didn't have the luxury of choosing from a wine cellar as extensive and interesting as this one. He ordered a Chateau d'Yquem, promising Elena she would enjoy it.

"It's sweet and memorable, just like you," he said with a wink.

She laughed, sensing he was being sappy on purpose. Normally she would find his comments cloying, but tonight she found them charming. If she was honest, she enjoyed Glen's company far more than she'd expected.

When the wine arrived, she made a little sound of pleasure as she sipped. It was a rich golden color that wrapped around her tongue like syrup. She was still savoring its sweet fruit notes when the waiter returned to take their order. Glen ordered a foie gras appetizer and a platter of Roquefort cheese with pear tart to share.

"To go with the wine," he explained.

The combination sounded decadent to her. For her main course, she ordered roast chicken with caramelized chanterelle mushrooms, while Glen selected braised rabbit in mustard.

"I'll order us a red, later, to pair with our main course, if you like," he said, sipping his wine and cutting a sliver of pear tart.

"Two bottles of wine! Are you trying to get me drunk?" She raised her eyebrows.

"Maybe," he laughed. "Or maybe I'm just trying to take full advantage of the amazing wine cellar here. Not to mention: I want to dazzle you with my knowledge."

"Consider me at least somewhat dazzled. I had no idea you were so knowledgeable or interested in wine or food. You seem like a burger and fries kind of guy," said Elena. The sharp taste of the Roquefort on her tongue brightened the flavor of the pear tart. It was a lovely combination. She could already feel the wine's warmth and was surprised to find that she was on her second glass.

"I never turn down a good burger and fries, but there's more to me than meets the eye. I love good food. I'm always open to trying new things and learning about new dishes and cooking methods. I don't often have the budget to eat in places like this, though. When I have the time, I cook well at home—it's more budget-friendly."

"You cook, too?" She sipped her wine again, following it with a nibble of foie gras.

"Yeah, I'm pretty good, if I do say so myself. My specialties are Italian and Korean. When I go out to eat, though, I love getting Thai food. I find it hard to replicate the magic at home."

They continued to chat, and the bottle of wine was finished before either of them realized. Glen couldn't take his eyes off Elena. Her cheeks were a deep pink, her eyes shining above the candlelight. She'd relaxed, and her smile came more easily and frequently than it had at the beginning of the evening. And yet, she remained distant and a little aloof, like part of her wasn't present or available to him. He reached across the table and put his hand on hers.

"You look incredible tonight, Elena, beautiful. Your work clothes are a little…severe, but tonight—well, it suits you."

She blushed and looked away. After a moment, she pulled back her hand and tucked it in her lap.

"Thank you," she said. "You're different than you seem at the airport, too."

She hadn't taken the compliment quite the way he'd hoped, so he was relieved when their waiter arrived with their main course. He asked for the wine list again and quickly selected a light red. Elena raised an eyebrow but didn't object.

The food was wonderful and they both ate in silence for a while.

When the red was poured, Elena exclaimed at how good it was.

"It's like you can read my mind. Both wines tonight are exactly what I like."

"Lucky guesses. Or, perhaps we share similar tastes. I also think they are both fantastic."

Elena drank her first glass of red quickly as she worked through the roast chicken. Her mushrooms were golden yellow and cooked to perfection. She could have eaten an entire plate of them.

They sampled each other's main courses and agreed that everything was perfect.

"You've been here before?" asked Glen.

"A few times. I usually stay nearby when I'm in town, so it's become a bit of a favorite."

"With dates?" Glen smiled to show he was jealous, hoping to provoke her.

"Yes, occasionally, but not always."

Glen dropped his voice and lowered his eyes. "And did you take them back to your hotel room after? For dessert?"

Elena blushed more deeply, but her response surprised Glen. "No, never."

Glen bit his tongue and managed not to push further. He didn't want to offend her, but he was curious. And perhaps disappointed. He wouldn't deny that he'd gone out with Elena tonight in the hopes of having sex with her. After his quick romp with Amy this afternoon, he'd been looking forward to something with more substance.

A few minutes later, Elena declared herself full, though half of her chicken remained on her plate. She offered it to Glen, who was more than happy to accept.

"I'm a growing boy, after all," he said.

Elena shook her head. "I hope you don't get any taller. You're imposing enough as it is."

The waiter cleared their plates, but they declined dessert in favor of slowly sipping their wine. Glen tried to read Elena's eyes, but she looked away whenever their eyes met. The wine made him bold. He reached across the table and took her hand, stroking her wrist gently. This time, she did not pull away. She shivered and closed her eyes.

Her skin was warm and soft beneath his finger. He could feel her trembling. She shifted in her seat, moving her legs under the table until her calf brushed against his. She opened her eyes.

"Let's get the bill. Then, walk me back to my hotel?"

Elena paid, leaving a generous tip. Outside, she found that she was a little unsteady and gratefully took Glen's offered arm, standing closer than she had on the way to the restaurant.

They walked slowly, enjoying the cool evening air and each other's company. Neither was quite ready to say goodbye when they found themselves in the parking lot, standing beside Glen's car.

"I had a nice time," said Elena, hugging herself against the growing chill.

"I did, too."

Elena looked up at Glen, her eyes searching his face. "Aren't you going to kiss me?"

"I thought you'd never ask," he said. He wrapped his arms around her and bent to her upturned face.

It was a polite kiss at first, only their lips touching. His tongue gently sought hers and as the kiss deepened, her body responded. She arched her back and pressed her breasts against his chest. His hand worked its way into her silky hair, cupping the back of her head. She grabbed the front of his shirt and with a sudden motion, pulled him down toward her.

He broke the kiss and stepped back, allowing both to catch their breath. Elena adjusted her hair and looked at him steadily, though she seemed hesitant to speak.

"Maybe," she said slowly, "you could come up to my room for a nightcap. Or dessert."

He nodded and took her hand, letting her lead him into the lobby. The vivid yellow and green decor seemed brighter after the darkness outside. Elena paused at the front desk to request a bottle of champagne be sent up to her room. She cast a glance at Glen, considering, before adding strawberries to her order.

As they waited for the elevator, he put an arm around her shoulder and felt her stiffen.

"Strawberries and champagne is such a cliché, I know. But I really do love them together."

"It's a classic for a reason," said Glen.

They were alone in the elevator and Glen took the opportunity to steal another kiss. This time, her mouth opened to his eagerly. He ran a hand over the bare skin of her back eliciting a sigh of pleasure. He grew excited at the thought of having her. She'd been so oddly cold and inaccessible over the course of the night, but he was happy that his suppositions might be wrong.

Her room was at the end of the hall. She hesitated before unlocking the door, but Glen waited patiently, allowing her time to get comfortable. He followed her in and closed the door gently, leaving them in the dark.

With a practiced step, she walked to the bedside table. She set down her clutch and clicked on the light before turning to face him. The lamp cast only a pale golden circle of light, but Glen could see that she was smiling nervously. They each took a step forward and met in the center of the dim room. He put his hands on her hips, enjoying the silky fabric that clung to her firm flesh. She reached out and stroked his tie, meditative.

They leaned in to kiss, but a polite knock came at the door.

Elena darted around Glen to open the door. She returned a moment later balancing a tray laden with an ice bucket, a bottle of champagne, two flutes, and a bowl of strawberries. She slid it onto the desk next to her laptop.

"He wanted to carry it in, but I sent him away," she said. "I like my privacy."

She started to fumble with the champagne bottle. Glen rescued her, popping the cork with a practiced gesture. She gave a startled jump at the sound, but held out both glasses. He pretended not to notice that her hands were trembling again.

Elena took a sip and picked the biggest, reddest strawberry from the bowl. She bit into it, her eyes half closed.

"So good," she said.

He imitated her, chasing each sip of champagne with a bite of strawberry. He could feel the effect of the alcohol, building on the two bottles of wine shared earlier. He drank slowly and was surprised to see Elena pouring herself a second glass before he'd half finished his first.

She finished the second as quickly as the first, then abruptly set her glass down on the desk. She nibbled another strawberry and watched him in silence.

"Elena, something's clearly bothering you. If you don't want me here, I can leave."

"No. I want you here. Really. In fact, I think you're just what I need tonight."

He considered this. "What do you mean? What do you need?" "All that flirting we do at the airport—I always just thought you were a kind of handsome, cocky jerk. I thought it would be a bit of fun to go out with you. A distraction. But you weren't really what I expected tonight."

"I think that's a compliment," Glen said with a grin.

"I've been on a few dates in the last few months, but I haven't brought anyone back to my hotel room and things have certainly never gotten serious. I've just been trying to keep things very light since...Well, since my life changed."

Elena lapsed into silence, nervously twisting a strand of her hair between her fingers. Glen waited for her to continue, but she seemed to be at a loss as to what to say next.

He set his champagne flute beside hers. "How did your life change?" he asked gently. "Did you get divorced?"

"No. Well, yes, I did get divorced, but that's not what's making me anxious tonight." She sat on the edge of the bed, bending forward to undo the straps on her heels. She slid them off and stood them up carefully to one side. She had an impeccable pedicure, her toenails a deep golden shade that perfectly complimented her skin.

She crossed the room to stand before the floor-length mirror. She smoothed her hair before methodically removing her jewelry. When she was done, she put everything away in a small zippered case. She turned back to face Glen, eyes wide.

"I want you to know that it's fine if you want to leave after I show you. I wouldn't blame you. My ex-husband couldn't handle it. I couldn't handle it either, but I didn't have much choice."

Glen fought the urge to run, or to shake her and make her spit out her secret. Dread settled over him, though part of him believed that she must be exaggerating the severity of whatever she was about to reveal. He swallowed hard and tried to wipe the sweat from his palms without Elena noticing.

She reached behind her neck and undid the one small button that held her dress closed. The sleek fabric immediately slipped down her shoulders. She crossed her arms over her chest and held it up while she took one trembling breath. With an effort, she kept her eyes open and looked straight at Glen as she carefully pushed the dress off her shoulders. It fell, puddling around her bare feet.

She kept her arms raised for a few seconds. She was trembling, but in the dim light, Glen couldn't see why. She lowered her hands and waited.

Glen let shock show on his face for a brief moment before he managed to assume a carefully neutral expression. The skin of her chest was dimpled and uneven. Two long horizontal scars started from beneath her armpits and almost met in the middle of her chest. They were fully healed, but still red and stood out against her pale skin.

He didn't stop to think. He was surprised and saddened, but not repulsed. He crossed the room, stopping only inches from her. Her eyes shone with unspilled tears and her lips quivered. He bent and kissed her gently, his fingers brushing gently against one scar. She tried to move away, to cover herself, but he held her and kissed her more deeply.

He buried his face in her shoulder, inhaling the bright floral scent of her shampoo and feeling her pulse beat rapidly in her throat.

"You're beautiful, Elena. Thank you for being brave enough to show me this. I'm not going to bolt."

He bent further and lifted her up, sweeping her off her feet and into his arms. He carried her to the bed, still nibbling and kissing her neck, and laid her on the coverlet. She tried to hide herself again, but he captured both her wrists in one of his hands and held them above her head. With his other hand, he slowly pushed down her underwear. He dropped them on the floor. She was naked, her dark hair fanning out beneath her.

"I want to see every inch of you and appreciate just what a gorgeous woman you are."

She made a small sound, halfway between a whimper and a moan.

Still holding her wrists, he traced a finger down her body, touching each of her scars for just a moment. The skin there was puckered, but the rest of her was smooth and soft and she moaned again when his hand reached between her legs. He stroked her thighs until she parted them with a sigh, closing her eyes. He was only a little surprised to find her already wet.

He teased her, drawing a few gasps before he stood. She opened her eyes and watched as he removed his tie. He knelt on the bed and bound her wrists together and then to the headboard with the tie. Her breath quickened, but she made no move to stop him.

He joined her on the bed, lying beside her, propped up on his elbow. He leaned toward her and she lifted her head to meet him, eager. As he pushed her back down to the bed, his hand found her pussy again and he slipped a finger inside. She moaned into his mouth and moved her hips. Her hands tugged uselessly at his tie. She was wet and tight and he thought that if he continued to play with her like this, she would cum within minutes. She raised her hips off the bed, trying to push his finger deeper inside her. He shook his head and smiled at her.

"Not so fast, darling. I want this to last."

He kissed her again and ran his hand up her side. He followed the curve of her hip to her shoulder and continued higher, caressing her arm. When he reached her bound wrists, he gave them a little tug. She relaxed into him. Her eyes were closed and his touch made her moan. He sat up and stroked her legs. He wanted her let go of everything holding her back. Nothing turned him on more than a woman who had given herself over entirely to her sexual desires.

He slid to the bottom of the bed and took her left foot in his hands. He massaged gently, working out the pain he was sure she had from walking around in heels all night. She sighed contentedly, finally seeming to forget her nakedness and her scars. He pressed his thumbs into the arch of her foot rhythmically, then moved his attention to her toes. She turned her head to the side, resting it on her raised arm, and Glen wondered if she was about to fall asleep.

He took up her other foot and gave it the same treatment. She stayed limp, completely willing to let him make her feel good. Her breathing had slowed and deepened. He lifted her foot to his lips and gently kissed one of her perfectly pedicured toes. She didn't stir, but he thought her breathing might have quickened. He kissed another toe, then licked it. She opened her eyes and stared at him.

"What are you doing?" she asked, with a nervous, high-pitched laugh.

In response, he licked her toes again and sucked on one gently, running his tongue over the sensitive underside. She shivered with pleasure and made no move to pull her foot away. He continued until her breathing quickened again and she was squirming on the bed, pulling at her bonds and giggling in between sighs of pleasure.

"I never imagined that would feel so good," she said.

"I know a few tricks," answered Glen. He smiled when he said it, but his serious tone made Elena shiver.

He put her foot down and massaged her legs, gradually working them apart. He could see that she was soaking wet. He wanted her bad. His cock was painfully hard, but tonight would be about Elena and her needs. He slipped two fingers easily inside her and crooked them upwards. His thumb found her clit and she moaned desperately.

He continued to touch her, his pace deliberate and slow, building her excitement gradually. As she began to pant and buck her hips, his free hand explored her body. He lingered on her chest, tracing the shape of the scars, trying to discover if there were any particularly sensitive spots to be found there. It only took a few minutes to bring her to orgasm. When she came, she cried out so loudly that Glen actually wondered about the guests in the neighboring rooms. Her orgasm lasted a long time, and Glen didn't stop stroking her until the last of the tremors had subsided, though she clenched so tightly around his fingers that it hurt.

He lay down beside her and kissed her cheek. There were tears in Elena's eyes and as she looked at him, they spilled onto her cheeks. He untied her and she curled towards him, burying her face in his chest and sobbing. She wasn't the first woman he'd been with who had cried after sex, but this time, he knew the weight of the emotion she'd released was more than anything he'd ever dealt with. For once, not knowing quite what to do, he held her, stroking her hair until they both fell asleep.

Elena woke in the dark, surprised and happy to find Glen still beside her, holding her tightly. She could feel his erection pressing against her insistently through his clothes. It didn't take her long to free his cock. She smiled to find it was much larger than her ex- husband's, and she knew what to do with it. Glen woke when she started stroking him. To stifle his protests, she kissed him.

Her cool fingers felt wonderful on him, but it didn't take long before he wanted more than her hand. He grabbed her shoulders and turned her over onto her back. She knew what he wanted and spread her legs as she wrapped her arms around his neck. He plunged into her, groaning at the perfect warmth and wetness between her legs.

He fucked her hard, his face buried in her shoulder, and when they came, it was nearly simultaneous. They lay panting in each other's arms, recovering. The sheets around them were a sweaty mess and Glen's clothing was rumpled and damp.

"Thank you so much for all of that," said Elena, her voice soft. "I couldn't bring myself to believe that anyone would ever want me again."

He kissed her shoulder, "You're a very desirable woman. Scars aren't going to change that."

"My ex-husband..." she started, trailing off.

"If your ex couldn't get past scars that prove you've fought to stay alive and won, then he wasn't worth your time anyway. It freed you up to find someone better."

She made no immediate response to this and they cuddled in the dark, each reflecting on the evening they'd spent together.

"Glen, I know you must be right and that there is someone out there for me, but I'm not ready for that. I agreed to go out with you because I thought it would be a harmless little bit of fun. We'd eat, we'd drink, we'd kiss. And then I'd take refuge back in my hotel room alone, like I do on every other date."

"Are you upset that it didn't turn out that way?"

"No. I'm happy with how this turned out. But this has to end here. I'm not ready to really be with anyone. This was a first step I needed to take, but I'm not done getting over my surgery, my divorce, and all the rest of that mess yet."

Glen, who'd never intended to get embroiled in anything so serious, remained silent. He'd also been looking for a harmless bit of fun, although certainly hoped for a lot more nudity than Elena's plan. Still, he couldn't say that he regretted the night either.

"I hope you understand. It's not that you're not a great guy. I'm just not available for anything more right now. I didn't even realize I could go this far."

"Of course, I understand." Although Glen was relieved he didn't have to say it first, he was a little disappointed to be on the receiving end of the message.

He looked out the window and could still see the moon, though the sky was growing pale with the first faint light of dawn. He offered to leave and let her spend the rest of her night in peace, but she only snuggled into him more tightly until they both drifted off once more.

In the morning, they made love again. This time Elena initiated, pulling his shirt open and climbing on top of him. When they were done, she kissed him and shooed him into the shower. They had an unhurried room service breakfast together. When he left, there was an unspoken understanding that they wouldn't meet again, unless perhaps by chance at the airport.

At work that night, Sarge and Rashid caught him just before his shift started, both curious about how his evening had played out.

"Bro, I spent the night cleaning out my mom's rain gutters and listening to her complain about the neighbors. I need a juicy story," said Rashid.

Glen hesitated, unsure how much to share. Normally, he loved to regale them with all the gory details, but it didn't seem right this time.

"You totally hit that, right?" Rashid continued, elbowing Glen and giving him an exaggerated wink.

Sarge, possessed of slightly more tact, quelling Rashid with a look.

"Well, yeah, we fucked," said Glen. "But it wasn't how I thought it would be."

"Was she terrible or something? Did she turn out to be 500 pounds and just really good at tucking herself into her Spanx?"

Sarge shook his head at Rashid, disgusted.

"No, we had a good time, but it was just different. I'm not really sure I want to talk about it much."

"She had a cock!" said Rashid, laughing.

Some travelers approached their counter and both Sarge and Glen pushed Rashid to go serve them.

"Just keep him off my back, alright?" Glen said to Sarge. "I'm not in the mood to deal with him today. And I can tell an even better story about a girl I picked up at work yesterday."

Sarge whistled in admiration, then shook his head in concern. "You sure do get around. Don't you ever think you might want to settle down? Stop using girls strictly for sex?"

Glen shrugged. Something about last night had made him start wondering about that himself. He felt a little ashamed of what he'd done with Amy. He didn't think he'd done her any harm. She'd just wanted to get her mind off her ex, and he'd been in the right place at the right time. Maybe he'd helped both women, in a way.

He thought briefly of the flight attendant who'd crossed paths with him and Amy. She'd been looking at him like she had him all figured out. He supposed she might. He wasn't sure there was all that much depth to him.

4

Rebecca enjoyed a luxurious morning after sleeping in late. She wasn't expected at the airport until late afternoon. Her next route was taking her overseas and she was in for a long night. She made herself some instant coffee and found frozen waffles in the freezer. Topped with some strawberry jam, they made a decent enough breakfast.

She debated calling her mom and asking after Panopticon, but she didn't feel like enduring a lecture about her life and job choices. She settled on sending an email and curled up in front of her computer still in her pajamas. She'd only intended to write her mother a brief note, but a sudden pang of loneliness overwhelmed her and she ended up typing for nearly half an hour, talking about the places she'd been and how much she'd enjoyed them, but also how stressful and draining work was. She ended by asking how everyone was, surprised to find herself genuinely wanting to know.

After hitting send, she checked the time. She still had hours to spare, but nothing to do and no one to spend the time with. She logged in to her dating profile, knowing she couldn't do more than browse.

The first thing she noticed was that Mike had looked at her profile. She sighed and almost closed her laptop. If she'd told her mother about Mike—leaving out the sexy details, of course—she knew what response she'd get: Why couldn't she settle down with a nice guy like that? Didn't she want to be a

51

good wife and mother? Didn't she want to give her own poor mother the grandchildren she so deserved? Rebecca didn't feel old or like her time to find love was running out, but her mother always made it seem like she was mere months away from turning into a confirmed old maid. She sighed again and wished that Pan was curled up in her lap like he used to.

She'd had a lot of other visitors to her profile and quite a few messages, too. She sorted through them methodically, deleting any with dick pics or rude and misspelled sexual advances. It became a chore after a while, but it was the price you had to pay to put yourself out there online.

One message caught her eye and made her pause. It was from a woman. Her profile picture showed short brown hair in a tousled, spiky halo around her head and heavy makeup. She had two rings through her lip and one in her left eyebrow. She had her arm draped around the shoulders of a taller person who'd been cropped out of the photo.

Becky,

I saw you creeping on my profile. You don't look like the kind of girl I usually get attention from, so I got curious. So, what's a girl like you doing on a profile like mine?

Sam

Rebecca didn't want to click on Sam's profile and attract her attention again, but she vaguely remembered some details from when she'd visited it two days ago. Her username was TwitchyNose, which made Rebecca want to giggle. Her profile listed her as "30, emo, anime girl, and lover of morbid and slightly unsettling things." Rebecca felt drawn to some of Sam's profile details, impressed she'd had graduated from the University of Washington with a B.A in Women, Gender and Sexuality Studies. As Rebecca drifted away from thoughts of Sam, there didn't seem any point in answering. She closed the message and logged off.

She had her work prep routine down to a fine art. Her bag was packed, her uniform laid out on the bed. She showered and did her hair without rushing, pinning it up into the severe chignon she always wore to work. She chose a pair of simple pearl earrings and applied subtle makeup. The airline was strict. She needed to look perky and healthy, but not flashy or overdone. Her look was boring, but the rigidity of it was freeing, in a way. She never needed to think about it too much.

She thought of the girl at the airport, the one with the skycap. She'd had colorful hair and clothes. And a certain disregard for convention that Rebecca couldn't help but envy.

She toured the apartment once before leaving, putting away the few dishes she'd used and wiping an invisible crumb off the table. She checked that all the windows were closed and locked, all the lights and faucets turned off. Satisfied, she let herself out and gave the door a final hard tug.

In the cab to the airport, she pulled out her phone and checked her dating profile again. She reread the message from TwitchyNose and bit her lip in indecision. She typed quickly and hit send before she could change her mind.

I was curious, too. And scoping out the competition. Becky

Blushing, she shoved her phone back into her bag and spent the rest of the drive staring out the window. She had no idea why she'd sent TwitchyNose an answer, really. Perhaps it was the novelty of the situation. It couldn't hurt her to make a friend, either. There was more than one way to combat the loneliness blanketing her life.

She made it to the airport early, but didn't dawdle. She rolled her bag across the concourse, her stride purposeful, not letting her gaze stay to either side. As she walked by the skycaps, she couldn't stop herself from taking a peek. The tall, dark-haired jerk from the bathroom incident was there, chatting and laughing with a couple of his coworkers. She pulled her bag off to one side to watch him.

A group of older women wearing t-shirts and sun visors approached and starting to ask him questions. She couldn't hear what they said, but the skycap grinned and took a look at their boarding passes. Banter seemed to come easily to him and when the women moved off, several of them were blushing and one was fanning herself theatrically. Rebecca gritted her teeth, both annoyed and oddly jealous. She clenched the handle of her bag and stalked off, angry at him for being so handsome and smooth, and angry at herself for thinking about him at all.

She was halfway to her gate, cheeks aflame, when she stopped abruptly. She hadn't the faintest idea why this man had taken such a hold over her. Maybe talking to him would break the spell. He looked like a dumb jerk, so why not give him the chance to open his mouth and prove it?

She turned and started back. She swerved to avoid a group of confused teenagers and nearly slammed straight into someone going the opposite direction.

"Darn. I'm sorry. I wasn't looking," as she spoke how true her words were. She hadn't been paying attention at all.

"No problem. Given our size difference, if we'd hit any harder, I imagine you'd be the injured one."

Rebecca started and dropped her bag. It clattered to the floor behind her. She bent to retrieve it, stammering apologies and cursing herself silently. It was the skycap. She straightened to face him, tilting her head up to take in his grin.

"So sorry," she said again, pointlessly.

"It's really nothing. Though I'll admit that you seem to be taking it rather hard, for some reason." He put a hand on her shoulder and gently guided her out of the flow of traffic towards a bench. She sat down without thinking, and he towered over her even more.

"Oh, well, I guess I was just thinking about something. Something personal. I'll be fine." She made a move to stand, but settled back when the skycap filled the space on the bench beside her.

"You do seem preoccupied. I hope it's nothing serious," he gave her a winning smile that she found simultaneously charming and irritating. "By the way, my name is Glen. It's a pleasure to meet you."

She took his proffered hand and shook it. "Rebecca. Nice to meet you, too. I really should be getting to work, though." She cast a glance over her shoulder at the departures board. She still had time to spare, but was desperate to escape the awkward situation in which she found herself.

"I think I've seen you around here recently. Do you come through this airport often?"

"Oh, I'm sure you could have seen me," she said, feeling a fresh blush rise to her cheeks. "This is my home base. I'm here all the time."

"I never forget a pretty face," said Glen. "I can't believe we've never spoken before. I like getting to know the people who work here."

She made up her mind and stood. "I really should be going. I'm sure I'll be passing through again soon."

"Wait. I remember now. I saw you over by the washrooms near baggage claim a few days ago."

Rebecca stiffened. "I have no idea what you are talking about."

"I think you might." Glen stood. He grinned and gave her a wink. "Actually, I'm pretty sure you remember it quite well."

She resisted the urge to kick him in the shin.

"Have a safe flight, Rebecca. And be sure to stop by when you're back in town. I'd love to take you out for a drink." He winked again.

She scowled and nearly spat. "I don't have time for drinks. Have a good day." She turned on her heel and left, hoping she wouldn't further embarrass herself by tripping over her bag or colliding with another stranger.

Once she'd turned a few corners and felt she was safely out of Glen's view, she slowed her pace and sagged her shoulders. She was mortified. Why had she been so ridiculously awkward and prickly? And what were the odds that he would recognize her and remember where he'd seen her? She shook her head and ducked into the nearest washroom, intending to fix her hair and makeup. She felt rumpled and disoriented.

One glance in the mirror was enough to tell her that her outside appearance did not reflect her inner turmoil. Not a single hair was out of place and though her cheeks were red, the blush was attractive and didn't betray the panicky shame she felt. She locked herself in a stall and sat on the toilet, breathing slowly and trying to gather her wits.

So, I can stop calling him the perverted skycap, she thought. His name is Glen.

She raised a hand and lightly touched her shoulder where Glen's hand had rested. Then she thought about the brief second when their bodies had been a mere fraction of an inch apart. Her heart thumped and she felt a pulse of heat between her legs. He really was incredibly handsome, and his stupid grin was charming, despite how much it annoyed her.

She looked around the stall and imagined Glen and the blue- haired girl. What had they done together? Had he pushed her up against the wall? Had he kissed her and undressed her? Had he turned around and lifted her skirt? Had they fucked? What would it be like to be held by those big hands and fucked hard by a man who looked that strong? She shivered, picturing his cock, proportional with the rest of him. How had that tiny girl handled it?

Did it hurt just a bit, but feel so good at the same time?

Rebecca was nearly panting. She'd been in the stall far longer than she intended. The warmth between her legs was more intense and she knew if she touched herself, she'd be wet. She shivered. She ached to touch herself, but now was not the time. She stood, straightened her skirt and blazer and walked out the bathroom.

Thirteen long hours later, she wearily closed the door of her hotel room behind her and collapsed on the bed fully dressed. She could hear the bustling mid-morning Paris crowds outside and sunlight streamed cheerily through her window. She was exhausted, but sleep would not come easily. She'd been on this job for years, but had never really adjusted to the long hours and constant time changes. She wondered for the zillionth time if she was cut out for this life.

She kicked off her shoes and let them fall to the ground. Resigned, she stood and forced her feet to carry her to the window. She pulled the heavy curtains shut and sighed. She felt better in the darkness. She carefully removed her uniform and hung it over the back of a chair. It was blissful to roll off her nylons and let the skin of her legs breathe. It was almost orgasmic to remove her bra. She stretched, enjoying the freedom of movement. She slid off her panties next and dropped them unceremoniously to the floor.

She eyed the bed, wanting to tuck herself in and try to sleep, but she felt dirty, as she always did after a flight. She needed a shower first.

The water was so hot it was almost painful, but she reveled in it. Clean, her muscles warmed and unkinked, she slipped into bed ten minutes later, a towel wrapped around her damp hair. She still felt lethargic, but also more awake. She turned on her phone for the first time since boarding and scrolled through all the emails she'd received while in the air.

The one from her mother was long and reproachful, touching on all the things her mother always nagged about. She rolled her eyes, but didn't delete the message, instead flagging it for attention later. She could put off answering for a few days before her mother would start calling and leaving frantic messages. Her mother had included a photo of Panopticon sunning herself on the deck and Rebecca made

it her new background image. She felt a twinge of guilt at the thought that the news about her cat interested and pleased her far more than the news about her human family.

Her inbox yielding nothing else of interest, she logged in to her dating profile again. There was a new message from Sam.

Your profile says you're straight and mine says I'm gay, so what are we competing for, exactly? Cute ass, by the way, 'straight' girl.

Yours in lesbianism, Sam

Rebecca stifled an outburst of shocked laughter. She wasn't sure Sam had the right idea about her, but this exchange was the best thing that had happened to her all day. Smiling, she typed out her reply.

I promise, you're barking up the wrong tree. I was just browsing idly and not pondering switching teams. Thanks for noticing my ass, though.

Yours in heterosexuality, Becky

She hit send and dared to hope for an immediate reply. Back home, it was either very late at night or very early in the morning, depending on the kind of person you were, though. Sam was probably in bed. Rebecca sighed and chuckled again.

She fished around for the remote and switched on the television. She found a talk show featuring a pair of French hosts with soothing voices and turned the volume down low so she couldn't make out any of the words. They appeared to be interviewing a small woman about a book she'd written. Rebecca closed her eyes and let them lull her to sleep.

When she woke, her brain was fuzzy and the remnants of a dream about Glen clouded her consciousness. She found herself aroused again, but tried to dismiss any sexual thoughts. She was only in Paris for one night and she intended to take advantage of it. She was dressed and out walking half an hour later.

The City of Lights was busy and beautiful, as always. She'd had the pleasure of coming to Paris a couple dozen times over the years she'd worked as a flight attendant, yet it never failed to enchant her. She could feel the history of the city in a way she never could at home. There were buildings here older than

America. It was fascinating how a centuries-old, gargoyle-covered church could co-exist so peacefully with so many modern things. And she loved the way Parisian women dressed. They all looked as though they spent an hour putting together their outfits every morning. Bright colors somehow never clashed, flowing scarves, gorgeous purses...She felt out of place in her jeans and sneakers.

She wandered for a few hours, watching people and visiting small shops. Her last stop was a small bakery where she bought a cheese sandwich on the best baguette she'd ever tasted. She sat in a church courtyard and ate, sipping from a small bottle of wine. Such a simple way to spend an evening, but it was perfect. The only thing missing, it suddenly occurred to her, was someone to share it with.

She chided herself for letting her mother get to her. She didn't need a boyfriend or a husband to be happy. She just needed to work harder to make friends, to get along with the other flight attendants. She knew they were all staying at the same hotel, yet she hadn't made any effort to socialize with them.

Despite the beauty of the night and her desire not to waste one minute of Paris, thoughts of missed opportunities at friendship made her pull out her phone. As she'd half hoped, there was a message from Sam.

You don't have to switch teams. I have it on pretty good authority that being bisexual is a thing. I won't keep flogging a dead horse, though. If you're straight, you're straight.

So, what's a fully heterosexual woman up to tonight? Something really straight, I'd guess.

Queerly, Sam

Rebecca stood up to snap a selfie, hoping the church would show up in the background. She grinned at the camera and held up her free hand in a little wave.

I'm in Paris! Just chilling with the gargoyles. Can't get any straighter than that.

Becky

She attached the picture and sent off her reply. She felt briefly self-conscious, but the stakes were low and it was too late to take it back. She didn't really care if Sam thought she was cute. It was nice to be able to share pictures with someone without worrying about lighting and makeup and whether or not she looked pudgy.

She finished her wine and headed back to her hotel. She needed to be at the airport bright and early the next morning and wanted to get a proper rest.

Back in her room, she found she couldn't sleep. She'd napped all day and the sounds of the people outside made it hard for her to go to bed as early as she knew she should. She switched on the television and browsed idly through the pay-per-view movies, skimming through the synopses of the romantic comedies. Nothing seemed appealing. She scrolled through the more serious films, but they all struck her as depressing and maybe too much for her to handle. She wanted something light and distracting.

On a whim rather like the one that had led her to click on TwitchyNose's profile, she selected "Adult Films." She scrolled slowly, reading the descriptions and looking at the cover images. She moved to the edge of the bed, trying to get a closer look. She couldn't see much, but began to feel slightly aroused anyway. Sex never seemed to far from her thoughts lately.

Despite her excitement, the porn was equally unappealing - a uniform parade of enhanced breasts, bleached hair and completely bald pussies. She resigned herself to a romantic comedy, something she could watch with half her mind as she fell asleep.

She stopped, about to click the back button. The next film had a different kind of cover than the rest. Instead of a girl with enormous breasts or an immense ass shoving her assets at the camera, this one featured a black and white photo of a woman wearing a blindfold. Her breasts were bare and crisscrossed with heavy black rope. Her lips were parted in a breathless, slightly anxious look. Beside her stood a fully clothed man whose face was hidden in shadow. The movie's title, Submission, flowed across the image in red cursive.

Rebecca moved even closer, until she was kneeling right at the edge of the bed, leaning forward. The man was tall, with wide shoulders. She imagined that Glen would look like that if he was wearing a dark, perfectly tailored suit, instead of the loose shirt and navy pants of his work uniform. Mesmerized, she selected the movie and authorized the exorbitant charge to her room.

Immediately skeptical and regretting her hasty decision, Rebecca moved back and reclined against the pillows. Her hair was tied back in a messy ponytail and she was wearing only her panties and an oversized T-shirt. She stretched out her legs and flexed her toes languorously as she watched the film's opening scene.

The heroine of the story was a woman named Miranda. She worked at a law firm along with several other equally attractive women. Some were lawyers like Miranda and others were assistants or secretaries. There wasn't a man in sight. Rebecca rolled her eyes and sighed at the labored dialogue.

Miranda's firm was bringing in a new partner and everyone seemed to think that what they need was an infusion of masculinity to revitalize the practice. Enter Nathaniel, tall, dark and brooding. He took an immediate interest in Miranda, but she rebuffed him, citing the firm's anti-fraternization policy.

Predictably, Miranda and Nathaniel eventually found themselves working late one night, the only two in the office. Miranda was wearing a very low cut blouse and a miniskirt. Not exactly professionally appropriate, Rebecca reflected.

Nathaniel couldn't keep his eyes off Miranda, stealing glances whenever he thought she was looking away. When she had her back to him, leaning over her desk looking for a document, he moved up behind her. Rebecca watched breathlessly as he grabbed her and turned her around. Before she could do more than begin to protest, he lifted her onto the desk, parting her legs and pushing up her skirt. The sex scene that followed was typical enough, but the details fascinated Rebecca.

Nathaniel was one of the most handsome men she'd ever seen in porn. The way he lifted Miranda and positioned her exactly where he wanted her made Rebecca shiver in excitement. She felt her pulse quicken when he held Miranda's hands above her head, tightly and inescapably in one of his. Miranda squirmed and moaned as he fucked her, utterly helpless but loving every second of it.

The next scene showed them awkwardly interacting at work the next day, Miranda doing her best to pretend that nothing had ever happened and Nathaniel subtly pursuing her. Rebecca skipped forward, eager to find out what would happen when he finally got his way again.

Their next sexual encounter was far less vanilla. Nathaniel revealed to Miranda that his lavish house contained an entire room devoted to his preferred sexual activities. He led her there and after a brief seduction, tied her hands behind her back, ordered her to kneel, and then looped the rope around her ankles. Bound that way, she looked very naked and vulnerable. Rebecca envied her.

The scene progressed rapidly. Nathaniel fucked Miranda's mouth roughly, making her eyes water and her mascara run. When she tried to pull away, he slapped her breasts until they were bright red. Demonstrating his strength again, he lifted her and deposited her over a vibrator so that she was forced to orgasm again and again as he continued to use her mouth for his own pleasure.

Rebecca was both horrified and fascinated by the violence and coarseness of the movie. As she watched Miranda, body shining with sweat, straining against her bonds, crying and squirming, her hand crept between her legs. Rebecca's pussy was wet and her clit already swollen and sensitive. She touched herself softly and moaned.

She closed her eyes, allowing the soundtrack of the movie to fade into the background. She pictured herself and Glen in Miranda's and Nathaniel's roles. She wondered what it would feel like for him to bind her like that and force her to her knees. She shivered as she imagined him pushing his cock into her mouth and using her until he came down her throat. Her fingers circled her clit slowly and she began to pant. She spread her legs wider and slipped two fingers inside herself, pressing the heel of her hand against her clit.

As Miranda and Nathaniel continued the elaborate sexual escapades onscreen, Rebecca's hand moved between her legs more and more quickly. She couldn't remember ever feeling so needy in her life. She couldn't get Glen out of her mind. She wanted him to fuck her so badly. More than that, she wanted him to tie her up and use her. She wanted to be taken and owned. These desires were new and exciting. They consumed her.

A flush spread over her breasts and face. Her breathing came fast and shallow. Her free hand lay limply on the bed, but in her mind, she imagined it bound, held securely in place. She pictured her ankles bound as well, and though she writhed on the bed, she didn't move her feet. The imaginary restraints spurred her on, increasing her excitement.

She wished she'd brought along something bigger than her fingers to fuck herself with. She was certain Glen had a huge cock. She very much wanted to know what it would feel like to be filled and stretched by him. She slipped a third finger inside herself, moaning and shuddering, frantically grinding the palm of her hand against her clit. Her orgasm came suddenly. She came hard, her hips lifting off the bed as she groaned. She fell back to the bed and lay shaking and panting as the little aftershocks of pleasure faded.

She opened an eye and looked at the screen. The movie was still playing. Nathaniel had invited another woman to his dungeon and had both her and Miranda tied up together. Rebecca had just enough energy left to feel intrigued by the idea, but she shut off the television anyway. The coverlet was damp where she'd been lying, so she crawled under the sheets. Her thighs were slippery, but she was too tired to do anything about it. Yawning, she clicked off the light and was asleep within seconds.

The return flight in to RDU was as long and uneventful as the flight out to Paris had been. She found herself constantly distracted by thoughts of Glen. She couldn't decide if she hoped he'd been on duty when she landed. Her curiosity about him was becoming overwhelming.

When she finally found herself on the concourse again, walking towards skycap counter, she was dismayed to realize that her mouth hand gone dry and that the palms of her hands were sweaty. She hated the effect that Glen had on her, but she was resolved to follow through with her desires. She wanted to get this guy out of her system so she could move on. She was tired of having him constantly invade her thoughts. And she was even more tired of being constantly horny because of it.

She approached the counter, looking left and right. Her heart sank. He wasn't there.

"Hi," she said, trying to keep her voice casual and light. "I'm looking for a skycap named Glen. Is he working today?"

The man she'd spoken to looked familiar. He was older, with salt and pepper hair, and a tired and unhappy look that seemed to be an essential part of him. His name tag read Addison.

"I know Glen, but he's not in today. I can give a message if you like, though."Rebecca hesitated for a moment. "No message. I'll come by some other time." She turned and started to walk away.

"You wouldn't happen to be Rebecca, would you?" asked Addison.

Startled, she turned back to face him. "Yes, I'm Rebecca." "Rebecca the flight attendant. Glen mentioned you a couple of days ago. You know, if you really want to talk to him, I'm sure he'd be fine with me giving you his number. More than fine, probably." Without waiting to see if she would accept his offer, Addison grabbed a pamphlet from the display on his counter and quickly jotted down a number. He held it out to her.

"He mentioned me?" she asked, letting the Addison's hand hang awkwardly between them.

"Yup," said Addison simply.

She took the pamphlet and stared at it, uncertain if she should tuck it away in her bag or hand it back.

"Thank you," she said, after a pause that had started to grow uncomfortable. "Maybe I will call him."

5

Since his date with Elena, Glen tried to keep a low profile. Of course, he had still flirted with that strangely awkward little flight attendant, whose name turned out to be Rebecca, but flirting was merely his default mode for talking to women. To men, too, if he sensed they might be gay, or straight but flattered by male attention.

He wasn't surprised that Elena hadn't reaching out to him, but he was a little disappointed. The evening hadn't turned out at all as he'd expected, but he'd felt good about how things had gone - even if he hadn't been able to spill all the steamy details to Addison and Rashid the next day. He had both Elena's number and the rare desire to see her again, yet his gut told him he might be crossing some kind of line if he called.

He lay in bed, not wanting to get up for work, and thought about the women he'd been with recently. He was surprised to find himself hoping they were better off for having met him, and wondered what he could do to ensure that was always the case. Rashid would laugh at this newly aware Glen, but Sarge might be more receptive. He pushed himself out of bed with a groan. These were not the kinds of thoughts he was used to, and certainly not on a workday.

The day was long and boring. Rashid was off and Sarge called in sick, so Glen was working with two guys whose names he barely knew. The airport was busy enough to keep them constantly running, but Glen didn't meet anyone particularly interesting. He got good tips off the ladies, per the usual, helped by a group of retired friends heading off on vacation who happened by. His coworkers groused about it all day.

"Yeah, if I was seven feet tall and built like a Greek god, I'd get good tips, too. Why do you have to hang out here, making the rest of us look bad?" one of them asked, only half joking.

"Don't forget: I'm charming, too, "said Glen, grinning. He offered to split his tips, which encouraged their enthusiasm as they helped him lift the group's overstuffed luggage, but didn't earn them much success in their flirtations with the retirees.

Glen was busy helping a family visiting from Oregon when he caught a familiar head of blue hair out of the corner of his eye. He immediately recognized Amy, noticing that her friend Briana was at her side a few seconds later. The girls hauled their luggage with the determined gait of the travel-exhausted travelers, but both grinned from ear to ear. Amy was more tanned than when Glen had last seen her, but the biggest change was the smile.

There was no one waiting at his counter and Amy and Briana headed straight for him. Amy dropped her bags unceremoniously on the floor and heaved a huge sigh.

"Hi, Glen. I'm glad you're working today."

"Hi, Amy. If I had to guess, I'd say your trip went well. And if I had a second guess, I'd say that you probably didn't spend a lot of time thinking about Josh."

"Josh who?" both girls said in unison, laughing.

"Seriously, though, you're absolutely right," said Amy. "I didn't spend much time thinking about him and even less time missing him. I had a lot of other things to occupy my mind."

Briana grinned and threw Amy a sidelong glance.

"So, I take it you found someone to keep your mind off Josh?" "Several someone's," answered Briana as Amy blushed. "When I saw you at the airport, I have to admit I thought you were just some perverted asshole player. Turns out, you were pretty good for Amy."

Glen felt a small twinge of shame. He hadn't wanted to do Amy any harm, of course, but his intentions had definitely been selfish when he'd seduced her. He was glad things had turned out well, better than he'd planned. He could get used to feeling like this.

Briana leaned forward and pitched her voice low, so only Glen could hear. He leaned down toward her.

"I really appreciate what you did for Amy, even if you didn't mean to. And...her story of what happened between the two of you is, ah, intriguing. I think both Amy and I would like to thank you."

"You're both very welcome. It was my pleasure, truly," said Glen, though he didn't miss the suggestive look Briana leveled at him.

"If you're interested, we'd like to thank you again, more privately and personally, if you get me." Briana gave him another grin. When he looked up, Amy winked and smiled, too.

"That sounds like a fun time," said Glen.

Briana grabbed a pamphlet off the counter and leaned even farther forward to take the pen out of Glen's pocket. She jotted down a telephone number and pushed it toward him. Glen took the opportunity to admire her dark, smooth skin and the ample cleavage her low-cut T-shirt revealed. Her nails were freshly manicured, bright red and long. He wondered if she was the kind to leave scratches.

"Tomorrow would be great, if you're free. Our place? There's plenty of room. Though, I hear you're pretty good at operating in small spaces."

Glen thanked her and promised he would call that night. Assertive girls like Briana were rare in Glen's experience, and he had no intention of passing on the offer. Whether she turned out to be a pussycat or a tigress, he was sure he'd enjoy himself. And he'd make sure they both did, too.

He carried their bags out to the taxi stand and saw them on their way. They were eager to get home and Glen suspected they'd pass out as soon as they reached their beds.

Back at his counter, his coworkers approached him curiously. "You seemed cozy with those two. Make a good tip?"

"No tip," said Glen. "But I did get a phone number."

Both of the other men sucked their teeth and eyed him in disbelief.

"Which one?"

"Both," answered Glen. "The three of us are going to get together tomorrow."

"Some guys have all the luck..."

Glen enjoyed boasting, normally, but he was glad when they dropped the topic and returned to work. His newfound appreciation for how his actions benefited others didn't prevent him from looking forward to whatever carnal pleasures Briana and Amy had in store for him, but he felt inclined to keep his thoughts to himself. Maybe he'd feel different talking about it with Sarge and Rashid tomorrow.

Back home after his shift, he sat on his couch in an old pair of sweatpants. His naked torso was beaded with water from the shower. He had Briana's number in one hand and his phone in the other. He was about to dial when his phone rang, displaying an unknown number.

"Hello?"

Only silence greeted him, though he thought he heard faint breathing and rustling.

"Hello?" he said again.

Again he heard something that was almost certainly the hiss of indrawn breath. He waited.

"Hi," said a hesitant female voice, finally. "This is...This is Rebecca."

He'd recognized her immediately, but before he could speak, she rushed on, her voice growing gradually more frantic and nervous.

"Maybe you don't remember me. The flight attendant you saw that day, outside the washroom. And then you ran into me, literally. And I dropped my suitcase and...well. That's me. Rebecca."

He waited to see if she was done, laughing silently at her discomfort.

"Never mind. I don't even know why I called, you probably don't remember or care. Or whatever. I don't know. Sorry. Bye."

"Wait!" he said. "Don't hang up. Of course I remember you. Cute. Blonde. Always way too nervous. Rebecca the flight attendant."

"Yeah, that sounds about right," she said.

When she didn't say anything further, Glen realized he'd have to do all the work if he wanted this conversation to go anywhere. She'd apparently exhausted all of her nerve merely dialing his number. He was curious how she'd wound up with his number, since he certainly hadn't given it to her himself.

"So, what can I do for you Rebecca?"

There was a long silence, during which Glen could hear Rebecca breathing again. He imagined her biting her lip, perhaps twisting a strand of her long blond hair between her fingers. He found her anxiety strangely charming, a sharp contrast with Briana's equally charming forthrightness.

"I was wondering if you might like to, well, get together some time. For a drink, maybe." She spoke quickly and sighed heavily when she was done, apparently relieved.

"Are you asking me out on a date?" He couldn't resist teasing her. She seemed like a very easy, and enjoyable, girl to tease. He smiled as he spoke, hoping she'd be able to hear it in his voice.

"Is that bad?" she cried.

He could tell she was getting ready to unleash a torrent of apologies and attempt to back down from her invite, so he cut her short.

"No, of course not. I was just teasing. I'd be happy to meet you for a drink. And maybe even more than a drink." He would have winked if she'd been able to see him. He enjoyed the overwhelming effect he had on Rebecca and was suddenly eager to put it into full force.

She sighed again and seemed to regain some of her composure. "When are you free?"

Glen thought quickly of Amy and Briana. They wanted to see him tomorrow, which sounded just about perfect to him.

"I'm free the day after tomorrow."

"Oh, good," she said. "Thursday works for me, too."

"Instead of going for a drink, though, why don't you come by my place? I can do better than an overpriced cocktail in a stuffy lounge. I've also been told I'm an excellent cook. You can judge for yourself. I'm thinking... Korean. How does that sound?"

She didn't respond and Glen wondered if he had somehow overstepped. Perhaps drinks was all nervous Rebecca could handle. He gave her a few more seconds.

"That sounds lovely," she said, finally. Glen heard something different in her voice, but couldn't quite tell what.

He promised to text her his address right away. She seemed pleased, yet eager to get off the phone. Her goodbye was almost as awkward as her hello, and he imagined her wiping sweat off her brow after she finally ended the call.

After sending Rebecca the promised text, he dialed the number Briana had given him. After two rings, she picked up, her voice bright and eager.

"Hello?"

"Hello Glen! I'm glad you got back to me so promptly. Have you thought about my little proposition?"

"I've done hardly anything but think about it, to be honest," he said, laughing. "Just tell me when and where tomorrow and I'll be there with a bottle of wine and a positive attitude."

"Perfect." Briana gave him the address for the apartment that she and Amy shared.

"Briana, you seem like a girl who knows what she wants and knows how to get it. If Amy told you what happened between her and me, you probably know that I'm also the kind of guy who knows what he wants and how to get it."

"Oh, I'm well aware," said Briana, her tone friendly but with a bit of an edge. "I'm not so easy to handle as Amy. Are you up for a challenge?"

Glen felt his eagerness grow at her words. He liked a compliant girl who enjoyed being under his control, but he liked wilder girls who fought being tamed, too. He couldn't wait to see if Briana lived up to her claims.

"I'm sure I can handle you. I very much look forward to the challenge."

Briana laughed as she hung up and Glen found himself wishing he were headed to see them immediately. He was a little surprised to realize that he was physically excited. Two dates with three women in two days was a little unusual for him, but not completely out of the ordinary. He had always been successful with women. But these three were something else. He shifted on his couch, adjusting himself. He had a lot to look forward to.

He arrived at Briana's and Amy's apartment the next day with a good bottle of white wine, as promised. He'd aimed for a relaxed and casual look and wore jeans with a white v-neck T-shirt. He knew how good his chest looked and played to his strengths.

Amy's shy smile greeted him at the door. She wore a short sundress and when she turned to lead him to the living room, it fluttered up to give Glen an alluring peek at her underwear. Briana sat on the couch, remote in one hand and a big red apple in the other. She greeted him almost off-handedly, then took a big bite of the apple, her eyes fixed on his as she patted the cushion beside her.

Glen set the bottle on the coffee table and sat.

"Thanks for the wine," said Amy. "I'll get us some glasses."

She disappeared into the kitchen, her skirt lifting in her wake. From his seat on the couch, the view was even more enticing. She returned focused on carrying three tumblers and a corkscrew, leaving Glen free to appreciate her rather low-cut dress. She didn't appear to be wearing a bra and her breasts moved freely as she walked. He could see her nipples poking at the light floral fabric.

"Sorry, all our wine glasses seem to have gotten broken."

Glen opened the bottle and poured for all of them. He handed a glass to Amy, who sat down next to him, close, but not quite touching. Briana took her own glass and sipped at the wine appreciatively. While Amy seemed tense and nervous, Briana was perfectly relaxed. She wore an old band T-shirt and a pair of yoga pants that looked equally well loved. They drank in silence for a few moments and Glen looked back and forth between them, trying to get a firm handle on the situation.

Amy drank her liquid courage quickly. She poured herself a second glass of wine and when she sat back down, her hip was a fraction of an inch away from Glen's. She rested a light hand on his thigh. On his other side, Briana lowered her glass and moved closer to him. She put a hand on his chest. She gave his pecs a few appreciative squeezes, making no attempt to be subtle.

"You look a lot better in this T-shirt than you did in that dorky uniform yesterday," she said. She took another sip of her wine and then set her glass aside.

"You look pretty good in a T-shirt, too," he said, putting down his own glass.

Amy's hand was still on his thigh, but he suddenly had more immediate sensations to attend to. Briana climbed into his lap and straddled him, her hands running over his muscular arms and shoulders. She bent to kiss him, pressing her soft lips against his, insistent. He opened his mouth to hers and wrapped his arms around her waist, pulling her in close.

She leaned back and grinned at him. "What do you say we head straight to the bedroom? You on board with that, Amy?"

Amy gulped at her wine at nodded. She was the first to stand and led the way to her bedroom. Glen was surprised to see a king- sized bed.

"Take a seat, big boy," said Briana, patting Glen lightly on the ass and pointing towards the bed.

Normally, he might have grabbed her wrist and pulled her in for another kiss, but he was curious to see where she intended to take things. He sat on the bed, back resting on the headboard, hands behind his head. Briana waited until he was comfortable, then turned to Amy.

"Come here. Let's give him a show."

Briana pulled Amy close and started to kiss her. At first she was gentle, running her fingers through Amy's hair and lightly stroking her arms. She cupped one of Amy's breasts through the thin fabric of her dress and played with the nipple. Glen felt his cock start to grow hard when Amy moaned. He remembered how perfect her breasts had felt and suffered a small twinge of envy. He said nothing and continued to watch them.

Amy seemed completely absorbed in kissing Briana. Her eyes were tightly closed and her arms were wrapped around Briana's neck. She made no move to pull away, moaning louder when Briana moved aside the hem of her dress and pushed down her underwear. Glen watched eagerly as Briana's fingers found Amy's pussy. Amy shuddered and clutched at Briana fiercely.

They continued, their passionate embrace. Briana fingered Amy until it seemed inevitable that she would cum, but stopped suddenly. Amy stood panting, a bewildered look of disappointment on her face. She glanced over at the bed and seemed almost surprised to see Glen.

Briana lifted her fingers to Amy's mouth. "Taste yourself," she whispered.

Amy obediently sucked on Briana's fingers, her eyes closing again. On the bed, Glen shifted his weight, fighting the urge to stand and join them. His cock was rock hard and watching Amy suck on Briana's fingers made him long to have her on her knees, her mouth on his cock.

When Amy was done, Briana began methodically undressing her. She pushed her underwear down until they fell to the floor. Her sundress soon followed, leaving Amy standing in the middle of the room, completely naked, vulnerable. She cast another glance at Glen and blushed. He'd already seen her mostly naked, but not on display like this. She was gorgeous and Glen ached to touch her.

Briana hooked an arm around Amy's waist and turned to Glen. "I bet you are rock hard and just wishing you could join the fun, right?"

Glen laughed. "That is one hundred percent accurate."

"You should touch yourself while you watch us. Make sure you're ready when we are. I'm just about done with Amy and then, I promise, we'll come join you."

Not normally one to follow orders, Glen wasted no time obeying Briana. As he unzipped his jeans and freed his cock, he couldn't help but wonder why he was being so completely biddable. He'd meant to give her a run for her money. He wrapped his hand around his cock and started stroking slowly, stifling a groan. He'd have time to turn things around later. For now, he was truly content to watch Briana tease Amy.

Briana guided Amy towards the bed and told her to sit, but warned her not to touch Glen. The bed was huge and there was plenty of room for both of them to sit side by side. Up close, Glen could see that Amy was flushed and glistening with sweat. Her breath was a shallow pant and her gaze darted from his cock to his face. She licked her lips and shivered. He remembered how impressed she'd been by his size and how incredibly tight her pussy had been. He made no move to touch her, but obediently sitting and stroking himself was growing difficult.

Briana pulled open the drawer of the nightstand and produced two pairs of black leather cuffs lined with fur. She dangled them suggestively in front of Amy and winked at Glen.

"How did those get there?" yelped Amy. "They aren't mine."

"I brought them in earlier this afternoon. I thought they might come in handy for what I had in mind. So...what do you say, guys?

Shall we try out my nice cuffs?"

Amy brought them in earlier this afternoon. I thought they might come in handy for what I had in mind. So... what do you say, guys? Shall we try out my nice cuffs?"

Amy's voice shook as she answered in the affirmative. Glen nodded his enthusiastic consent, but could only manage a groan of anticipation and pleasure by way of verbal response. He wondered if Briana intended to use them on him. His heart skipped a beat and he held his breath until she bent forward and closed the first cuff around Amy's right wrist.

Working quickly, but still taking the time to stroke and tease Amy's quivering body, Briana cuffed her wrists to the headboard and her ankles to the footboard. Amy's legs were spread, exposing her dripping wet pussy. Glen was losing his urge to touch her. He was about to give in to his impulses when Briana climbed onto his side of the bed and claimed his attention.

"I bet you want to fuck her very badly, don't you?" she asked as she sat in front of him, watching him stroke his cock.

"Yes, I do."

Briana made no reply, but slowly took off her T-shirt, allowing him, finally, to see her beautiful breasts. Glen could barely form a coherent thought. He groaned at the sight of her. He let go of his cock and reached for her, intending to pull her into his lap, but she batted his hands away.

"I'm in charge, remember?" she said, almost sweetly.

Surprising himself, he leaned back and looked at her beseechingly. Once he was settled, she moved forward, her hands trailing slowly up his legs until she reached his inner thighs. He jumped at her touch, his cock twitching. A drop of pre-cum fell slowly from his cock onto his belly. Briana reached a hand out and wrapped it around his cock, stroking slowly. He closed his eyes and moaned. It felt amazing.

"Why don't you touch Amy while I touch you?" said Briana. He'd been aching to touch Amy since he entered the bedroom.

He was more than happy to accept Briana's direction. As she

continued to stroke him and draw moans from his lips, he put a hand on Amy's belly and felt her jump. He moved his hand lower, until he found her pussy. Her clit was swollen and so sensitive that she whimpered when he first brushed against it. He could tell that she was dying to cum, but guessed that Briana wanted her to stay needy for a while yet. He played with her, stroking her softly, just enough to make her writhe on the bed, but not enough to bring her to orgasm.

"Oh, that's good," said Briana. "You're doing such a good job of teasing Amy. I think you deserve a reward."

Glen gasped when she leaned forward and took his cock into her mouth. She was enthusiastic, seeming to enjoy sucking his cock as much as he enjoyed having it sucked by such a gorgeous, talented, girl. She surprised him by taking almost all of his considerable length into her mouth and down her throat. As her head bobbed, he couldn't resist moving his hips slowly, fucking her willing mouth.

It was very hard to concentrate on touching Amy, but he suspected if he stopped, Briana would stop, too. He could feel himself getting close and groaned at the thought of cumming down her throat, of feeling her swallow every drop. On the bed next to him, Amy moaned and twisted, her cuffs clanking against the bed.

Briana raised her head and looked over at Amy, leaving Glen to groan with disappointment.

"Are you feeling neglected, Amy? Would you like some more of our attention?"

Amy nodded vigorously and rattled her bonds. "Yes, please," she gasped.

"Come on, Glen. I know you want to fuck her tight little pussy just as much as she wants to get fucked by your massive cock."

Glen didn't wait to be asked twice. He straddled Amy and fondled her breasts, teasing her pussy with his cock. She twisted and begged him to fuck her. Her eyes were closed tight, her voice was filled with desperation. Glen loved seeing a girl so needy and had to admire Briana's ability to bring Amy right to that precipice. Unable to hold back any longer, he plunged his cock into her, finding her just as warm and wet and tight as he'd remembered. He didn't restrain himself, fucking her hard and enjoying how her breasts bounced as she moaned beneath him.

Briana watched them both for a moment, enjoying their passion and Glen's focus on satisfying his need. She stood up and removed her pants, then walked around the bed, completely naked. Neither Amy nor Glen paid her any attention. She climbed back on to the bed beside Amy, quickly straddling Amy's shoulders, her back towards Glen. She settled back, muffling Amy's moans by pressing her pussy to her mouth.

"Use that talented mouth to make me cum, Amy," she said, as she started to move her hips, grinding herself against Amy's face.

Glen looked up to see Briana's perfect ass moving back and forth right in front of him. Though muffled, Amy's moans were still audible and had become even more desperate and needy. He could see Briana's juices dripping down Amy's chin, wetting her chest. Amy was bucking wildly beneath him, raising her hips off the bed to meet his every thrust. He groaned, wondering how much longer he could possibly hold back.

He pulled out of Amy suddenly and heard her moan despairingly. He knew she'd been close, but she was his toy to use and he was done using her for the moment. He moved up her body until he was so close to Briana that his hard, glistening cock was resting against her ass as she continued to grind herself against Amy's face. He reached around Briana to grab her breasts, feeling immensely gratified when she moaned and arched her back. Her nipples were hard, nudging insistently against the palms of his hands as she moved. He pinched them, enjoying how she squirmed. Amy seemed to enjoy it, too, pulling furiously against her bonds and raising her head from the bed to plunge her tongue as deeply as she could into Briana's pussy.

Glen slid his hands down Briana's sides. Her skin was silky against his and he could feel her sleek muscles clenching. When he reached her hips, he gripped them tightly, then slowly slid his cock into her ass. She moaned again and arched her back even further. He moved gently, allowing her to adjust to the feeling of his massive cock, but he didn't stop pushing until he was buried completely inside her. Knowing he was fucking her ass just inches away from Amy's face made the experience even more exciting. Amy squirmed and moaned beneath them as Glen began to fuck Briana in earnest, driving his cock into her over and over, pushing her down so that her pussy pressed into Amy's face even harder.

Briana tensed suddenly and then started shuddering. Her hands seized the headboard and held on so tightly that her knuckles turned white. She groaned loudly and panted as her ass began to clench rhythmically around Glen's cock. The sight and feel of her orgasm was more than Glen could resist. A few seconds later, he reached his own climax, thrusting hard and deep into her one last time before pulling out and spilling his cum all over her lower back and ass. He rolled off Amy and fell back on to the bed, panting.

He watched in fascination as Briana turned around and offered her cum-covered ass to Amy, commanding her to lick her clean. Amy obeyed instantly, craning her neck and moaning, doing her very best to get every single drop. When she was finally done, Briana rolled over and collapsed next to Glen. The both lay still for a few moments, allowing their heart rates to return to normal and their breathing to slow.

"Wasn't Amy a good girl?" asked Briana sweetly. "Yes, very," said Glen.

"Do you think we should allow her to cum?"

Glen looked over at Amy, who was flushed and drenched in sweat. Her pussy was still swollen and wet and he didn't think he'd ever seen a girl more needy.

"Maybe not right away," he answered, enjoying the way that Amy moaned as she closed her eyes and pulled on the cuffs that bound her.

"I like the way you think, Glen," said Briana. "Let's rest a little. If she pleases us well enough, perhaps we can allow her to cum during round two."

Leaving Amy in her cuffs, Briana went to fetch the wine from the living room. While Glen was alone with Amy, he bent to kiss her, tasting Briana on her swollen lips. He lay back down, hands behind his head, content, but still excited. He couldn't help but wonder what the rest of his afternoon might hold.

6

After she ended the call with Glen, Rebecca stared at her phone. She was waiting for Glen to text her his address, but a little part of her believed she'd imagined the whole conversation. When the phone buzzed in her hand, she jumped and almost dropped it.

She'd been nervous and the call had started off badly, but in the end she'd gotten what she'd hoped for. More than she'd hoped for. She was surprised to learn he could cook, but delighted his skills extended to Korean food. Perhaps there was more to him than met the eye. She decided to head to out the liquor store and buy a bottle of her favorite Korean black raspberry wine. It wasn't easy to find, but she knew a place that almost always had some in stock. If he really did appreciate Korean food, he'd be impressed. And a little alcohol would definitely help her be less awkward and nervous.

The next night, she sat in front of her laptop in her bathrobe, a towel wrapped around her damp hair. The black raspberry wine sat in a bag next to the door and her couch was littered with half of the dresses from her closet. She couldn't decide what to wear tomorrow and had finally started to feel silly. Her date was almost twenty hours away and she was already starting growing frantic with anxiety. She hated how much of an effect Glen had on her when he was seemingly just a big, dumb skirt chaser.

In a forced attempt to relax, she checked her email. Her dating profile had attracted some attention today, but nothing that seemed interesting. She also had a message from Sam.

What's up tonight, straight girl? And where in the world are you? Reykjavik? Beirut? Detroit?

Rebecca logged in to her account and fired back a reply.

I'm not anywhere special tonight. I'm off work and lounging around in my living room.

She hit send and went back to her email, doing a little housekeeping, blocking and reporting any guys who'd seen fit to attempt to break the ice by sending a picture of their cock next to a can of Coke or shaving cream. She wondered if Glen ever did anything that off-putting.

Her computer pinged and one of her browser tabs flashed. She had an instant message on the dating site. Curious, but ready to block and report if it was a dick pic, she clicked over.

TwitchyNose: Becky, you online?

Rebecca hesitated, her fingers hovering over the keys. She still didn't know why she was talking to Sam—or why Sam was talking to her. The sporadic and casual chatting had been fun, but she wondered if it was wise to have a live chat with her. The message stared back at her, the question mark a challenge. She decided she was overthinking and typed a quick answer.

MileHighBecky: Yeah, I'm here.

Panic sunk in after she hit send. All thoughts of Glen were driven from her head. What was she getting herself into? Or was she just being paranoid?

TwitchyNose: Just lounging around your living room, huh?

MileHighBecky: Well... the lounging part might be a bit of a lie.

MileHighBecky: I'm getting ready for a date. A date that's tomorrow. So I might be over-preparing...just a bit

TwitchyNose: Would I be right to guess you're a little high-strung?

MileHighBecky: You certainly aren't wrong. I'm a nervous wreck about this guy.

TwitchyNose: What's so special about him?

Rebecca leaned back, uncertain. What was so special about Glen? He was tall and good-looking, certainly, but she met handsome men all the time. She'd wanted to dislike him from the moment she laid eyes on him but his unflappable confidence had cast some kind of spell over her.

MileHighBecky: I don't know. He's a total player who works at the airport. He's maybe a complete jackass, but my brain turns to mush around him.

TwitchyNose: LOL. So, he's a bad boy?

MileHighBecky: Not the leather jacket-wearing kind.

TwitchyNose: What makes him a jackass?

MileHighBecky: I saw him take a girl, practically a teenager, into a bathroom at the airport and they came out all disheveled ten minutes later.

TwitchyNose: Oh, so you're jealous cuz you also want to get fucked in a public bathroom stall.

MileHighBecky: What? No!

MileHighBecky: Maybe...

Sam didn't answer for a full minute and Rebecca had ample time to imagine her laughing and shaking her head at her computer screen. Fidgeting, she almost closed the lid on her laptop and walked away, back to her obsessive search for the perfect dress for tomorrow.

TwitchyNose: Naughty, naughty.

TwitchyNose: So where are you in the getting ready process?

MileHighBecky: Trying to choose a dress to wear, mostly. Once I know what I'm wearing, then I can start to worry about makeup and hair and jewelry.

MileHighBecky: I've already removed every stray hair from my body. I even plucked my eyebrows, which I almost never do.

MileHighBecky: Sigh.

She cast a glance over her shoulder at the couch. There were at least a dozen dresses laid out and none of them seemed right. She couldn't decide what message she wanted to send to Glen, or if she even owned the right dress to send it.

TwitchyNose: Why don't you try a few on for me and let me pick? ;)

The words leapt off the screen at her. The suggestion sounded innocent enough, but the winking emoji Sam appended to it made Rebecca's heart beat faster. Was Sam flirting with her? She found herself nervous in the same way she'd been on the phone with Glen. Her fingers trembled as she typed out her cautious reply.

MileHighBecky: Okay. Why not? BRB.

She chose three dresses off the couch, her top contenders, and put them on one after the other, taking a series of tame pictures in her full-length mirror. She sent them off to Sam, telling herself not to think too hard. She didn't find any of them particularly flattering, but if she allowed herself to start worrying, she'd never send anything.

The first was a demure black cocktail dress with lacy three quarter sleeves and a hemline that hit just above her knees. It was pretty, but probably too reserved and formal. The second was navy blue sundress. It had a conservative cut and hemline, but a more casual feel thanks to a sleeveless top and simple folded collar. The third was the shortest, and she had to resist the urge to tug at the hem as she posed. It was a bright red with a tinge of orange, featuring a pattern of white and yellow daisies above bright green stems. It had a plunging neckline and capped sleeves.

She waited impatiently for Sam to receive the photos and send her comments. She drummed her fingers on the table, counting the seconds as they ticked by. When her computer pinged, she jumped and suddenly found herself hesitant to read what Sam had to say.

TwitchyNose: Nice. You have a great body. You could wear anything and this airport guy will think he's lucky.

Rebecca blushed, pleased.

MileHighBecky: Oh, you. You're just saying that to be nice.

TwitchyNose: I most certainly am not. You look great in all those dresses.

TwitchyNose: Sooo, tell me about this date? Where are you going?

MileHighBecky: He's cooking me dinner at his place. Korean.

TwitchyNose: Impressive. Well, I vote for the red one, then. The others seem... kind of formal.

TwitchyNose: And I sense you need to cut loose a little, Becky.

MileHighBecky: Maybe...

MileHighBecky: And thanks. I think I will wear that one. I'm tired of trying to pick. I'm going to give myself an ulcer.

Again, there was a long pause before Sam replied. Rebecca was about to ask her if she was still there when a new message popped up on her screen.

TwitchyNose: It's a pretty short dress. You'd better wear some cute underwear.

Rebecca felt a twinge of sexual excitement. Sam was flirting with her after all. Suddenly brave, she ran back to her bedroom and put on the red dress again. She chose a pair of white lace boy shorts from her underwear drawer and pulled them on. Turning her back to the mirror, she flipped up the hem of the dress, exposing the lacy edge where the underwear hugged her firm, round ass. She took a picture and sent it faster than she could change her mind.

MileHighBecky: How about these?

She gasped at herself, shocked at her newfound audacity. She took off the red dress and sat in front of her computer in only the white lace panties and a matching bra. Without thinking, she slipped a hand between her legs, enjoying the way the soft lace clung to her skin. The panties were damp and she shivered as her fingers traced lightly over her pussy. Was it thinking about Glen that had turned her on? Or was it Sam?

TwitchyNose: Yeah... Yeah, I think those will do just fine.

TwitchyNose: Damn. That airport guy really is one lucky jackass.

MileHighBecky: Thanks, Sam. I'm glad you approve.

TwitchyNose: I approve alright.

TwitchyNose: I hope you have a good time on your date. You'll have to let me know how it goes.

MileHighBecky: I will, I promise.

TwitchyNose: Okay. I'm gonna sign off for tonight. Sleep well and try to stop worrying so damn much. I'm sure everything will be fine.

MileHighBecky: Thanks again. And you sleep well, too.

The little green circle beside Sam's name turned red and she was gone. The end of the conversation felt abrupt and Rebecca wondered if she'd done something wrong. Her cheeks were flushed and she was still aroused. Conflicted, she allowed her hand to slip beneath the waistband of her panties. She pushed it between her legs and touched the slippery wetness there. She teased herself briefly, spreading her legs and letting her head fall back against her chair. She imagined Glen suddenly slipping inside her and she gasped. Would she be in his arms this time tomorrow night?

Her excitement continued to build and her thoughts turned to Sam. What would it be like to have Sam between her legs instead of Glen? Would Sam touch her like this, soft, slow, teasing? She wondered if Sam owned a harness and a strap-on cock. What would it be like to be taken that way?

She'd never pictured herself having sex with a woman and the thoughts made her head spin, but her fingers didn't stop moving between her legs. She moaned, her imagination combining Sam and Glen together until her fantasy wasn't anything concrete, merely a series of intense sensations. Her toes curled and uncurled against the carpet and she shuddered as her orgasm swept over her.

She lay in the chair for a few minutes as her breathing slowed. She didn't understand what was happening to her, but she pushed the confusion out of her mind. Tomorrow she'd see Glen, they'd talk, they'd eat. And perhaps she could put an end to this strange and overpowering little crush. She stood and stripped off the bra and panties, dropping them on top of the red dress lying on the couch. Naked, she padded into the bedroom and slipped into bed, her thighs wet and her mind still filled with thoughts of Glen and Sam.

Briana returned to the bedroom carrying the bottle of wine and two glasses, as well as a big bowl of strawberries, with a neatly folded washcloth beneath the bowl of strawberries. Glen felt a twist in his gut when he saw the berries, remembering Elena. Briana was completely unashamed of her nakedness and walked as confidently as if she was striding down the street fully dressed. He smiled at her as she sat on the bed next to him, pointedly ignoring Amy as she rattled her cuffs against the bed frame.

"Here, have some more to drink, big boy," she said, grinning and handing him one of the glasses.

She watched him drink and silently ate a few strawberries. She bit one in half and held out the remaining fruit to Amy, letting her lick at the juice that dripped from it. She brushed it across Amy's lips, turning them briefly red before Amy's tongue darted out.

"I think we should try something different for the rest of our time together. What do you think, Amy? Glen?"

Amy nodded vigorously and answered immediately. "Yes, whatever you like, Briana."

Glen raised his eyebrows. He was starting to learn what kind of things Briana had in mind and they were surprisingly outside his comfort zone. He was curious what would come next. Briana used the damp washcloth to carefully wipe Glen clean and prepare him for Amy. The warmth of the soft cloth helped stabilize and comfort Glen. Amy's submissive enthusiasm was contagious, but part of him wanted only to grab Brianna and make her submit to him. Instead, he dipped his head once in a nod.

Briana smiled, satisfied. She offered a strawberry to Glen, batting his hand away and putting it directly in his mouth. It was sweet and juicy, but he barely tasted it. His heart was beating hard. For the first time in years, he was nervous in a sexual situation.

She turned away from him and began to uncuff Amy. It was almost like she'd forgotten him. He watched her intently as she gently stroked Amy's body, making her shiver as she lay docilely on the bed. When all four cuffs were removed, she piled them on Amy's belly and turned back to Glen.

"How are you feeling? Recovered? Or is your cock still too sensitive to play again?"

He was surprised at her directness but it was still appealing. She cast an appraising glance between his legs and waited for his answer.

"Um, I could maybe use a bit more time to recover. If I want to be at my best, I mean."

"Well, I'm not going to let you just sit there and take a nap. You need to keep busy."

He raised an eyebrow at her, wondering how she would react if he turned the tables on her now. He thought of the cuffs and wondered how quickly he could get them on her. He glanced over to the other side of the bed, wanting to grab them off Amy's belly, but she was gone. He turned back to Briana, opening his mouth to speak. She moved forward suddenly, wrapping her hand around his limp cock.

He squeaked as she held him, her grip firm as she ran her thumb over the head of his cock. The sensation was an overpowering mix of pain and pleasure.

"Stay very still, unless you want me to stroke you a lot harder," she whispered.

Already, his cock was growing hard in her hand, but it only made the pain worse. He wasn't ready to be touched yet and certainly not so insistently. He raised a hand to push her away, only then noticing Amy standing beside the bed, holding the cuffs. Deftly, she closed one around his outstretched arm and buckled it shut. She pulled his arm back and attached the cuff to the headboard before he'd fully registered what was happening.

"What...?" he asked, twisting his body to the side to look up at his trapped wrist.

He hissed as Briana stroked his cock. He was rock hard now but he was still desperately sensitive.

"Stay still," she said. "Hold out your other hand for Amy." Bewildered at his own obedience, he did as he was told and

Amy quickly cuffed his other hand to the headboard. He tested his

bonds with a series of swift tugs. He thought he might be able to break free if he needed to, but he wasn't entirely sure. Another wave of somehow pleasant fear and nervousness rushed through him.

He allowed Amy to cuff his ankles to the sideboard. When she was done, she returned to the bed beside him and kissed him. Her lips tasted of strawberries, and he ached to touch her ample breasts when they pressed against his chest. He pulled at the cuffs again and was rewarded only with a series of merciless and deliciously painful strokes on his cock. He gasped against Amy's lips.

"Please, Briana. That's a little bit too much."

LIVING GRY

Amy sat back so Glen could see Briana's twisted grin. She continued to stroke him, enjoying his twitching and grimaces of pain.

"That's kind of the point, big boy. You seemed to enjoy torturing Amy. Now I'm going to let her get a little revenge. I, of course, will enjoy that thoroughly and will also take advantage of your delightfully compromised position."

He stared back at her, refusing to give her the satisfaction of watching as he tried to squirm away from her touch. He was uncomfortable, but part of him was curious how far she would go. And he couldn't deny that despite his wincing, he was rather enjoying what she was doing to him. When she stopped and sat back on her heels, he sighed with a mixture of relief and disappointment.

Looking devious, Amy moved to kneel on the bed between his legs. Her hands were cool on his thighs and he couldn't quite hold back a shiver when she moved them higher. She wrapped one hand around the base of his cock and then leaned forward to take it into her mouth. He groaned and leaned his head back, closing his eyes. She was far gentler than Briana and though he was still over- sensitive, her mouth felt amazing. With each stroke, she flicked her tongue over the head of his cock. Soon he was lifting his hips from the bed in time with the bobbing of her head.

Suddenly, he felt a cool pressure on his chest. He opened his eyes and looked down to find one of Briana's feet resting there. She wiggled her toes and then moved her foot upward until they rested against his lips.

"You seem like the kind of guy who has a decent appreciation for a woman's feet. Why don't you show me how much you appreciate mine?"

Obediently, he parted his lips and allowed her to slip her toes into his mouth. He knew she meant for him to feel submissive, but as his tongue moved along her tender skin, he enjoyed the way she shivered. It was hard to concentrate on

92

what he was doing with Amy still stroking and sucking his cock, but he did his best, focusing on each of Briana's toes in turn, feeling a flush of triumph and pleasure when she moaned.

He was unable to suppress his own moans when Amy's free hand crept between his legs to cup his balls and gently squeeze. She was careful not to hurt him. The slight pressure felt good, but also reminded him of how vulnerable he was. If she decided to squeeze harder, there was not much he'd be able to do about it. His attention drifted away from Briana's toes to focus on what Amy was doing. It felt amazing, and the small knot of fear in his belly only added to his pleasure.

"Amy, stop. You're distracting him from his work."

Amy lifted her head, lips red and glistening, but disappointed. Glen groaned and bucked his hips, trying to gain some friction from her hand, which was still holding him loosely, but with a look from Briana, Amy settled both of her hands primly into her lap. He wanted to speak, to tell them to stop teasing, but Briana's toes were still in

his mouth and he understood that his best chance at getting what he wanted was to please her.

Her toes trembled in his mouth. He moaned when he saw her move a hand between her legs. She was wet and her fingers slipped easily into her pussy. She caught his eye and smiled.

"Don't you wish you could be fucking me?"

He nodded his head, eager. He wasn't sure how much more teasing he could take. He pulled on the cuffs, recalling how Amy had squirmed and pulled earlier.

"Amy, I think he needs to be taught the same lesson in patience that you have learned."

Briana sat up and moved her foot away from Glen. She trailed a hand up his leg slowly, pausing to brush just one finger across the tip of his cock. He moaned and raised his hips but she didn't give him the touch he craved. Her hand continued up over his belly and chest. The contact was subtle, but he shivered. When she reached his face, she grabbed his chin firmly and turned his face to hers. She kissed him deeply, pushing her tongue past his lips and into his mouth. He kissed back eagerly, wishing he could grab her to pull her gorgeous body against his. He wanted to feel her silky skin and the weight of her breasts. When she broke the kiss, he moaned.

"Now, I'm going to do something that you will enjoy, but I'm also going to ask you for something that's very hard. Obey me and you will be rewarded. Disobey and you will regret it. Do you understand?"

He nodded, flicking his eyes to Amy, trying to guess what they had in store for him. She smiled and winked. Briana pinched his chin hard, forcing him to turn his gaze back to her.

"No matter what I do, don't move unless I give you express permission. Got it?"

He nodded again and she let go, turning her back to him. Shooing Amy towards his feet, Briana straddled him. He looked hungrily at her perfect ass, remembering how good it had felt to fuck her earlier. Her pussy was only inches away from his rock hard cock, and the urge to move his hips, to try to slip inside her, was overwhelming. He resisted, unwilling to test her authority. She lowered herself until she came to rest on top of him. He could feel her wetness and his cock strained against her. He wouldn't even have to move his hips now, he thought. Merely flexing might be enough to slip his cock into her tempting pussy. He moaned and balled his hands into fists, but otherwise didn't move.

"Lay back, Amy. I think you finally deserve to cum. I'm sure Glen agrees that you've been very, very good."

Eager, Amy lay back and spread her legs, draping them over Glen's. She rested her hands lightly on his calves. She moaned when Briana leaned forward and buried her face between her legs. Glen trembled and his cock twitched. Briana's dripping pussy was even more exposed now and he would have given anything to be able to touch her. Amy was shivering even harder than him, her hands clenching spasmodically on his legs.

She'd been so close to cumming earlier that she only needed a few moments of attention from Briana's tongue to reach orgasm. She cried out and dug her nails into Glen before going limp.

Amy was panting and shivering, but Briana didn't stop. Soon, Amy was moaning again, gripping Glen's legs painfully. He knew he would find marks there later - red half-moons made by her fingernails, perhaps even bruises. He watched the two women, rapt, trying to control his own excitement. He didn't know how much longer he could remain still.

Briana reached between her legs and grabbed Glen's cock. He jumped, then groaned as she angled it back so that she could slip it inside herself. Her pussy was warm, wet and tight, and he thought he'd never felt anything more glorious. He wanted desperately to move his hips, to fuck her, to feel any kind of friction, but Briana stayed completely still. He feared she might withdraw if he disobeyed her, so he tried to slow his hammering heart and forced himself not to move.

Amy was writhing and moaning as Briana continued to lick and suck at her pussy. Glen tugged at his bonds again and wondered briefly if he might be able to cum even without the friction he wanted so badly. Just being buried inside Briana while Amy twitched and cried out was almost more than he could bear. He licked his lips.

"Please, Briana."

Neither woman reacted to his voice, but Amy's trembling intensified and her fingers dug like claws into his skin. He hissed, but she only gripped him tighter.

"Oh, God, I'm going to cum," she said, her voice ragged.

Her cries were even louder this time and as she bucked her hips, Glen felt Briana's pussy clench even tighter around him. He groaned, absolutely desperate.

"Please, please, Briana. I can't take this anymore. I just can't. I need you to touch me, I need to fuck you, I need to cum."

She turned to look at him over her shoulder. Her face was wet and he suddenly yearned for her to kiss him again. He wanted to taste Amy off her lips. The thought made his cock twitch inside her and she grinned.

"You seem to be having a hard time staying still, big boy."

"I'm sorry, I can't help it," he moaned. He shook his head. The power Briana had over him was incredible. He'd never been in this position before. He was usually the one listening to his partner plead and beg for his touch.

Laughing, Briana finally started rocking her hips. She moved slowly, gliding up and down the considerable length of Glen's cock. He gasped with pleasure and tugged at the cuffs. He wanted to grab her ass and pull her down onto him, to be as deep as possible inside her. She ignored his needy gasps and moans and continued to move slowly and deliberately.

"Amy," she said. "Why don't you go entertain him a little?"

Glen could hear the tension in Briana's voice and knew that she was enjoying this as much as he was. He could feel her excitement building.

Amy came to sit beside him. Her face and breasts were flushed and when she cuddled up against him, he felt her nipples poking into his skin. She reached a hand between her legs and dipped two fingers into the wetness there. Smiling, she pressed the fingers against his lips. He lapped at them hungrily, loving the taste of her and wishing he could have been in Briana's place.

Amy continued to tease him until Briana suddenly sat up straight. She settled against him, impaling herself deeply on his cock.

Her hand was between her legs and she was touching herself. She was completely intent on what she was doing, ignoring both Glen and Amy. Her pussy tightened like a vise around him and he groaned. She was going to cum around his cock. He wanted badly to buck his hips, to fuck her so that he could reach orgasm at the same time, but Amy guessed his intentions and shook her head at him. He groaned and pulled at the cuffs in frustration.

A few seconds later, Briana shuddered and her pussy clamped his cock so tightly it almost hurt. She moaned and let her head fall forward, her whole body shaking. Before Glen could say anything or even begin to beg for his own release, she lifted herself off him and turned to face him again.

"Oh, God, please, you have to let me cum." "Do I?" she asked, grinning impishly.

"Please." He didn't like how raw and needy his voice sounded, but he was helpless to control it.

"Very well. You were obedient up until now, so I'm going to give you another set of instructions. How does that sound?"

He had no idea what she could possibly expect of him now, but he nodded.

"Good. It sounds good."

"I'm going to wrap my hand around your cock, quite firmly. And I'm going to stroke you, up and down, exactly twenty times. No more, but not less. After that, I will let go, no matter what. If you haven't cum, that's just too bad. You can go home and jerk off later. Do you understand?"

Again, he nodded. He didn't trust himself to speak.

As she'd promised, she wrapped her hand around him. He moaned happily as she started stroking. It had seemed like a daunting prospect at first, but he was desperate to cum. She counted out loud as she moved.

"One. Two. Three. Four. Five. A quarter done, big boy."

He groaned. He ached. He'd never wanted to cum so badly in his life. Beside him, he heard Amy laugh.

"Six. Seven. Eight. Oh, I can feel it coming. Are you close?"

"Yes, yes," he gasped.

"Nine. Ten. So much precum..."

"Fuck. Don't stop. I'm going to cum," he cried.

As Briana reached eleven, Glen tilted his head back, the cords standing out in his neck, and came explosively. The mess was incredible, cum spilling over Briana's hand and shooting across his belly, a few drops even landing on his chest. She counted twelve and then thirteen as his cock continued to spurt. His entire body was tense and the headboard creaked ominously as he pulled at his bonds again.

"Fourteen. Fifteen."

Suddenly, her touch was unbearable. He'd cum so hard that his ears were ringing, but now he was too sensitive once again.

"Stop. Please," he said.

"Oh no, not 'til I'm done," she said, smiling. "Sixteen. Seventeen."

He gasped and bucked, but he could not stop her. She concentrated her strokes on the tip of his cock, mercilessly torturing him. Her hand was slick with his cum but the friction was still far too intense.

"Eighteen. Nineteen."

He trembled uncontrollably and begged her to stop through gritted teeth. Only one more stroke, he thought.

"Twenty," she said. She gave him one last squeeze and then sat back, looking satisfied. "That was a lot of fun, guys."

Glen's cock twitched against his belly and he jumped. He closed his eyes as both women laughed.

7

Rebecca spent all afternoon getting herself ready to go to Glen's, spending far more time on her makeup and hair than normal. Fussing over her appearance gave her a distraction to save her from focusing the events of the previous night off her mind. She studiously avoided her laptop, an embarrassed blush spreading over her cheeks every time she glanced at it, or even walked past the desk.

Although she'd spent what felt like forever perfecting the details, her makeup was light. She wanted to look casual and confident, even if she was a nervous wreck in her head. She'd already considered calling Glen to cancel more than once. The thought of hearing his particular brand of deep-voiced playful mocking in was enough to make her reconsider. He had a strange way of rendering her unable to say no.

She swept her hair into a loose ponytail, teasing a few artful strands out to frame her face. She slid in a few strategic bobby pins for insurance. As she patted everything into place, followed by a quick spritz of hairspray, an image flashed, her hair, tousled and sweaty, bobby pins tumbling out as Glen grabbed her. Was that how the night would end? Was that what she wanted?

She found her carefully selected outfit on the sofa where she'd left it and picked up the now soiled white panties. She shivered as she slipped them on, her thoughts shifting abruptly away from Glen. Could it be Sam that she really wanted to see tonight? She shook her head to push the thoughts away. She wasn't gay and she'd never even met Sam. She was just confused, lonely. Maybe her mother was right. Her eyes drifted to the photo of Panopticon and she wished— for the umpteenth time—that her job hadn't forced her to give Pan up. She sighed. How pathetic, mere steps away from a crazy cat lady.

Her phone pinged, interrupting her reverie. The notification told her someone from the dating site had sent her a message, but Rebecca resisted the urge to check it. She had the uneasy feeling it might be Sam, and she wasn't prepared to talk to her right now. She dismissed the notification and dropped her phone back onto the table after checking the time. She slipped the dress over head and zipped it

up. It flared prettily as she twirled in front of the mirror. She'd drawn out the process as much as she possibly could and it was time to admit she was ready. She hesitated, but was determined to get out the door.

She collected her purse, phone and the bottle of blackberry wine before heading out the door, closing it decisively behind her.

Rebecca's heels clicked as she walked down the hallway toward Glen's apartment. Her steps slowed until she was barely moving. Her heart thundered in her chest, so loud she feared the doors around her would start opening one by one as Glen's neighbors came to investigate the disturbance. Her cheeks reddened and the wine almost slipped from her tingling and sweat-dampened fingers. The walls loomed, pressing in on her. She tightened her grip on the bottle and turned to walk away.

Suddenly Glen's door opened. He stood in the doorway, a cocky grin spreading across his face.

"I heard you clacking up the hall but you didn't knock, so I came to check on you."

Her flush deepened and she opened her mouth. When no particularly brilliant response occurred to her, she closed it with an audible snap, leaving her staring back at Glen lamely.

"Here," she said, holding out the wine.

He took it and examined the label with interest. Rebecca was acutely aware of the sweaty finger marks she'd left around the neck of the bottle. She again contemplated turning tail and running, but with her luck, she'd probably twist an ankle and wind up falling flat on her face. Graceful exits were not her specialty.

"We can stay out here in the hall if you want, but it is customary for guests to actually come inside my apartment," said Glen, smiling. "You might even find it comfortable in here."

"Yes, alright," she answered, her voice weak. She couldn't tell if he was making fun of her.

She edged past him into his brightly lit apartment. It was smaller than her place, but much less spare, more like a home. None of the furniture matched, and books and DVD cases were strewn everywhere. A PlayStation console sat beneath the television and a controller on the coffee table. Rebecca spotted the red light winking on the controller and knew that he'd been playing before she arrived. She followed Glen into the galley kitchen and nearly bumped into him when he stopped to put the wine in refrigerator.

"I figure we can save that to go with our meal. But if you'd like a drink now, I have some soju."

Still clutching her purse and wondering if she could pull off leaning casually against the doorframe, Rebecca nodded. In his tiny kitchen, Glen appeared even more massive than she remembered. He moved easily and confidently around the kitchen, cutting a slice of crisp apple into matchsticks and dropping a few into a pair of tumblers. Next, he added several paper-thin slices of lime and some ice cubes. He poured in a generous measure of soju and topped the glasses up with soda.

Rebecca smiled delightedly as he handed her one of the drinks. They clinked their glasses before taking a sip. "Wow.

You did that like a pro." She eagerly sipped the drink again and made an appreciative sound. "It's lovely."

He set his drink down on the counter and turned to the stove. "Come and see what I'm making for us."

Her anxiety, which had started to recede, roared back as she stepped closer. His presence was overwhelming. They were almost touching. Rebecca held herself rigid and took a gulp of her drink.

One of the pans on the stove held slices of chewy rice cake in a thick red sauce. A large pancake, studded with pieces of shrimp, squid and green onion, filled the other. She watched as Glen stirred the rice cakes and added a cupful of green onion before sprinkling on a generous amount sesame seeds. He held out the bamboo spoon.

"Here, have a taste. I hope you like spicy food."

Rebecca leaned forward, suddenly awkward. It felt strangely sensual to allow him to feed her, but she told herself to focus on how delicious the food looked and smelled. The sauce was sweet and rich and the rice cake perfectly chewy. Glen watched her, gauging her reaction.

"It's so good," she said. "I would never have guessed you were so talented in the kitchen."

Glen quirked an eyebrow and she winced, belatedly catching the backhanded compliment.

"I'm sorry... I mean, you just don't look like the type who'd be into food." She stopped. That was even worse. "What I'm trying to say is that I'm pleasantly surprised. Let's leave it at that..." Her cheeks were burning again and she was acutely aware of how silly she must look standing in his kitchen, clutching her drink in one hand and her purse in the other, sputtering like a fool.

Glen laughed. "Don't worry, I'm not that easy to offend."

He put a hand on her shoulder and gently guided her out of the kitchen. He suggested she drop her purse on a side table near his front door and she gladly accepted. When she opened her hand, her fingers ached from white-knuckling her bag. His hand weighed warm on her skin through her light sweater. It made her heart race. This close to him, and away from all the spices in the kitchen, she could smell him, too. She didn't think he was wearing any cologne or aftershave, but she caught herself leaning closer to him.

They sat on the couch, Rebecca awkwardly crossing and uncrossing her legs, unable to find a comfortable position. Glen seemed perfectly at ease and she frowned when he arched an eyebrow at her again. His constant self-possession irritated her.

"Have you had a good week so far?" she asked inanely, to cover her nervousness.

Glen grinned and took a long swallow of his drink. "Yes, as a matter of fact, I have. It's been a lot better than I expected."

Pleased that she'd found a safe discussion topic, Rebecca relaxed. "Anything you'd like to share?"

Glen's eyes sparkled. "I'm not sure you really want to hear about it. You strike me as a little bit prudish. At least on the surface."

Rebecca bristled. "What makes you say that?"

"Well, remember our first encounter? I haven't forgotten that expression you had on your face. It was a perfect mix of flustered and disapproving. I nearly expected you to waggle a finger at me."

She hid behind her drink, giving herself a moment to think. "What if you'd gotten caught? I'm fairly sure whatever you were up to in there, with that girl, is against some sort of airport regulation. Probably it's even against the law."

Glen laughed. "Yup, probably. But I like to enjoy myself. And I wasn't about to pass up the chance to make an unhappy girl a little happier."

Rebecca stared at him, remembering how terribly curious she'd been at the time. She wondered again what exactly had happened while she'd stood outside the restroom, stuck in the agony of indecision. She swallowed the rest of her drink in one gulp, nearly choking on an apple matchstick.

"I'm not quite the prude you think I am," she said when she'd recovered. Trying to maintain her dignity, she crossed her legs and looked at Glen as evenly as she could. "What did you two do in there, exactly?"

"You really want to know?" he asked. She nodded.

"Even if it's a dirty story?"

She nodded again, exasperated. Did he think she was a blushing virgin?

Glen shifted until his knee was lightly touching hers. She repressed a shiver and waited for him to speak.

"Well, first, she dropped to her knees and sucked my cock," said Glen. He paused, gauging the reaction of his words on Rebecca. Her eyes widened, but she didn't pull away from him. "Then I told her to touch herself while I watched. It was an entertaining show, but the main point was to make sure she was extremely needy."

Rebecca felt a surge of warmth between her legs and she leaned closer to Glen, pressing her thigh against his.

"Why?" she asked, her voice barely a whisper.

"I wanted her to beg me to fuck her. And she did, eventually, when she couldn't stand it anymore." He paused again, enjoying Rebecca's quickened breathing. Her breasts had already drawn his eyes more than once, but they drew his gaze more insistently now as they rose and fell against her dress.

"Then what?"

"When she begged, I picked her up and fucked her while holding her completely off the ground. She's a small girl, so it was easy to manhandle her."

He gazed into Rebecca's face, recognizing the unmistakable haze of desire in her eyes. He knew she was still uncertain about him. He leaned forward and kissed her parted lips, making her gasp. Despite her initial surprise, she returned the kiss enthusiastically.

After a heartbeat more than a second, he sat back. "I think supper must be ready by now. Shall we eat?"

She blinked, trying to focus on his words. He'd kissed her and she felt like she'd nearly lost her mind. One more second and she might have climbed into his lap.

"Yes, of course, let's eat." Dazed, she watched him stand up and walk to the kitchen. For the first time, she really looked at him, admiring the way he appeared so at home in his body, moving far more gracefully than she ever did. His jeans and T-shirt fit him perfectly but she didn't imagine that he'd spent anywhere near as much time agonizing over his outfit as she had.

She stood and moved around the small apartment, taking in as many details as she could. In the kitchen, plates and cutlery clanked. There were no pictures anywhere that she could see, but the living room looked lived-in in a way her own apartment never had. Several books on the coffee table sandwiched bookmarks between the pages, but none looked dusty or abandoned. Below the television, she saw three more PlayStation controllers and a big stack of games. In one corner of the room, a cluttered table held what looked to be a disassembled computer monitor and a bunch of delicate-looking tools. She picked up a tiny screwdriver and hefted it in her hand.

"Come and get it while it's still warm," Glen called from the kitchen.

Rebecca jumped and nearly dropped the screwdriver before replacing it carefully, exactly where she'd found it. She felt guilty for poking around his things.

"Coming," she answered, hurrying to join him.

A small round table and two chairs sat tucked away at the back of the kitchen. Glen had moved the rice cakes onto a serving plate, dressing them with extra sesame seeds and a drizzle of sesame oil.

On another plate, he'd sliced the pancake into perfect wedges. As she approached the table, he pulled the blackberry wine from the fridge.

"Chopsticks or fork?" he asked.

She saw that he'd put both at one of the place settings. "Chopsticks."

He whisked the fork away and twisted the cap off the wine bottle. He filled both glasses in a smooth, adept motion, not spilling a single drop of the dark red, almost purple, liquid.

Rebecca squeezed past him.

"You're so big. This kitchen is a pretty tight fit for you," she said.

"I manage," he laughed. "When I'm on my own, I mostly eat in the living room anyway. The couch is more comfortable and I've got Netflix on the PS3."

"The bachelor life," she said, unable to keep a critical note out of her voice.

"And what's wrong with that? I'm young, I'm single. And I paid a lot more for that couch than I did for this kitchen set. Priorities, you know."

"I guess that makes sense. I spend so little time in my apartment, I guess I just don't think about it much."

"Well, I do spend a lot of time here, so I put the money and effort into the things that matter to me." He stopped and grinned. "I didn't skimp on the bed."

Rebecca blushed and looked away. She picked up her glass. "A toast."

"A toast to what?" asked Glen, raising his own glass. "Um... to the airport."

Glen looked quizzical.

"Yeah, the airport. We met there and it sounds like you've had at least one other pleasant experience thanks to the airport."

They clinked and drank.

While Glen served the food, Rebecca grew aware of exactly how small the table was. Although he was keeping his long legs to one side as much as possible, their knees still brushed. Every time they touched, Rebecca had to suppress a quiver.

The rice cakes were delicious, still perfectly chewy and wonderfully spicy. She discovered, hidden in the thick red sauce, several peeled hard-boiled quail eggs. She concentrated on eating, sipping at her wine whenever her tongue needed a little soothing. Glen seemed to be enjoying the wine, too, and kept both of their glasses full.

As they ate, they spoke about their jobs and their younger lives. Though curious, Rebecca avoided asking any more questions about women. She knew Glen probably had many more intense, erotic stories to tell but she wasn't sure if she wanted to hear them. The earlier story had had an unexpected effect on her. She'd been intensely aroused, but had also felt an unfair twinge of jealousy. Glen certainly didn't belong to her, and his sexual confidence and experience was part of what drew her to him, even if it also made her uncomfortable.

The element of dominance in Glen's story intrigued her. The way he told it, he'd taken control of that girl so easily, using his power in a way that Rebecca hadn't experienced. She looked across the table at Glen, trying to imagine what it would be like to be at his mercy like that, to allow him to tease her until she resorted to begging.

Glen looked up to find Rebecca staring at him. Intrigued, he asked, "What's on your mind?"

Caught off guard, she diverted from her mental fantasy. "The food is amazing."

Glen didn't buy it, but didn't press her.

When the last wedge of pancake and bite of rice cake were gone, Glen stood and cleared the table, piling the dirty dishes in the sink. The wine bottle and both glasses empty, and they both felt the effects.

"I neglected to make any dessert, since Korean desserts are not really my strong suit, but I do have this," said Glen, pulling out a small bottle of Korean plum wine.

"Oh, wow. I think you might be trying to get me drunk. But, I love that stuff, so pour me a glass. But just a little one." She pinched her fingers together for reference. They moved back to the living room and sat on the couch, hip to hip. Rebecca had enough wine in her not to worry about awkwardness anymore. The food had been delicious and Glen was more easygoing and less overwhelming than she'd imagined. She picked up his PS3 controller and pressed the power button.

"What were you playing? Call of Duty? Battlefield? Some other game where you run around trying to shoot a bunch of teenagers with really big guns?"

To her surprise, Glen actually looked embarrassed.

"You might tease me for this, but I'm actually playing a game called Katamari Damacy. Have you heard of it?"

She shook her head. "What's it about?"

"Well, technically, it's about restoring all the stars and the moon to the sky and avoiding annoying the King of All Cosmos. But the plot isn't very important. What you actually do is roll up really big balls of stuff."

She lifted both eyebrows. "Stuff?"

"Well, you start with tiny things. Bugs, paperclips, coins. And then you move on to bigger things like shoes and chairs and traffic cones. Eventually you can roll up people and then cars and, well... just bigger and bigger things."

"Maybe I've had more to drink than I realized. Because...what the fuck?"

He laughed and took the controller from her. He grabbed the remote and turned on the television. The soundtrack of the game, upbeat and melodic, filled the room. On the screen, a tiny green figure with a large horizontal cylinder for a head stood in front of a colorful knobby ball.

"Watch," said Glen.

The little green figure start to push the ball around a room scattered with an array of eclectic objects. Rebecca watched, fascinated as the ball grew larger and larger, picking up all sorts of strange junk. The soundtrack was catchy. Full of liquid confidence she made up lyrics and sang along, teasing Glen as he rolled and collected more objects into his massive ball.

"What's the goal?" she asked, pausing her operetta.

"Mostly just to roll the biggest ball possible. Though, on some levels you have goals related to the number and kind of objects in the ball."

She watched him play until the end of the level. The victory cinematic was even stranger than the rest of the game.

"You try," said Glen, queuing up the first and easiest level and handling her the controller.

It took her a few tries to catch on to the control scheme, but once she got the hang of it, she beat the level easily. She moved on to the next one, playing attentively, her tongue poking out of the side of her mouth as she swerved around tight corners, rolling up everything from broccoli florets to rolls of toilet paper. She hadn't played a video game since she was a kid. She'd forgotten how much fun it could be.

She'd just collected a toothbrush when Glen slipped an arm around her shoulders and gently kissed her shoulder. She turned to face him but he nudged her back towards the game.

"Don't stop playing. You're so cute and you look like you're having a really good time. But you're winning too easily. I'm going to make it a bit more challenging."

She gasped as he nuzzled her neck, nibbling gently at the sensitive skin there. He dropped his other hand to her knee and squeezed. She tried to return her focus to the game, but he moved his hand higher until his fingers slid beneath the hem of her skirt. Her body trembled and she felt herself growing excited.

"Is that distracting?" he asked, his voice teasing. "Yes," she said, her voice already breathless.

"Do you want me to stop? Or do you want me to keep going?"

She bit her lip. On the screen, she guided her ball straight into a wall and bounced away, postage stamps and lollipops flying off in all directions.

"Keep... keep going." Her cheeks, already flushed from the wine, grew warmer.

Glen pushed her thighs apart and brushed his fingers against her smooth, soft skin.

Rebecca knew Glen wanted her badly, his cock already straining

against his jeans, but she needed and wanted something different from him tonight. He pulled her body close, his erection pressing against her thigh. Her eyes flicked away from the screen to look at him.

"Keep your eyes on the screen and keep playing. As long as you keep that ball rolling and growing bigger, I'll keep touching you. But if you stop playing, or if you fail the level, I'll stop. Understood?"

She nodded and licked her lips. "Yes, I understand."

"I also want you to keep your face pointed at the TV, eyes open and on that screen. Is that clear?"

She nodded again and let out a faint moan. Her hands, clutching the controller, had grown slightly sweaty. On screen, she continued to roll her ball, attempting to make up for her lack of concentration with an abundance of caution.

Glen kissed her neck again, pushing the collar of her dress out of the way so he could kiss her collarbone. She shivered and parted her thighs further. She wanted more than kisses, but she wasn't going to ask for it so quickly. He slid his hand higher on her thigh until he found her soft, white panties. She moaned when Glen's fingers brushed the fabric and she smiled when she felt his breath quicken against her neck.

She considered putting down the controller and turning to climb into his lap and kiss him. She could feel his erection against her leg and he felt huge. A desperate surge of desire and curiosity shot through her. She craved to know what it would feel like to be fucked by him. Still, she believed he would stop touching her if she stopped playing. She wasn't ready to test him. She blinked and brought the game back into focus.

As he nibbled on her earlobe, Glen carefully pushed aside her underwear. He was pleased to find her already soaking wet. The little blonde flight attendant looked so prudish, but she was, as he'd suspected, in need of some satisfaction. He savored the way she gasped as he pushed his fingers inside her. She was tight, but her slickness made it easy. He knew if he wanted to, he could make her cum within a minute or two. He checked the screen to make sure she was still playing and had to suppress a laugh when he saw that she was guiding her ball into the same outraged clown riding a bicycle over and over again. She was clearly not paying that much attention to the game.

"You should pay more attention to what you're doing," he whispered as he started moving his fingers inside her, stroking her slowly and deliberately.

She moaned and bucked her hips, trying to force him to penetrate her more deeply. "I'm trying, I swear, I'm trying." Her whole body trembled and she almost dropped the controller. Her hands were damp with sweat.

"Keep trying, Rebecca. Remember: if you stop, I stop."

She moaned. "You wouldn't really stop, would you?" Her voice was filled with need and he loved it. Holding back was going to be very hard, but he had the feeling that the eventual release would be worth it.

"Oh, I never joke about things like that," he said, and nipped sharply at her earlobe. "As long as you keep rolling that ball around and growing it bigger, I'll keep teasing you. If you beat the level, if you make a ball big enough to win, then I'll reward you. If you lose, you won't get anything."

She shuddered. He didn't sound like he was joking, though he was obviously enjoying himself. Still, Rebecca couldn't believe he'd actually put a stop to things if she failed to complete the level. She kept playing.

Her panties soaked through quickly and her hips moved rhythmically as she fucked herself with his fingers. He slipped another finger into her, loving how tight she was. He desperately wanted to knock the controller out of her hands, flip her over so her ass was in the air and take her, right there on the couch. Teasing her was torture for him, too, but he enjoyed her need far too much to give in to his own.

He put his thumb over her swollen clit and stroked it gently. She shivered and arched her back. Her eyes slipped closed and her left hand dropped away from the controller. On screen, the little green figure stopped moving.

"Keep playing, darling. Or else."

She lifted the controller again and opened her eyes. "Oh, please don't stop," she moaned. She was surprised at how desperate she felt. "I'm so close."

"Don't you dare cum until you've beat this level. As long as you're playing, I'll keep teasing you, but no orgasm until you're done."

"Oh, please..." she breathed, unsure what she was even asking for. She guided the ball around the screen erratically, vaguely looking for the objects she needed. But she could hardly focus, and lost more objects to collisions than she gathered.

Glen moved his hand from her shoulder to her hair and gently massaged her scalp. It was incredibly sensual but also unbelievably distracting. She closed her eyes again and heard the sound of her ball colliding with a vehicle. She opened her eyes to find her ball had lost a huge proportion of its volume. Her eyes flicked to his face again. He was smiling. It occurred to her that he wanted her to fail. The thought was perplexing, but exhilarating.

His touch between her legs had grown light. He knew she was close, but refused to help her go over the edge. She tried to focus more intently on the game, but it was starting to look like a lost cause. The countdown timer would be running out soon and she was still nowhere near the target size. She moaned in frustration and clamped her thighs around his hand. He wouldn't really stop, would he?

Glen fought his urge to simply allow Rebecca to cum. When it became clear she was going to lose, she'd tried to trap his hand between her legs, but that wouldn't be enough. Her pussy grew even tighter around his fingers and he knew that despite his gentle touch, she was only a few seconds away from cumming. On screen, a warning sound played and then the countdown timer ran down to zero. The screen went black, except for the little green figure falling to its knees in failure in the bottom right corner.

"Oh no, how unfortunate," said Glen. He pulled his hand out from under her skirt, his fingers wet.

"What? No. Please don't stop," she gasped. "I want to cum. I need to. I'm so close."

"No, not tonight."

"What? Please. I can feel how hard you are. I know you want

me."

"I do want you, Rebecca. I want you bad. But what I want even more is for you to feel what submission feels like. For you to understand denial. And for you to know how much better it will feel when I do allow you to cum."

Outrage flared and she turned to face him, anger clearing her head. "You don't own me, you don't get to make decisions for me."

"That's quite true," he said. He raised his wet fingers and pressed them against her lips. She tasted herself and squirmed. "But if you allow me this power, if you grant me this control over you, I promise you will find it worthwhile."

She stared at him, lips parted, her eyes searching his face, trying to read his intentions. She wanted to defy him, but his words had made her feel strange.

"Okay," she breathed. "Fine. I grant you control over me."

8

As soon as the words left her lips, a strange mixture of apprehension and excitement washed over Rebecca. She absolutely still wanted to crawl into Glen's lap and grind her throbbing pussy against his hard cock, but her desire to please him with her obedience was even stronger. She shivered and searched his face for some hint of what he might want from her. Her entire body quivered with need and she hoped he would relent.

"Very good," he said. He kept his voice steady, but his own need was hard to resist. He stroked the soft skin of her thigh, enjoying the tremors it sent through her. He kissed the side of her neck, eliciting another moan. He had to be careful. She was so aroused that the slightest touch might be enough.

"What now, Glen?" she asked, her voice husky, but tinged with a delightfully submissive note that he loved.

"Do you have any plans tomorrow?"

She shook her head and a stray strand of her hair escaped from a bobby pin to fall into her eye. She didn't seem to notice, but Glen smiled and tucked it behind her ear.

"I'm going to give you two choices and I promise that I don't mind which you choose. Either one will be very enjoyable for both of us, though in very different ways. However, they will involve sacrifice on your part. Do you understand?"

Rebecca nodded breathlessly, the strand of hair freeing itself again, bringing several friends along with it. Her carefully arranged her was now in disarray and Glen thought it only made her look more beautiful.

"Your first choice is as follows: I will give you a kiss good night that will make your toes curl, and then I will send you home. I won't tease you anymore and you can sleep in your own bed tonight. Your dreams might torture you a little, but I will be kind and let you have peace. While we're apart, you'll agree not to touch yourself and not to make yourself cum. Tomorrow, we'll meet up again and pick things up where we left off. I will kiss you, I will tease you. I will make you

beg for release. I do not promise you will receive it. I might give it to you. I might not. Do you understand your first choice?"

Rebecca nodded again, though she pressed her body against his and he could tell she was hoping her second option would be more immediately satisfying.

"And here's your second choice: You'll spend the night here, with me, in my bed. You haven't earned the right to cum yet, so I will use your body and pleasure myself as I see fit. It will be very hard for you, I promise. You will be constantly hoping for release, but I will not grant it, not until the morning. However, once morning arrives, you'll be allowed to cum and I swear it'll be worth the wait. Do you understand your second choice?"

She licked her lips and nodded again.

"Just so I'm sure you understand, explain them to me."

"Either I can have an easy night, but no guarantees of an orgasm tomorrow," she said, her voice trembling. "Or, I can have a harder night, but with guaranteed satisfaction at the end." She stopped and bit at her lip.

Glen sat back, breaking contact with her. Her eyes darted down and she saw that his cock was still hard.

"The choice is yours," he said, grinning. "I'll give you a few minutes to think about it." He stood and walked to the kitchen, leaving her alone on the couch.

Rebecca breathed deeply and pushed the hair out of her eyes, her mind racing. She craved him, he'd made sure of that. Away from his gaze, she began to feel rebellious. If she chose to leave, how could he stop her from touching herself and cumming a dozen times if that's what she wanted? And if she stayed, would he really have the self- control and expertise to keep her on the edge all night long? The timid part of her was leaning toward going home. Maybe she wouldn't even come back. As she'd said, he didn't own her.

At the thought of ownership, she pulsed between her thighs. The idea of being owned, of being controlled, was tantalizing. She picked up the PS3 controller and remembered how much effort she'd put into obeying his instructions and how good it had felt. She'd failed her first challenge and hadn't been allowed to cum, but he was offering her a greater challenge now and she sensed that the reward at the end would be worth the effort. Her decision made, she restarted the first level of Katamari Damacy and waited for Glen to return.

Glen had taken their glasses to the kitchen and then stood in the hall, watching Rebecca weigh her options. He'd told her he'd be happy with whatever she chose, but when he saw her relax, her decision clearly made, he felt a little twinge. His desire for her was bordering on overpowering, but it was obvious he would have to hold off for a little longer. Assuming as neutral an expression as he could, he stepped behind the couch, lowering a firm hand onto Rebecca's shoulder. She twitched, but she kept her eyes on the television, faintly defiant.

He bent forward and spoke so softly she had to strain to hear him.

"Have you made your decision?"

"Yes," she said.

She paused, poking her tongue out as she guided her ball of miscellaneous junk up a ramp and into a wide-open vista of matchsticks, spare change and thumbtacks. "I'm going home. Mayeb I'll come back, maybe I won't."

Glen smiled and pressed his lips to the hot skin of her neck. His hand left her shoulder and crept down her body. He pushed her dress up as high as it would go and slipped his fingers beneath her damp panties. He stroked until she moaned and trembled, then pulled his hand away.

"You'll be back," he said, grinning.

With a triumphant cry, Rebecca dropped the controller on the sofa next her bare thigh. "Beat it," she said, breathing harder than the video game warranted. She stood and smoothed her skirt, trying to ignore the discomfort of her damp underwear and the way Glen was smirking at her.

"Too bad you didn't beat it earlier. You might be flushed and breathless right now for an entirely different reason."

"Thank you for a lovely evening. The food and the drinks were wonderful. And you...you were just terrible." She smiled ruefully as she retrieved her purse and stood by the door with what dignity she could muster.

Glen opened door for her, but before she could dart out, he put a hand on her elbow. She stopped, looking up at him expectantly. He could tell he had her, but he'd allow her this defiance. For now.

"I'll text you tomorrow. Until you're back here, you're not allowed to cum. And don't think you can lie to me. I'll be able to tell."

She started to scoff, but he silenced her with a kiss. Her lips parted easily for his tongue and he could feel how much she wanted him to relent and allow her to stay. He wanted it too, but he forced himself to break the kiss and guide her out the door. He watched as she walked away, unsteady on her feet.

All the way home in the cab, Rebecca debated texting him. He'd proven himself every bit as arrogant and cocky as she'd expected and she knew she should tell him off, delete his number and forget she'd ever met him. Shouldn't she?

It wasn't what she wanted, though. She felt an almost perverse desire to disobey him out of spite. He'd turned her on, teased her, tormented her and now he expected her to keep up the torture all by herself because he'd commanded it? She huffed so loudly the cabbie turned his head to ask if she was alright.

"Yes, yes. I'm fine. Just... tired."

She squeezed her thighs together, but it only made her feel more needy. She pulled out her phone, not sure what message she intended to send. Her thoughts were interrupted by the message icon flashing on her screen. Sam, she realized. She couldn't bring herself to read what Sam had written. She dropped the phone back into her purse and watched the dark scenery spool past the car window. The rest of the ride passed quickly and in complete silence.

Opening the door to her apartment, she missed the silky feeling of Panopticon twining around her ankles. Normally, she would spend some time on her laptop or find a late-night movie on TV, but instead she undressed and crawled straight into bed. She was annoyed to find that she felt like a child on Christmas Eve. She wanted to fall asleep as quickly as possible to bring the morning faster. If she were good, there'd be a text there from Glen in the morning. Maybe she could rush over immediately and finally relieve all this sexual tension.

Eyes wide open in the dark, she gritted her teeth. Why was she even thinking this way? She could relieve her tension now, if she wanted. He'd never know, despite his arrogant assertions to the contrary. Sighing with pleasure, she pushed up her T-shirt and cupped one breast, squeezing the nipple lightly. Her other hand slid under her panties, her fingers circling her clit eagerly. She groaned. It wouldn't take long, just a few flicks of her fingers and she'd be able to sleep, satisfied and defiant.

Her toes curled and her hips rose slightly off the bed. Just a few more seconds and she'd be there. It would be so sweet, so perfect. Her whole body trembled.

With a frustrated groan, she stopped, pulling her hands away from her body and balling them into fists.

"Fuck," she muttered into the darkness.

She felt something akin to guilt, but it was exactly guilt that had stopped her. She wanted to please him. She wanted to see him tomorrow and hear him praise her for her obedience. She kicked her feet under the covers and the rolled over onto her side, her shoulders hunched.

"Fuck," she said again, resigned.

Sleep was a long time coming. She could think of nothing but sex. Her eyes kept drifting to the clock on the bedside table as the night ticked slowly away. Her desire did not abate quickly, but part of her savored it. She really was like a kid at Christmas. She couldn't remember the last time she'd felt this eager, this full of anticipation. It drove out all her anxiety and self-doubt. Finally, she drifted off, her head still full of thoughts of Glen. In her dreams, he didn't hold back or tease her.

Glen closed the door behind Rebecca, then stood pressing his forehead against the cool wood for a few seconds. His cock was almost painfully hard. He knew if he opened the door, he could have her back in his apartment and pressed up against the wall, begging to be fucked, in less than thirty seconds. He imagined how satisfying slipping inside her would be and sighed. He was denying himself to tease her and it was proving to be a lot harder than he'd anticipated.

He went to the kitchen and washed every single dish, willing his erection to subside the entire time. He tried to concentrate on his chores, but his mind kept returning to the silkiness of her hair and the warmth of her body pressed against his. The kitchen was spotless when he stopped, every surface gleaming, every single tool in its place. He couldn't remember the last time it had looked so flawless and organized. Apparently sexual frustration was the secret to a clean house. What must Martha Stewart's sex life be like? He flicked off the light and escaped to the living room before he gave in to his urge to alphabetize his spice rack or sort his carrots by length.

He tried to play Katamari Damacy again, but the upbeat soundtrack seemed steeped in eroticism now. Every note reminded of him of how Rebecca had squirmed and panted beside him as he touched her. He dropped the controller and looked at the time. It was late, but he didn't think he could sleep. Was she still awake? Was she as consumed with need as he was?

He turned off the television and the PS3 and sat staring at the dark screen, trying to clear his mind. He wanted the delayed gratification to be worth it for both of them, but he was having trouble thinking rationally. There was something about Rebecca that got in the way of his usual cool detachment. He ran his hands through his hair in frustration.

He stood and stripped off his clothes, dropping them in a pile on the couch. He walked naked to the bathroom and turned on the shower as high and as hot as it would go. He stepped under the burning spray, letting the daggers of water hit his dark olive skin until it grew dark red. When he could hardly stand the pain any longer, and the air was so steamy he could barely see, he turned the temperature down until the water ran cool and gentle. Usually, the contrast was bracing and enough to clear his mind, but tonight nothing rid him of his thoughts of Rebecca.

He closed his eyes and wrapped a hand around his cock. Instantly, he was as hard as he'd been while he'd been teasing Rebecca. He groaned, vainly wishing it could be her hand on him or, even better, her perfect mouth. Her kisses had been such an arousing combination of soft and aggressive, he could only imagine how she would go down on him. He stroked himself slowly as the cool water sluiced over his reddened skin. He braced himself against the tile wall as his legs started to shake.

Had she obeyed him or had she given in to her urges and

touched herself before bed? Either alternative was unbearably arousing. He pictured her hair a sweaty, tousled mess, her dress partially undone but not removed, her panties tangled around one ankle. His fantasy could have continued down any number of exciting paths, but merely thinking of her naked and touching herself was enough. His orgasm came over him with shocking strength and speed, and his knees nearly gave out as he spilled thick strands over his hand and into the swirling water at his feet.

"Fuck," he said, his voice as unsteady as the rest of him.

He stood under the water, leaning against the wall, until the trembling in his legs subsided. The edge of his desire had dulled, but he still felt completely unsatisfied. Not since he was a teenager had he been more tempted to start stroking himself again so soon after cumming. He knew it would be pointless. He wouldn't be satisfied until he could have that strange, awkward little flight attendant in his bed.

Soon, he thought as he stepped out of the shower. Now that he'd regained a bit of equilibrium and self-control, he started planning what he'd do the next day. However defiant she'd tried to be as she was leaving, she'd put herself in his hands, and he wanted to make the most of it. Before tucking in for the night, he made sure his phone was charging next to his bed. Grinning in a way that would have made Rebecca shiver if she could see, he set an alarm for 6 AM.

Rebecca's sleep had been restless, punctuated by intense sexual dreams and brief periods of wakefulness during which she alternated between cursing Glen and wishing he were next to her, naked, huge, hard. Dawn lightened the sky and birds twittered happily when her phone pinged loudly, drawing her from yet another sexually charged dream. She raised her head from her pillow and dug her fists into her sleep gummed eyes. The sheets and blankets were a tangled sweaty mess around her. It took a few moments for her become consciously aware of what had woken her. Dreading what she might see, she picked up her phone. She was in no shape to be called into work suddenly.

She was relieved to see it wasn't the airline contacting her, but sat bolt upright as she recognized Glen's number and the full force of last night's memories hit her. All the self-assurance she'd felt while in the clutches of alcohol and sexual desire had left her. She was suddenly convinced Glen had changed his mind about her and was texting to tell her not to bother coming over, he'd made other plans. Plans with a girl who wouldn't run away when he tried to fuck her.

Her hands shook. She couldn't bring herself to open Glen's message. Last night, she'd felt confident and desirable and like she played his game well. For a brief while, she'd even fancied she might be able to beat him at his own game. But in the cold light of dawn, with her sweaty hair straggling down her back and her mouth reminding her that she should have had a big glass of water before bed, she could only think how frustrated he must have been to watch her refuse him and walk out of his apartment.

She deliberated for too long and the screen of her phone went dark again. She dropped it on the bed and buried her head in her hands. He'd said he'd be fine with either decision, but of course, obviously, he'd wanted her to stay. How could it be otherwise?

Resigned, she picked her phone again and unlocked it, going straight to Glen's message.

Did I wake you, darling?

She stared, puzzled. There was only one message and it said nothing about how she'd left. Her worry surpassed her confusion, she answered.

Yes, but it's okay.

She combed her hair with her fingers and tried to pat it into place while she waited, unsure what to expect next. She hugged herself against the growing chill of her bedroom.

Did you sleep well?

She couldn't bring herself to admit her sleep had been fractured by constant thoughts of the delicious things she wished Glen were doing to her, so she sent back only a curt "yes" and looped a few strands of hair around her index finger as she waited for his next message.

I'm going to send you something by courier in a few hours, if you send me your address. I promise you'll like it.

Fighting the insecurities threatening to overtake her, she typed and sent her address. She waited ten minutes, shivering in her thin T- shirt, but there were no further messages from Glen. She got up and paced around her bedroom, trying to decide what to do next. All signs pointed to him wanting to see her again, but she couldn't help but fear she was misinterpreting things. Maybe his intentions would become clear when the courier arrived. Until then, she'd have to find a way to keep busy and not allow her worry to consume her.

She caught a glimpse of herself in the mirror and flinched. She couldn't answer the door to anybody looking like this. Grateful for something to occupy her time, she rushed to the shower and spent the next hour bathing, washing away the night before.

When she emerged, she wrapped herself in her bathrobe, made a cup of tea and curled up on her couch. It was still annoyingly early and she couldn't find anything interesting on television. She clicked from channel to channel, bored with the options. She inhaled the faint lavender of her tea and put her head down, idly watching a popular music video countdown. Her mind whirled, caught between her eyes soon grew heavy. She'd only had a few hours of sleep and her body was desperate for more.

The sound of her doorbell jolted her awake. A group of overly tanned twenty-something's chattered away on the TV and bright, buttery sunlight streamed in through her window, blinding and disorienting her. She flailed, spilling her forgotten cold tea. She cursed at the puddle and flew to her front door, adjusting her bathrobe to make sure she was covered.

A bored bike courier stood outside her door holding an unremarkable brown box about the size of thick paperback book. He tilted his head and read off the label.

"It just says Rebecca, no last name. You Rebecca?" "Yes," she said.

"Good enough. Sign here, he said, holding out a clipboard.

When she was done, he slipped the clipboard back into his bag and handed her the box. He jogged off down the hall before she could even thank him. She watched him go, hefting the box curiously in one hand.

She closed the door and forced herself to clean up the spilled tea before she opened the box. Her stomach twisted as her anxiety crept back. She couldn't really imagine that Glen would go to the expense and trouble of hiring a courier only to deliver her some form of cruel rejection, but her angst wouldn't allow her to dismiss the possibility entirely.

She carried the box into her bedroom. It felt like the appropriate setting as she sat on the bed, holding her breath and thinking again of a child on Christmas morning. She slit the tape open with a nail and pulled open the flaps. Inside she found a small blue envelope with her name, and a black box with fine matte finish. Buzzing with the thrill of anticipation and hot rush of arousal, she picked up the envelope and drew out the single creamy sheet of paper it contained.

Rebecca,

I want you to be thinking about me all day, so I sent you a gift that will be a potent reminder. Wear it, starting right now, and come to my place at eight tonight. And don't forget: I'll know if you disobey.

-Glen

Her urge to defy him on principle rose up, but was quickly squashed by her excitement and the craving to please that he'd woken in her. She lifted the black box and opened it with care. It was lined with bright pink satin and the lid was hinged with black satin ribbon. Nestled in the lining was something that

Rebecca initially mistook for some kind of abstract jewelry. She picked it up, surprised at the substantial weight. The metal was cold against her hand and she shivered as she recognized what she held.

It was a buttplug, but made with such an elegant swooping design that it looked more like art than a sex toy. It was small, but heavy, and made entirely of smooth stainless steel. Though alone, she blushed and closed her hands over the plug, as if someone might see. A flash of color caught her eye and she found the box also contained a handful of sample packets of personal lubricants. Her blush deepened.

Glen's instructions had been clear and she wanted to follow them, but she faltered. She opened her hands and looked down at the toy. She traced an appreciative finger over it, enjoying the smoothness and elegant design. She tried to imagine what it would feel like inside her, but she'd never used anything like it before and had no frame of reference. The thought of wearing it all day, of revealing it to Glen when she saw him tonight, made her squirm. She felt herself growing wet. She glanced at the alarm clock and saw it wasn't even noon. So many hours to wait.

She lay back against her pillows and spread her legs. She wished Glen were there, hard and ready to take her, but it occurred to her that he'd sent this proxy to satisfy a little bit of her urge to be fucked. The knowledge made her hot. She opened one of the packets and coated the toy with lube. She reached between her legs and ensured that she was equally slippery and ready.

The toy had grown warmer sitting in her hand, but it was still cooler than her skin when she pressed it against herself. She shivered and gulped, then started applying gentle pressure. Initially, her body resisted, but she breathed and did her best to relax, focusing on her eagerness to please Glen. She gasped as the plug slid into her, almost popping into place. She adjusted her hips and tugged gently on the ring that remained outside of her body, a moan she couldn't suppress escaping her lips. The pressure was subtle but undeniable and her desire was immediately inflamed. Her fingers drifted upwards and brushed over her swollen clit. It would be so easy and he'd never know, would he? Groaning, she moved her hand to her side. No, maybe he wouldn't know, but she'd know and her need to obey was genuine and seemed to be growing stronger.

Determined to go about her day as he'd instructed, she stood up and started dressing. The weight and pressure were enough that she couldn't ignore them. When she sat down to pull on her socks, she gasped and squeezed her thighs together. It was going to be a challenging few hours.

Once dressed, she moved around the apartment tidying and arranging her few belongings. She couldn't remember the last time she'd paid this much attention to her apartment. Everything felt so much more vivid than usual. The minutes ticked by slowly, each heavy with her anticipation. Every so often, she'd bend or twist in just the right way and the plug would shift ever so subtly, making her gasp and reach out to grip the nearest solid object, her knuckles turning white.

When the apartment was nearly spotless, she wandered back into her bedroom and opened her closet. It was not quite 1 PM, but she couldn't stop thinking about what the evening had in store for her. She wanted to pick out what to wear. It had to be perfect.

She discarded all the other options she'd considered for her first date with Glen. None of it suited her current mood or her expectations for the evening. She chose a casual dress that fitted her like a comfortable T-shirt. It was a soft blue, complimenting the blue in her eyes and highlighting the pink in her cheeks. The dress hit her mid-thigh, so she pulled on a pair of boy-short underwear, blue with white dots, cute and comfortable. She turned and looked at her butt in the mirror, checking that the underwear hid her secret.

She didn't bother with a bra, liking the way her erect nipples showed through the thin fabric of the dress. She sat and brushed her golden hair until it flowed like silk, then pinned it up into a messy chignon with a large clip. Makeup and jewelry seemed superfluous, so she completed her simple outfit with a pair of white leather sandals. She felt comfortable and confident and every time she moved, she was reminded Glen was waiting for her. She had so many hours left to wait and no idea how to distract herself from her gradually increasing arousal.

She flipped open her laptop and immediately saw she had several messages from Sam.

Hey. Good luck on the big date.

I guess I didn't catch you early enough. I hope you're having fun with the player.

Let me know you're okay. Haven't heard from you in a while.

And the final one:

Okay, I guess I did something wrong the other night...

Rebecca felt a surge of annoyance. What right had Sam to expect immediate answers from her? But, it was true that she hadn't gone this long without replying to her before. It was also true that she still felt awkward and conflicted about what she'd done after Sam had signed off. All Sam had done was flirt a little and Rebecca had flirted right back—and built a fantasy around her. Added to the general awkwardness and confusion of her feelings about Sam, Rebecca suddenly felt guilty. She'd finally succeeded in distracting herself from her need to fuck Glen, but it was by fantasizing about someone else.

She opened a new window and hovered her hands over the keyboard. She needed to send Sam and answer, it was only polite, but she had no idea what to write. None of the possibilities seemed right and the more she thought about both Sam and Glen, the more she squirmed in her seat. She was still hesitating, wishing Glen would put an end to her indecision by suddenly appearing by her side and fucking her silly, when she heard her phone ping loudly in the other room.

9

Rebecca minimized the empty chat window and ran to look for her phone in her bedroom. She knew the message could be from her mother or even work, but she hoped it was Glen. Despite his earlier request that she arrive at his place at 8, she wished he'd summon her earlier. Or maybe announce he was standing outside her door, unable to wait a minute longer to have her.

Another courier should be arriving in about an hour. While you're waiting, download this app.

Appended to the message was a link. Intrigued, Rebecca clicked and followed the instructions to download and install the app. She opened the app, confused and excited, but decided to wait for the courier to arrive before exploring further. She clenched her pelvic muscles, enjoying the weight of the plug inside her and wondering what interesting sensations the new package might contain. She guessed that Glen had decided to make the day more challenging for her than she'd expected, but she couldn't claim she wasn't enjoying it.

She returned to her computer. Without allowing herself any more time to overthink, she sent Sam a message.

The date went well. I was nervous beforehand and I didn't spend much time on the Internet, then I came home and went straight to bed. I'm not upset about anything if you aren't.

She hit send and then waited, though Sam didn't appear to be online. When she didn't get an answer after a few minutes, she closed her laptop and resumed wandering around her apartment looking for things to keep her occupied.

Glen enjoyed all the planning and organization he'd put into his interactions with Rebecca today. He was looking forward to seeing her, but focusing on all the little details allowed him to keep his desire in check. As tempting as it was, he didn't want to masturbate again. He wanted to be needy, full of desire, nearly as much as she would be, when they finally met again.

After texting Rebecca about the second courier, he packed up another box, sliding in a note. He wished he'd told her to arrive earlier. It wasn't until he'd checked the time on his phone for the third time in the ten minutes that he realized how anxious he was for eight o'clock to arrive. He convinced himself it gave him more time to prepare and build up the sexual tension.

If he handled things well, the night would be explosive.

He gave the courier a big tip in exchange for his promise to let Glen know as soon as Rebecca had received the package.

"And if you could let me know how she looks, I'd appreciate that, too. I'm setting up a big date for us tonight and I'm hoping she's excited for it."

"Sure thing," said the courier, eyeing the small package curiously. Normally, he didn't care for special instructions or requests, but Glen's energy and demeanor made him curious about the girl who would receive the package.

After he was gone, Glen paced around his apartment. He looked at his phone, opening the app he'd instructed Rebecca to download and hoping that she'd done as he'd instructed. He checked his messages, knowing there was no way the courier had yet delivered the package, but hoping anyway.

It was just past two when Rebecca's doorbell rang again. She jumped up from the couch where she'd been failing at watching television and rushed to the door, gasping as the plug shifted inside her. She greeted the courier, out of breath, a flush spreading across her cheeks.

"Rebecca?" he asked.

She nodded, her embarrassment growing. His knowing smile made her uncomfortable. She could swear he was examining her from head to toe. Had he guessed her secret? The thought was both terrifying and exciting.

She signed for the package and retreated into the apartment, closing the door with a sigh of relief. Though her hands were shaking, she went immediately to the bedroom and sat cross-legged on the bed, shivering when the pressure of the mattress pushed the plug deeper inside her. Glen was certainly making it hard to have the peaceful day he'd promised, but she didn't think she could hold it against him.

This package, like the last, contained an envelope and a smaller box. Inside the box was a small purple object she could only guess was another sex toy. It was made of silicone, only a few inches wide, with two bulbous ends, one smaller than the other, and a flexible, curved middle. She turned it around in her hands, flexing it and squeezing various parts of it. Suddenly, it sprang to life, vibrating fiercely. She gave a little cry and dropped it before laughing at her own skittishness. She found the part she'd pressed and applied pressure for a few seconds until the vibrator shut off. She put it down and opened the envelope, pulling out another hand-written note.

Follow the instructions in the app to pair the vibrator to your phone. You'll also find information on how to wear the vibrator. I want you to wear it for the rest of the day and to show up here with it tonight. And make sure to keep your phone close at all times. Enjoy the rest of the day. You can be quite sure I will be thinking about you nearly constantly...

-Glen

Rebecca opened the app and followed the instructions, but the shaking in her hands had intensified so she needed to start over twice before she succeeded in pairing the vibrator to her phone. She was tempted to explore the app further, trying to guess what Glen might have in store for her, but she knew he wanted her to be surprised. Her curiosity and her sexual desire were building, but she found them both overpowered by her need to please him. She imagined it would be very satisfying to have him compliment and congratulate her on her self-control and obedience. Some part of her still wanted to rebel, but that part was getting weaker. The idea of trusting Glen, of giving herself over to him, of pleasing him with compliance, was more appealing than anything else. Why should she deny herself this harmless pleasure?

After consulting the instructions again, she figured out how the vibrator was designed to fit her. One half slipped inside her and the other pressed against her clit. In her already aroused state, even that minimal pressure was enough to make her squirm. After inserting it, she pulled up her panties and made sure they were nice and snug, ensuring the vibrator would stay safely in place.

She got up and walked to the living room. The plug had been a mild distraction, but the vibrator was much more intrusive, especially at first. She found herself struggling to do anything besides think about it. She kept her phone in her hand as instructed, but nothing happened. She paced around her apartment until the friction and pressure of the toys was too much to bear. She sat at her computer, voicing an indignant moan as she shifted her weight on the chair, seeking a position that wouldn't stimulate her any further.

She opened her laptop and logged in to the dating site to check on her message to Sam. Several messages waited in her inbox, most from men she had no interest in. Glen was more than enough to keep her busy at the moment. There was also a message from Sam, and she was still online. Rebecca clicked on Sam's message.

Glad to hear things went well. Tell me about it?

Rebecca was debating what, if anything, to reply when a chat window flashed open.

TwitchyNose: You really there?

MileHighBecky: Yeah.

TwitchyNose: So the date went well? Did he like your carefully chosen outfit?

MileHighBecky: Yeah, it seems like it.

Rebecca hesitated. Her fingers hovered over the keys and she chewed her lip anxiously. She shifted in her seat, but the movement did nothing to clear the fog of sexual arousal that had settled over her mind. Glen certainly had her exactly where he wanted her: needy, distracted, and unable to focus on anything but him and the release he'd surely provide.

MileHighBecky: Things got pretty hot and heavy. And... um... kinky.

TwitchyNose: Kinky? I kinda had you pegged as vanilla.

MileHighBecky: I guess there's more to me than meets the eye.

TwitchyNose: I guess there is.

MileHighBecky: I'm seeing him again tonight.

TwitchyNose: Oh, well then it must have been a very good time indeed.

MileHighBecky: And he's been kind of teasing me all day

long...

She was relieved Sam couldn't see her. After hitting enter on her last message, she blushed a deep red. She could feel the blood burning in her cheeks. Waiting for Sam's answer, she fussed with her hair and rearranged the pencil and two paperclips that she found on her desk. Annoyed at how much even such a minor confession had flustered her, she tried to change the topic to something less anxiety inducing.

TwitchyNose: Teasing you? That sounds... intriguing.

MileHighBecky: Just sending me messages and things. Building anticipation for tonight, I suppose.

TwitchyNose: Is it working?

Rebecca giggled and squirmed in her seat, unable to suppress a gasp and a moan. It was working, alright.

MileHighBecky: Yeah. I'm looking forward to seeing him again.

TwitchyNose: Good.

MileHighBecky: What about you? Did you do anything fun last night? Or do you have any big plans tonight?

TwitchyNose: Well, I spent some time with a girl last night. She reminded me of you. Blonde, a little nervous and jumpy. New to the queer scene. Cute as a button and with an absolutely amazing ass.

Rebecca's blush deepened as she got the distinct impression Sam was flirting with her again. Her pulse quickened. She hadn't thought it possible to be more aware of the toys inside her, of their subtle yet insistent pressure against her most sensitive spots, but she was suddenly unable to think of anything else. She almost blurted out her situation to Sam, but the impropriety of it all stopped her. Fighting her growing arousal, she directed her attention back to the screen.

MileHighBecky: That sounds nice.

TwitchyNose: Yes, it was nice. Very nice.

MileHighBecky: What did you two do?

TwitchyNose: We went out for drinks. Neither of us had eaten any dinner, so the alcohol went to our heads pretty quickly. I ended up inviting her back to my place. So your things weren't the only ones that got hot and heavy last night.

Though she'd wanted to avoid the topic of sex, Rebecca found herself overwhelmed with curiosity. Her aroused state made her brave, desperate to find out what had gone on between Sam and her nervous blonde date.

MileHighBecky: Oh yeah?

TwitchyNose: She really did remind me of you. Even more so when I pulled her dress over her head. She was wearing cute little white lace panties like the ones you showed me. She didn't keep them on for long, though.

MileHighBecky: Oh?

TwitchyNose: No, not long at all. I gave her a lot of attention and made sure she was well taken care of. It was quite delightful… and quite loud.

As she read Sam's last message, Rebecca suddenly felt the vibrator nestled in her pussy buzz to life. It throbbed against her twice and she cried out in surprise and pleasure. It was almost like Glen knew what she was doing and . Or warn her, reminds her who was in charge today. Gasping, she held on to the edge of the desk and looked back at the screen.

TwitchyNose: We fell asleep after that, but we did wake up for round two, which was even hotter, in the middle of night.

MileHighBecky: Wow. Good for you. Sincerely.

Rebecca struggled to type, her heart hammering in her chest. Thoughts of Sam and this mysterious girl who was like her flashed through her mind. And what had Sam done to take care of the girl, exactly? She pictured Sam by the side of a bed, on her knees, the blonde girl's legs dangling over her shoulders. Strengthening her belief that Glen was somehow looking over her shoulder, the vibrator turned on again. This time the buzzing was insistent and constant and lasted at least thirty-seconds. She panted and moaned, her eyes clamped shut. She squeezed her thighs together as her whole body shook. She wanted to obey Glen, but it was too much, she couldn't bear it. She fought against her orgasm but knew she would not be able to keep it at bay for long.

Just as she was about to either surrender to her pleasure or pull the toy from between her legs, the buzzing stopped. Relief and frustration washed over her in equal measure. She pushed her hair

out of her eyes, finding it damp from the sweat at her temples. A new message from Sam was already flashing on her screen, demanding her attention.

TwitchyNose: I hope your evening was as exciting. And satisfying.

MileHighBecky: Sort of. In a way. Or not…

TwitchyNose: Hmm. What does that mean?

MileHighBecky: Nothing, really. Let's just say that tonight can't possibly come fast enough.

TwitchyNose: Haha.

MileHighBecky: I should go, I guess. I should get ready for tonight and let you go about your day. We can talk again later.

TwitchyNose: Sure thing. Have a great time. I'll be thinking about you. ;)

Normally, Rebecca would have spent some time worrying about the ambiguity of Sam's final words, but she could barely think. She closed her laptop without bothering to log out of the dating site, and pressed a hand to the damp crotch of her panties. The desire to make herself cum was overwhelming. She considered going to the bedroom and taking care of herself regardless of Glen's instructions. Then, she thought of messaging him and begging for permission.

As much as she wanted relief, both options bothered her, but for different reasons. She stood and wandered around the apartment on shaky legs, cell phone in hand. She wondered if Glen was at home right now. He'd been plotting, messaging and sending packages all day long. Surely he was there, waiting for her, perhaps thinking up even more ways to tease and torture her.

She remembered how hard his cock had been the night before. He'd wanted her as bad as she wanted him. He wasn't only torturing her today. He was forcing himself to wait as well. She frowned. He wasn't barred from orgasm, though. Had he indulged in the release he was denying her? The thought annoyed her, but the image of Glen touching himself, stroking what had felt to her like a huge cock, made her shiver with pleasure. Even if he had, he was probably desperately needy, too. Was he regretting how late he'd asked her to come over?

Would he be happy to see her if she appeared on his doorstep now?

The vibrator buzzed again, stronger than the previous times. This time it was a series of short, sharp bursts against her clit and inside her. Her pussy clenched and she nearly came instantly. Her knees buckled and she sat down on the floor abruptly, moaning. She lay down on the carpet and dug her fingers into the thick pile as the pulses continued. She wasn't going to be able to hold back this time. He was pushing her too hard. She couldn't resist.

She nearly sobbed when the vibrator quieted again. She'd been so close. Despite her desire to obey him, she would have been happy to cum. She was desperate for release and having it taken away at the last second was unbearable.

She lay on the ground, watching the sunlight move across the ceiling. It was better not to move. She knew that standing or walking would only stimulate her more. Gingerly, she pulled her soaked panties away from skin and moaned when the cool air touched her swollen pussy.

She didn't know quite what time it was, but she knew she simply couldn't wait any longer. The cab ride out to Glen's was fairly long and she could hardly imagine surviving that long. Perhaps he would forgive her for arriving early. Or perhaps his own desire was overwhelming, too, and he'd be nothing but happy to see her, to use her, to grant them both the pleasure they so badly needed.

Her dress was damp and wrinkled, but she didn't care. She found her purse and hooked it over her shoulder, calling a cab as she let herself out of the apartment and locked the door. The vibrator had become so slippery that she had to adjust her gait to walk down the stairs and out the front door. The world felt artificial. She stared at the people walking down her street, living their lives, scarcely believing they were real.

She nearly lunged into the back of the taxi when it arrived, suppressing a moan when the leather seat pushed the plug deeper inside her. The driver raised an eyebrow at her when she gave him Glen's address, her voice breathy, her fingers digging into the passenger side headrest, nearly white with effort. He made no comment, merely acquiescing and pulling the car smoothly away from the curb.

After a few minutes, her nerves suddenly started to get the better of her. She rocked back and forth anxiously and bit her lip to stifle a moan. She leaned forward.

"Maybe you should, um, take the long way to get there. I'm going to be way too early."

He raised an eyebrow at her again but then just shrugged. "It's your money. We can drive around as long as you like."

The day was still bright and warm, the afternoon just drawing to a close. She was going to be several hours early no matter how much the cab driver dallied. She considered asking him to drop her off somewhere, but she couldn't imagine walking in her current state. Instead, she groaned and turned her face away from the glass. As much as she wanted to be good and obedient, she didn't think she was capable of waiting much longer. She'd have to take her chances. She was betting that Glen was equally as needy and he'd be glad to see her.

Twenty long and torturous minutes later, the cab stopped in front of Glen's building. With what felt like superhuman self-control, Rebecca paid the driver, carefully calculating a proper tip instead of throwing a few bills at him to make a quick escape. A teenage boy with an energetic cocker spaniel on a leash was entering the building and didn't even seem to notice Rebecca slipping through the door. She giggled nervously when the dog sniffed at her.

It took forever to rush to Glen's door, but once there, she hesitated, fist poised, ready to knock. Had she made a mistake? Though the thought made her want to cry, it still wasn't too late to leave. She could make her escape, unseen, and return at the appointed time. She'd find some way to survive and be all the more turned on when she finally saw Glen later.

She started to turn away but before she could take a single step, the vibrator began to buzz again. She gave a strangled cry and stumbled. She fell heavily against the door, bruising her shoulder and crying out again, this time in pain. The vibrator stopped immediately and she heard footsteps on the other side of the door. She stood up quickly, panicking, her eyes darting from side to side as if a perfect hiding place would suddenly appear in the nearly featureless corridor.

As the door opened, she resigned herself to her fate, staring down at her feet and irrationally hoping Glen somehow wouldn't recognize her. He was still for a few seconds, looking at her, his face blank. She peeked at him, surprised at his silence, expecting some kind of reaction.

"Rebecca," he said, his voice low and husky. It seemed like the beginning of a sentence, like he intended to fill the tense silence with words. Instead, he choked on his inability to express exactly what he was feeling.

Her fingers tightened on her purse, her nails leaving permanent marks in the pale leather. She felt like she should say something but she had no idea what.

"I..." she started.

Glen reached for her elbow and pulled her gently into the apartment. He wasn't rough, but his grip on her was firm almost to the point of pain. She didn't resist, but she started to tremble. He closed the door behind her and pushed her against it, the look in his eyes unreadable.

He kissed her roughly, parting her lips with his tongue and plunging it into her mouth. His hand on her elbow squeezed more tightly, pinning her against the door while his other pushed up her skirt and slipped beneath her panties. Glen broke the kiss, burying his face in her neck. He groaned when his fingers moved over the toys he found between her legs.

"Fuck," he whispered.

She could feel him against her leg, rock hard already, practically throbbing. She suddenly noticed his bare chest and low-slung sweatpants. She could just make out the elastic of his underwear over the waistband. Feeling brave, she dropped her purse and allowed her hands to graze his bare skin. When she touched him, he growled like a wild animal and pressed his hips against her.

Shaking his head, he pulled back. "You're a bad girl, Rebecca."

He walked into the living room, leading her by the elbow. She followed obediently, her steps careful and small. Her pussy was soaking and she was afraid the vibrator would slide free. She stood by the couch, expectant, nervous, her heart beating so hard she could scarcely breathe. Glen leaned forward and kissed her again, rougher.

The stubble on his cheeks abraded her skin, but she didn't care, kissing back fiercely and arching her back.

Abruptly, he broke the kiss and flipped her around, bending her over the back of the couch. He reached between her legs and pressed the subtle indent on the vibrator, turning it on. It was on the lowest setting, buzzing softly, but it was enough to make her moan and writhe. She pressed her ass against his hard cock, expressing her need wordlessly. When he didn't respond immediately, she spoke.

"Please. Please, Glen. Fuck me."

He might have had other plans, he might have wanted to continue to torture her, but holding back was no longer possible. He pushed down the front of his pants and underwear and freed his cock. With Rebecca's wet panties already out of the way, there was nothing to stop him. He pushed himself into her roughly, slamming his hips into hers and driving her into the couch. She cried out in pleasure and thanked him, over and over her.

He felt like a dying man who'd found water in the desert. Being inside her was pure bliss and relief. Her wetness eased his way, but she was already nearly painfully tight with her approaching orgasm. The vibrator buzzed against both of them.

140

He'd wanted to make their first time slow, building inexorably to an explosive finish, but there was no way he could deny himself anymore. He thrust into her frantically, completely overcome, his mind blank of any thought except the need to have her, to own her, to cum inside her.

He grabbed her arms, using them as leverage to fuck her harder and deeper. He could feel the heavy and insistent weight of the plug pressing against him. She writhed beneath him, lost in her own pleasure. He thought she was trying to speak, but her sounds were incoherent, animalistic moans and groans. Suddenly, she began to buck wildly, her hands opening and closing on thin air. Her pussy clamped around him so tightly that he couldn't help but gasp. Her orgasm was beautiful, perfect, the most arousing thing he'd ever witnessed. As she reached her peak, he joined her, thrusting one final time and grunting as the rhythmic clenching around his cock milked the cum out of him.

His vision faded to black at the edges and filled with stars for a few seconds. He'd never passed out from cumming, but it appeared to be a real possibility now. He pulled out of her, releasing her arms. The vibrator, wet and slippery, tumbled to the carpet, still buzzing. Must be a lot of room up in there...heavy equipment and sex toys. Rebecca hung over the back of the couch, only the tips of her toes touching the floor, panting and limp. Her dressed was flipped up as far as it would go, exposing her perfect ass with the steel of the plug clearly visible above her throbbing pussy and her slick inner thighs.

Glen knelt to retrieve the vibrator, turn it off and put it in his pocket. Rebecca didn't seem inclined to move at all. Her whole body still trembled, and he imagined she would simply fall over if she asked her legs to support her.

Still kneeling, he moved forward, putting a hand on each of her thighs and parting them gently. Her pussy was soaked and dripping with both of their fluids and he had a suddenly overwhelming urge to taste her. He knew she would be sensitive, still recovering from her orgasm. He leaned in and pressed his tongue against her swollen clit, enjoying the way she jolted and moaned. He dug his fingers into her thighs, hard, wanting to keep her still. He didn't care if he left in bruises. The thought excited him.

Once his mind had cleared enough, he thought about how she had disobeyed him. He'd been unable to resist her, or allowing her to orgasm, but she would need to be punished for her presumption and for her obvious, if successful, attempt to breach his self-control. His erection, which had started to subside, returned as he continued to lick her pussy, loving the way she tasted.

She was moaning wildly again, trying to press herself more firmly against his mouth, but he held her in a nearly helpless position. Until she released her thighs, she couldn't find leverage purchase on the floor. His tongue explored every bit of her, teasing gently at her sensitive clit until she felt ready to explode again. But Glen seemed able to read her perfectly. Every time she was about to reach the point of no return, he would back off, licking her pussy lips, or gently kissing her inner thighs. She moaned in frustration and writhed as much as she could, but he was in control and he clearly wasn't ready for her to cum again just yet.

When she was nearly sobbing with desire, Glen suddenly stood up and pulled her up, too. He turned her to face him and kissed her gently. She could taste both of them on her lips. It was intensely exciting. She wrapped her arms around him and pulled him close. She could tell he was still hard and the realization made her happy. With a sigh, he moved back a step, leaving her to stand unsupported on her shaking legs.

"I can see by your grin that you think you've gotten one over on me, you little temptress," said Glen, returning her smile. "I promise you I'm going to make you think twice about trying something like that again."

His threat made her shiver with anticipation. She found she craved his punishment as much as she craved his cock, his tongue and the sweet release only he could grant her. She smoothed her dress down over her thighs and tried to look chastened, but her eyes flashed. She had no intention of stopping her efforts to undermine his authority.

He laughed at her expression. Perhaps she thought she was being subtle, but her eyes revealed her devious thoughts as clearly as if she'd spoken.

"Go to my bedroom. Get naked, completely naked, and lay down on the bed. Wait for me there, as long as it takes. Even if I stay out here for an hour or longer, keep waiting. Don't get up off the bed, don't come looking for me and don't, under any circumstances, touch yourself. That pussy is mine and I'll be coming to claim it, but only when I'm ready. Understood?"

Rebecca nodded. "Answer me out loud." "Yes, I understand." "Yes, what?"

She hesitated, but realized quickly what he was expecting. "Yes, Sir."

Satisfied, he gave her a short nod and watched as she turned and walked carefully, on shaking legs, to the bedroom.

10

Nearly as shaky as Rebecca, Glen collapsed onto the couch after she left the room, pushing sweaty hair off his forehead. He let his head fall back and closed his eyes as he focused on his breathing and tried to slow his heartbeat. He didn't regret the amazing, explosive sex they'd had, but he did have to admit things hadn't gone according to plan. Not according to his plan, anyway. It was clear from the impish look that Rebecca gave him before leaving the room that she'd accomplished what she'd hoped to.

He opened his eyes and sat up. With her out of his sight, he felt a little more in control of his faculties and he needed to plan what was going to happen next.

He jumped when Rebecca's phone buzzed in the silence. He retrieved her purse from where she'd dropped it and held it. He didn't want to bring it to her and break the spell, but there was a chance the message was important. He hesitated, but set the purse down again. Whoever it was could surely wait a few hours. The phone buzzed again, and then a third time, but Glen had made his decision and ignored it.

He stood and paced around his living room. It was hard to resist the urge to go immediately to Rebecca, but he knew waiting was key. She was needy now, of course, but not as desperate as he wanted her to be. And he wanted to think of the perfect way to punish her for her disobedience. She might

145

enjoy rebellion, but he could tell she enjoyed submission just as much, if not more.

His pacing took him to the kitchen, where he poured himself a large Scotch on the rocks. He stood at the counter, sipping it and listening to the ice cubes clinking gently against the glass. He imagined her lying on his bed, naked, as he'd directed. Would she be shivering, cold and exposed? Was she struggling with the temptation to touch herself as much as he was struggling to resist going to her? It occurred to him that since she'd disobeyed him once, she might disobey him again. Perhaps she sat fully dressed in his chair, waiting patiently to raise a rebellious eyebrow when he came to find her. Or perhaps she was naked, but had her hand buried between her legs, giving herself the orgasm he had denied her. His hand shook as he continued to drink. In the living room, her phone buzzed again. Glen frowned.

In the bedroom, Rebecca couldn't hear her phone, though she had heard Glen's pacing steps and the sound of the refrigerator opening and closing. She folded her clothes and left them in a neat pile on the chair, then sat on the bed. Every few minutes, she changed her position, unable to decide if she wanted to look prim and composed, or seductive. Either way, she wanted to look in control, despite her slick pussy and the ever-present pressure of the plug.

Time ticked by slowly and there was only silence from the rest of the apartment. She leaned over carefully, not wanting to leave the bed, but hoping for a glimpse of something revealing down the hall. She wondered what Glen might have hidden in his bedside table or in the drawers of his dresser, but she didn't dare peek.

Finally, with nothing to do but wait, her lack of sleep caught up with her. Sighing, she rolled over to her side, resting her head on one of Glen's plump pillows, and closed her eyes. She still felt aroused, despite her heavy eyelids, and when sleep overcame her, her dreams were vivid and erotic. She moaned softly and flexed the muscles in her pelvis, her need mounting exactly as Glen had hoped it would.

He barely managed to hold back for an hour, pacing and pouring himself another drink. When he simply couldn't wait any longer, he filled a glass with ice and water and strode to the bedroom, his cock growing hard in anticipation. He froze when he saw Rebecca sleeping sweetly, one hand tucked beneath her head. Then he noticed her other hand had strayed and rested almost between her legs. When she moaned, a tiny, almost undetectable sound, his cock twitched in response.

Careful not to make any noise, he set the glass down on the bedside table and looked down at her, considering his options. She was beautiful and innocent in her sleep, and part of him wanted to lie down beside her and pull the quilt over both of them. She was small and delicate and he knew she would fit perfectly in his arms. When she moaned again, his dirty thoughts moved to the forefront of his mind. Sweetness and sleep could come later.

He stooped and slid his strong arms under her, lifting her from the bed in one smooth motion. She was light and, for a few seconds, remained limp with sleep. Her eyes fluttered open and she stared at him in confusion.

"What...?" she said, leaving her question unformed.

She felt so small and pliable in his arms. It was almost enough to change his plans. She shook her head and began to sleepily push the hair away from her face, still trying to get her bearings. He lifted her higher and bent his head to kiss her. Squirming happily, she twisted in his arms and kissed him back. He sat down on the edge of the bed, still cradling her almost tenderly. They kissed for a long time, longer than he'd intended. There was something so sweet and satisfying about her mouth that it took an immense effort to tear himself away.

"Rebecca. I love kissing you, but that's not why I'm here. You disobeyed me and it's time for your punishment."

She lowered her eyes, putting on a show of being chastised. Any attempt at looking sincere was ruined by the playful grin she flashed at him even while keeping her eyes downcast.

"I'm sorry. I just wanted you so badly. I couldn't wait."

Glen traced a finger gently over her shoulder, moving lower until her reached her nipple. He took her breast in his hand squeezed softly.

"You should use proper forms of address when you speak to me," he said, his voice casual, but tinged with authority.

She wiggled in his lap. "I'm sorry, Sir." Her laugh sounded more gleeful than repentant.

Glen sighed and shook his head. Rebecca started to reach for his neck, intending to kiss him again, and gave a shriek as he effortlessly flipped her over and laid her across his knees. Too surprised to speak, she merely stayed still, her bare ass raised and looking very tempting.

"You've been bad, Rebecca."

"Yes, Sir. I'm sorry, I promise." She didn't sound quite so self- assured and cocky anymore, but there was still amusement in her voice.

"Do you know what happens to bad girls?" As he spoke, he caressed the naked skin of her ass, his touch soft and almost absent- minded.

Rebecca cast him an impish glance over her shoulder, though he could sense her surfacing nervousness.

"They get spanked?" she said, making it a hopeful question.

Glen didn't answer, but leaned over and fished an ice cube out of the glass of water. He held it over Rebecca's back, allowing a few cold drops to land on her. She squealed and squirmed and started to protest. Her words turned to a shocked gasp as Glen first held the ice cube between her legs, pressing it against her clit, and then smoothly slipped it inside her. Quickly, he grabbed another ice cube and trailed it along her back before inserting it into her pussy to join the other.

Her breath came in quick, panting gasps as the chill of the ice spread. She'd never felt anything like it before and novelty of the sensation overwhelmed her, making it impossible to form a coherent sentence. Glen's hand, his fingers still cold and wet, crept into her hair and tilted her head back slightly.

"I'm going to give you that spanking now," he whispered gently in her ear. "And I want you to work very hard to keep those ice cubes inside you."

"Yes, Sir," she panted. She brought her thighs together and tried to concentrate on squeezing her pelvic muscles. She shivered and moaned as the ice shifted inside her.

She was so entirely focused on the sensation of the ice, she forgot what was about to happen. Glen raised his hand and brought it down sharply on her ass. The sound it made was louder than she'd expected and she jumped as much from that as the pain. Her whole body jerked.

The second blow was not a surprise, but the pain was more intense. Her ass felt so hot, she imagined it must be bright red, nearly glowing. Each time his hand connected with her stinging flesh, she cried out and trembled, trying not to lose focus and let the ice cubes slip free. She felt cool water dripping down her thighs as they grew smaller inside her.

The spanking continued as Rebecca writhed and squealed. She couldn't decide which was harder to bear, the pain or the humiliation. She hadn't ever been spanked as a child, but she still felt the indignity sharply. Her hands flew up to cover her face and she felt tears on her reddened cheeks.

"I'm sorry, Sir," she cried. "I promise I'll be good. Please stop."

Glen ignored her, applying several more bright red handprints to her pale skin before finally relenting. He reached and she parted her thighs willingly, nearly sobbing with relief. He slipped a finger inside and was pleased to find the remnants of the ice cubes still there.

He stood and lifted her easily. She hung limply in his arms, exhausted and marveling at his strength. He turned and laid her on the bed. Grateful, she pressed her warm and tear-stained face into the cool sheets. Her ass was still stinging and she hissed when Glen kneeled behind her and gently parted her thighs. Leaning his weight on her lower back and pinning her to the bed, he thrust his hips forward and pushed his cock into her dripping pussy.

The chilled sensation inside her was unusual, but arousing. He fucked her slowly, admiring her bright red ass, the shape of his hand clearly visible in several places. She lay completely limp beneath him, though her breathing was quick and she moaned every time he thrust forward.

His movements were slow and deliberate, almost teasing. The contrast between her warmth and the chill that still lingered from the ice made him shiver with unanticipated pleasure. He wanted her desperately, as badly as he had in the living room, but he had more control now. He tucked his hands under her hips and raised them off the bed, giving himself a better angle so he could penetrate her even more deeply. She groaned desperately but still didn't move.

After a few minutes of slow fucking, her pussy started to tighten around him and he knew she was getting close to orgasm. His own was fast approaching, but he wasn't ready for things to end. He moved back and sat on his heels for a moment, reluctant as he watched her pant. Her eyes were closed tightly and she seemed unaware of her surroundings.

"Rebecca, open your eyes."

She moaned like a sleeper woken too early and turned her face into the bed.

"Open your eyes. I'm not done with you. You still need to pay for your disobedience."

His voice was gentle, but firm, and Rebecca felt compelled to obey, even through the fog of pleasure clouding her brain.

She opened her eyes and turned to face Glen, though she didn't raise her head from the bed. It felt impossible. Despite the arousal and need burning through her body, she felt languorous, incapable of movement. She wanted Glen to keep fucking her, to keep using her. She could tell how much he wanted her and she ached to be filled by him again.

"I know you want to please me, Rebecca."

She nodded, incapable of speech. She heard some rustling and gasped as Glen pushed the little flexible vibrator inside her. He adjusted it to ensure it was secure, the outside half resting firmly against her clit.

"Get up and kneel beside the bed," he said. When she didn't immediately move, he swatted her reddened and burning ass. She winced and cried out, but found the will to push herself up off the bed.

Her legs trembled as she stood and looked down at herself. Her body was flushed and sweaty and she felt terribly exposed. Glen looked at her expectantly, cocking an eyebrow as if to ask what he was going to need to do encourage her to follow orders. She sank to her knees on the hard floor, knowing that it would be painful after a few minutes but she didn't care. She winced again when her ass touched her heels, but there was something enjoyable about the pain, about knowing Glen had left his mark on her.

Instinctively, she put her hands behind her back and lowered her head, closing her eyes and waiting. The floor was rigid under her knees, her muscles still trembling. She shivered as the sweat dried on her skin. She was content to be still and wait, though. She heard the floor crack as Glen stood, then she felt his hand in her hair. He caressed her head gently and it felt so good, she thought she might start to purr. She wanted to move forward and press her face against his skin.

He put a finger underneath her chin and gently tilted her head up and back. She opened her eyes and looked up at him. It was the first time she'd ever seen him from this angle and it struck her again how good-looking he was, tall, strong. The veins stood out in his arms and she longed to touch them, to run her fingers softly over the length of them. While she knelt, he'd gotten naked. Rebecca shifted her gaze from his arms to his erect cock. Up close, it seemed huge and she wondered how she'd been able to fit it all inside her. She shifted her weight, finally noticing that she was sore. Her need had been so great that she hadn't felt how full and stretched she'd been. She knew she'd be able to feel it for days. The thought was exciting.

"Open your mouth," Glen said.

Rebecca was so distracted with her thoughts that at first she was confused, but when he wrapped his hand around the base of his cock, she understood.

"Yes, Sir," she said. Her eyes darted to his other hand and she noticed he was holding his cell phone. The screen was lit but she couldn't tell what it displayed. She opened her mouth, eager, but apprehensive. She'd been able to manage that huge cock in her pussy, but what would it be like to have it in her mouth?

He pushed his cock past her lips and he moaned with pleasure as her tongue licked at him eagerly. She tasted herself on him. He stood almost still, letting her explore his cock, bobbing her head and sucking gently. She focused on the tip, never taking more than a third of him into her mouth. Glen flicked his thumb quickly over his phone screen and the vibrator in her pussy buzzed to life. It was on the lowest setting, but she still twitched and moaned, her attention shifting away from Glen's cock.

Noting her distraction, he laughed. "Stay focused, darling. Your job right now is to concentrate on sucking my cock, no matter what happens."

Rebecca managed a small nod despite her position and tried to make her moan of pleasure into a sound of assent. Glen moved his free hand to the back of her head, holding it firmly in place. Before, he'd been still, letting her do most of the work, but now he started moving his hips, thrusting his cock into her mouth. He went much deeper than she had, the tip of his cock just barely hitting the back of her throat, though only just.

She breathed slowly through her nose, keeping her mouth relaxed. Still, his size was daunting and she felt a sliver of fear every time he pushed a little more deeply. She blinked and looked up at him, watching his abs clench as he fucked her mouth. He groaned and increased the pace, though he was still very much in control of his movements. His cock was covered with her spit, sliding in and out of her swollen lips. He flicked his thumb over his phone again and the intensity of the vibrator increased. Rebecca moaned and squirmed, her attention again momentarily pulled away from Glen.

He jerked her head back firmly, tilting it at the perfect angle for his thrusts. She was shocked and scared when he started fucking her in earnest, his huge cock pushing farther and farther down her throat. She held her breath and struggled not to gag.

The demands on her attention continued to be divided. The vibrator buzzed insistently against her clit. Wetness dripped from her pussy, down her thighs and onto the floor beneath her. Glen's fucking grew primal. He groaned and grunted as he used her mouth and throat for his pleasure.

"I'm getting close," he said, his voice tight. He swiped at his phone again, and the vibrations grew stronger and began pulsing.

Rebecca would have cried out if Glen's cock hadn't been deep in her throat at that very moment. Her entire body trembled. Tears gathered in her eyes and slid down her cheeks. Every time Glen pulled back, she gasped and moaned, but she kept her mouth open eagerly, wanting him back inside her.

With one final grunt, Glen buried himself as deep as he could in her mouth. She struggled, her throat convulsing around his cock, squeezing it. She felt it twitch, felt the thick ropes of cum shooting down her throat. She did her best to swallow, but when he pulled out, her mouth was still full of his taste. At that instant, her own orgasm suddenly hit her, completely overwhelming her. She'd already been shaking, but as she came, she collapsed on the floor, shaking and moaning.

After the last wave of pleasure washed over her, she simply lay, unmoving except for the rapid rise and fall of her chest. Glen picked up the vibrator, which had fallen to the ground, and turned it off. Showing off his strength, he picked her up from the floor as if she were a small child and set her gently on the bed. He lay next to her and pulled her into his arms, kissing her softly on the back of the neck.

"How are you doing?"

It took her several seconds to gather herself enough to answer. "I'm good," she breathed. "But I've never felt anything like that before."

"You were amazing," he said, speaking close to her ear, his voice low and tender. "I've never felt anything quite like that either."

She wanted to thank him, or explain how exhausted she was, but her eyes were suddenly irresistibly heavy. She nestled herself into him and smiled when he pulled the blanket over both of them. Secure and warm, her body still trembling and aching in the most pleasant way, she was asleep in seconds.

Rebecca awoke in the dark. Glen lay next to her, breathing deeply and slowly, his arm heavy over her. She was warm and comfortable and closed her eyes again, hoping she could slip easily back to sleep. The apartment was completely still and quiet except for the sound of Glen's breathing so when her cell phone buzzed in the living room, she heard it.

Sighing, she squirmed out from under Glen's arm, reluctant to leave the bed, but feeling a pang of guilt over leaving her phone unattended for so long. She hoped neither her mother nor her supervisor had tried to reach her. Either way, she'd be in trouble and would have to deliver some sort of explanation for her unannounced disappearance. She padded quietly out of the bedroom, naked and shivering in the air-conditioned chill. She found her purse on the couch and couldn't remember if she'd put in there. The few minutes after her arrival were a blur of erotic sensation.

She fished her phone out of her purse and then stood indecisively in front of the couch. She was naked and cold, and the bed, and Glen's arms, beckoned her. She headed back to the bedroom and snuggled back up under the blanket, happy she'd managed to avoid waking Glen. Carefully, she dialed her screen brightness down as low as it would go and checked her messages.

There was nothing from either her mom or her supervisor, but there were a whole slew of messages from Sam. She opened the dating app and read, biting her lip.

TwitchyNose: Hey, have you left for your date yet? You are still showing up as online.

The next message arrived nearly an hour later.

TwitchyNose: Well, I guess you're gone and you just left your computer logged in or something. Darn. I wanted to talk to you.

Again, there was a long interval before the next message.

TwitchyNose: I really wanted to talk to you...

TwitchyNose: You know what, I've been a coward. I'm just going to come out and say it.

TwitchyNose: Even if you don't want to hear it.

TwitchyNose: I think you're really cool, Becky. And when I was with that girl last night, all I could think of was you. To be honest, probably the only reason I went out with her is because she looks like you.

TwitchyNose: And correct me if I'm wrong, but I'm pretty sure there's some... tension between us. And I'd like to explore that.

TwitchyNose: Ugh. That sounds so dumb. What I mean is that I think you're hot and I kind of think you think I'm hot, too. And I want to go on a date. With you. And see where it goes.

A half hour of silence before the next message, the one that had made Rebecca go and find her phone, arrived.

TwitchyNose: I'm sorry. I'm an idiot. You're straight and you're even out with some guy right now. Probably fucking him. I'm so sorry. Good night.

Rebecca stared at her phone, shocked. When the screen darkened and eventually blinked off, she stared out the window at the streetlight, hoping for some sort of clarity. With sudden resolve, she picked up her phone and typed an answer to Sam, her fingers trembling.

MileHighBecky: I think you're right. And I'd like to go out with you.

After hitting send, she felt a twinge of guilt about messaging Sam while she was in bed with Glen. She pulled away from him and curled up on herself. As excited and absorbed as she'd been just a few hours ago, she now felt disconnected from everything that had passed between her and Glen. Her mind was far away from the warm bed in which they both lay. She knew she should feel guiltier, but she was too busy panicking over what she had said to Sam. The prospect of meeting her in person, of going on a date, was both terrifying and thrilling.

If she'd been alone in bed, she would have tossed and turned, or maybe even gotten up to pace, but out of respect for Glen, she tried to stay still. Her heart was beating faster than usual and she fought off the impulse to bury her face in the pillow to hide her embarrassment. She tucked her phone under the pillow and closed her eyes, focusing on her breathing and trying to calm herself. Her physical exhaustion eventually won out over her emotional turmoil and she fell asleep.

Glen woke in the morning, crinkling his eyes against sunlight. He was surprised to find that he'd slept solidly all night. Normally, having someone in bed with him made him toss and turn for at least part of the night. He was even more surprised when he realized he'd even slept through Rebecca getting out of bed. The sheets where she'd been lying were disheveled and still warm. He sat up, suddenly worried she'd sneaked out on him. Not that he hadn't done the same in the past, and not that he'd minded when some women had done it to him, but he wanted more than a one-night stand with Rebecca. The feeling surprised him, but he wasn't the type to overthink. He liked her. He wanted her. What more was there to say?

The silence of his apartment was broken by the sound of the shower. The thought of Rebecca naked, under the water, in the steamy room, made him eager for her return to bed. She'd come out clean, her long hair still damp, maybe dripping water onto her perfect skin. It occurred to him that he was as sticky and sweaty as she'd been in the morning and that he could do with a shower, too.

He decided to join her. They could both get clean at the same time and maybe have a little fun in the shower before making it back to bed. He had nothing planned today, no work, no obligations. All he hoped to do was to coax Rebecca into staying with him all day and all night. And maybe tomorrow, too. He started to get up, but was startled by a buzzing sound coming from under the pillow that still bore the imprint of Rebecca's head. He retrieved her phone and stared at the notification on the screen. He recognized the logo of the dating site. He had an account there himself and he'd used it several times, though he preferred to meet women in person.

He felt uneasy, thinking about all the messages Rebecca received the night before. Looking guiltily over his shoulder, he tried to guess the code to unlock the phone. Like a lot of people, Rebecca hadn't been too original and her phone unlocked on his second try. He hesitated, knowing he could still just put the phone back where he'd found it and stop snooping, but he couldn't help himself. He clicked on the latest message Rebecca had received.

TwitchyNose: Wow. You don't know how thrilled, excited and relieved I am. I'm going to make this a date to remember, sexy.

His stomach sinking, he scrolled up further, reading through the whole all the messages that Rebecca had checked during the night and her response to them. Checking the time stamps, he realized she must have been lying right next to him, planning a date with someone else as he slept. His gaze hardening, he shut off the phone's screen and tucked it back under the pillow. He laid back down and pulled the blanket up to cover himself.

Ten minutes later, when Rebecca returned to the bedroom smiling, with a towel wrapped around her hair, she found him bundled up, his back to the door.

"Hey," she said. "Good morning, sleepyhead."

He didn't turn, but heard her footsteps come around the bed. As soon as her weight hit the mattress, he spoke without looking at her.

"Last night was fun. Thanks for coming over, but I've got a lot to do today. I've got to shower and stuff. You can take your time getting dressed and just let yourself out."

She froze, shocked. He looked at her then, sitting up and dismissively shrugging his shoulders. Her cheeks flushed bright crimson.

"Yeah. Sure. Of course," she said. Her voice was tight and cold as she quickly found her clothing and pulled it on. Her movements were abrupt, broadcasting her anger and embarrassment.

Glen regretted his attitude immediately, but still felt it was for the better. Obviously, he was the only one who felt like something special had been happening between them. When she was only half dressed, he got out of bed and walked straight to the bathroom, closing the door firmly and locking it behind him. He turned on the water, but didn't get into the shower. Instead, he stood with his back to the door, listening for her footsteps. She walked down the hall a few minutes later, stopped to find her shoes and purse in the living room and then was out the door, slamming it.

He stayed slumped against the bathroom door, looking damp imprints of her delicate feet on the floor, and cursed himself.

11

Rebecca flew down the hall, her cheeks burning. She knew she had no right to be upset with Glen. After all, only a few hours ago she'd been making plans to see someone else while in bed with him. But she'd expected more from him. She'd thought they had a real connection. He'd been so tender, so involved the night before, but now he was practically throwing her out.

Her hair was still wet, leaving trails where it dripped onto her rumpled dress. Despite the shower, she felt disheveled and out of sorts. She wished she'd had more time to organize herself, but right now she only wanted to get away from Glen and his apartment. Fuming, she stamped her foot and started to walk down the street, too heated to call and wait for a cab.

When she finally made it home, she was still irate. She felt duped and stupid. Glen had never pretended they meant something to each other and she knew he was a player. He hadn't lied to her, she'd lied to herself. As the afternoon wore on, her anger shifted to embarrassment and her thoughts moved away from Glen. Instead, she thought about Sam.

With great trepidation, she opened her laptop and logged in to the dating site. She clicked over to her messages from Sam and was confused to see that the most recent was marked as read. It had come in the morning, either while she was asleep or showering, but she certainly hadn't read it yet. With a sinking feeling, she realized that her phone had been lying unattended in bed with Glen. He was the one who had read Sam's excited message.

Her anger flared again. Glen had been snooping and if he'd found something he didn't want to see, he had only himself to blame. He had no respect for her privacy and she was better off rid of him. But her rage burnt out after a few sharp seconds. Glen had not been the one to change their dynamic. He had gone suddenly cold in response to the revelation that she was callously making plans to see someone else while lying naked in bed beside him. She would have been deeply hurt if she'd been in his shoes. He'd obviously been lashing out in response, but she couldn't blame him.

Feeling sick and guilty, unsure if she should try to salvage anything or leave bad enough alone, she was distracted by the little ping of a new message. She'd come to associate the sound with Sam, but instead of a little rush of pleasure, this time she felt a twinge of guilt.

TwitchyNose: I know you are probably busy and I'm probably going to seem over-eager, but I'm going to take a chance and invite you out tonight. So... Are you free?

Rebecca read the message and felt another flush of pleasure and excitement, accompanied by even stronger guilt. Only hours ago, she'd been hoping Glen would invite her to stay the day, that he would continue to show her the pleasures of submission. She'd hoped to spend hours more in his arms, trembling in ecstasy. Resolute, she tried to push Glen out of her mind. She'd made a mess of whatever that could have been. Time to move on.

MileHighBecky: As luck would have it, I'm completely free and clear.

TwitchyNose: That's the best news I've had all day. Can I pick you up at 7?

MileHighBecky: I'll be waiting with bells on.

TwitchyNose: I'd prefer those little white boyshorts to bells...

Rebecca blushed deeply, all her early shyness with Sam coming back in a rush. She sent Sam the little red-cheeked emoticon signifying embarrassment and then quickly logged off.

Glen slouched into his couch, shabby sweatpants slung low around his hips, chest bare. His feet rested on his coffee table and he held a half-empty glass of Scotch.

He knew he was acting pathetic, and he knew how different this was for him. He felt like he'd been becoming a new man over the last week, someone better, more empathetic, more open. But as he sat on his couch, miserable and half drunk, he wondered if he'd been happier when he hadn't cared so much about other people. Look what caring had gotten him. He took another sip and pulled his cell phone out of his pocket.

Both Rashid and Sarge were working today, but they'd be off in a couple of hours. He texted that they were long overdue for a boys' night out and received immediate replies from both of them. Rashid was enthusiastic in his response to the group, perhaps too enthusiastic, if Glen was honest. He wasn't sure what to make of Rashid's constant requests to hang out lately. Sarge seemed more guarded, asking Glen how he was in a private text. Glen sighed. Sarge had a way of seeing through his bullshit, but he didn't really feel like unburdening himself right now. He just wanted to get drunk, eat junk food and maybe pick up some air-headed little number who wanted a quick roll in the hay, no strings attached, no thought required.

Brooding, he tossed back the rest of his drink and pried himself out of the couch. He couldn't help but see signs of Rebecca's presence everywhere he looked. He closed his eyes, but that only brought her face to mind. He saw her so clearly: blond hair sweaty and messy, cheeks pink with exertion and pleasure. He'd never had trouble letting a woman go before and it irked him that he kept thinking about Rebecca.

His boredom and restlessness hung on him. He stalked around his apartment before finally getting dressed. He decided to meet Rashid and Sarge at the airport. It was a long way to drive, but he had nothing better to do. Besides, the sooner he met up with them, the sooner he'd be able to get his mind off a certain blonde flight attendant.

As seven o'clock drew near, Rebecca grew nervous. It was similar to the way she'd felt before her first evening with Glen, but she was self-conscious about putting too much time into getting ready. Sam had witnessed that whole painful decision-making process and Rebecca didn't want her to imagine that she'd undergone the same for Sam.

She pulled on a clean pair of lacy white panties, but kept the rest of her outfit simple and casual. She found a long abandoned basic short denim skirt in the back of her closet and paired it with a red T- shirt. To really cement the casual theme, she pulled on white athletic ankle socks and her only pair of sneakers. She almost gave in to the immediate urge to change into something else, worried she'd give the impression that she hadn't tried to look good at all. She might as well be going on a date in her pajamas.

Sam had messaged to request her address an hour ago. Knowing she was on her way brought a new sense of reality to the whole situation. She'd be here soon, they'd meet in person, and it would be a date. Rebecca shook her head, wondering how it had all happened.

She stood in the bathroom, applying lip gloss and trying to decide if she should tie her hair back, when the doorbell rang. She jumped and ran to the door while her heart skipped a beat before hammering in her chest.

Sam stood on the threshold, smiling and clearly nervous. Her short hair was parted and swept neatly to the side, and she didn't appear to be wearing any makeup. She'd dressed more soberly than Rebecca had expected, in dark wash skinny jeans, a plaid button down shirt and a dark blazer with three quarter sleeves.

They stared at each other for a moment, uncertain, before Rebecca started laughing.

"I feel so awkward!" She stood back to let Sam in.

Sam's eyes darted everywhere, taking in the details of Rebecca's small, antiseptic living space. Her gaze rested on the photo of Panopticon before she turned to face Rebecca.

"It's great to finally meet you in person. You're even more beautiful in the flesh." Sam's voice became hesitant on the last few words, fearing she'd overstepped.

"You're beautiful, too," said Rebecca, surprised to find that she truly meant it.

Sam was shorter than her and appeared compact and slim. She moved with a kind of repressed energy, very unlike Glen's sleepy languor. She winced as Glen crossed her mind. She wanted to focus on this moment, on this person.

They stood in the living room, questions and hesitation heavy in the air between them. Finally, Sam sighed.

"I had this idea that I wanted to do something crazy, ambitious, romantic. To take you on the most breathtaking date you'd ever experienced. But, when I was on my way over here, I started to realize how ...pointless that might be. I want to get to know you. And I want to kiss you. Those things don't require an expensive meal or a helicopter tour of the city or a string quartet playing Celine Dion songs." She laughed ruefully. "So, let's just do something casual...if that's ok?"

Rebecca, whose heart had leaped into her throat, relaxed and unclasped her hands. "I'd quite honestly prefer that."

"Well, then here's my suggestion: I know a little place that makes amazing pizza and it's just about a twenty minute walk from here. Let's go, pick some up and bring it back here. And maybe a bottle of wine if we pass a liquor store and you feel like a drink."

The plan sounded delightful to Rebecca and she said so immediately. She picked up her cell phone, keys and credit card and stuffed them into the pockets of her skirt. The evening already felt more like a night out with a friend than a date, but there was still something thrilling about it. She felt like the last few days had awakened her sexually in ways she'd never expected. She was ready for anything, nervous, but ready.

They strolled casually down the sidewalk, their small talk stilted for the first few blocks. More than once, Rebecca caught Sam looking at her, short glances so subtle she might have missed them. There was intensity in Sam's eyes and it made Rebecca blush.

They chatted about inconsequential nothings until Sam assumed a false, casual tone.

"So, did you have a good time with that guy last night?"

Rebecca's already red cheeks flamed brighter and she twisted a strand of her hair around her finger as she spoke.

"It was kind of incredible. The sex was so intense. But…things fell apart in the end and I don't think I'll be seeing him again."

"What happened?"

Rebecca paused, aware that she might already have said too much. She didn't want to lie, but she'd painted herself into a very awkward corner.

"I thought there was real potential there, although maybe I was just kidding myself. He saw the messages you and I exchanged, I think, and it upset him." An uncomfortable silence hung between them for a few seconds. "I'm not really sure what happened, to be honest," she finished lamely.

The pizza place was still a block or two away, but Sam stopped walking and turned to face Rebecca.

"I didn't mean to mess anything up for you. If you're feeling regretful right now, if you think you made a mistake saying yes to my invitation, please just tell me. It was a long shot and there won't be any hard feelings if you want to back out."

Rebecca looked into Sam's eyes. She was confused, overwhelmed. She'd been impulsive when she'd accepted this invitation, but she'd been excited, too. Sam's gaze began to cloud and she started to turn away from Rebecca, her posture slung with resignation and defeat.

Rebecca put a hand on her arm, "Wait. I'm confused, it's true, but I know I don't want you to walk away right now. I want to see where this goes, even if I still have no idea where it's heading." She took a deep breath. "What happened with Glen wasn't your fault, it was mine. And I honestly don't know what I want from either of you. I'm trying to figure that out, so please give me a chance."

Sam smiled. "I can respect that. You're an interesting girl, Becky. I don't know what the future holds either."

Impulsively, Sam moved closer to Rebecca and gave her a quick kiss on the mouth. It only lasted a fraction of a second and was almost chaste, but Rebecca experienced an unexpected burst of sexual excitement. They resumed their walk to the pizzeria, the energy between them more relaxed.

Glen collected Rashid and Sarge the second their shift was over, barely allowing them enough time to change out of their uniforms before dragging them to the closest bar that had an ambiance Sarge would tolerate. His friends were still settling in when Glen returned carrying a pitcher of beer and three glasses.

While he poured, Addison eyed him skeptically. "Are you going to tell us what's going on?"

Rashid raised an eyebrow, oblivious to anything out of the ordinary. He'd been oddly quiet during the short drive to the bar, preoccupied.

"Nothing, really," said Glen. "Just wanted to hang out, get drunk and maybe find an interesting young lady to spend the evening with. The usual, Sarge."

Rashid took a long swallow of his beer. "Sounds good to me."

Addison took a more restrained drink from his glass and gave Glen a measured look. "Whatever you say, kid. A few beers sound good, but you're on your own in the young ladies department."

Talk of women made Rashid's eyes light up eagerly. "Didn't you have something hot lined up for last night? That awkward blonde flight attendant?"

Glen's shrug wasn't exactly convincing, but only Sarge caught it. "Yeah, I did have plans with her."

"Any wild stories to share? You usually like to boast."

His taste for boasting had diminished over the past few weeks, and he found that he had no desire at all to talk about what had happened with Rebecca. The sex would be worth boasting about, but the prospect of describing it to his friends made him feel more gloomy than proud. And he didn't feel like bringing up the sour turn of events of the morning, either.

"I'd rather not talk about it," he said. He read immediate disappointment on Rashid's face, contrasting with worry on Sarge's. He deflected, "What about you guys? Any success with the ladies recently?"

Sarge shrugged and shook his head. "I haven't got your charm or your sex drive. I had a few dates with that neighbor I mentioned a while back, but nothing really came of it."

Glen nodded, hoping it would elicit more details, but Sarge was content to leave it at that. They both turned to Rashid, who flashed a grin. Constantly overshadowed by stories of Glen's latest conquests, he rarely got to be in the spotlight. He leaned forward and looked around the bar in a conspiratorial manner. Glen rolled his eyes. He knew if Rashid could somehow manage it without looking ridiculous, he would request the whole room's attention.

"I finally gave that phone app everyone's always talking about a try. I literally swiped right on every single girl, to get the most matches possible." Rashid spoke as if he was the originator of this brilliant idea.

Glen rolled his eyes dramatically. "Let me guess. Your profile pic is just your abs?"

"No, my face is in it, too," answered Rashid, missing Glen's mockery. "I got a decent amount of traction, but I wasn't into all the girls."

"That's what I don't get about always swiping right," interrupted Glen.

"I haven't got a clue what you two are talking about. I feel like I'm a hundred years old," said Sarge.

Rashid laughed. "You might as well be."

The conversation wasn't doing much to help Glen feel better. He looked around the bar as Rashid continued his story, detailing the variously lewd exchanges he'd engaged in with women, some successful, but most failing abysmally. He noted a woman drinking alone. Her long blonde hair gave him a twinge, but she was beautiful and he had the feeling he'd be able to charm her if he put his mind to it. She seemed lonely and the way she kept staring at her phone hinted that she might have been stood up. Though she was clearly annoyed, her demeanor was open.

He turned back to find Rashid using extravagant gestures to describe the generous hips of a woman he'd managed to hoodwink into an in-person meeting. Sarge was leaning back on his chair looking bored and contemptuous. Was that how he looked when Glen told his stories? He'd never paid enough attention to say.

The conversation dragged on with minimal participation from either Sarge or Glen until the older man finally pushed his chair away from the table and stood up.

"Okay, guys, I think I have to call it a night. I've got an early shift tomorrow." He paused and looked pointedly at Glen. "And I know you do, too. So don't do anything too stupid."

Glen thought about following him out, leaving Rashid to swipe right on his phone app, but he looked over at the blonde in the corner. She seemed to have given up on her phone and was staring at the bar display as she toyed with the straw in her drink.

"Sure thing. And thanks for coming out, Sarge. I'll see you tomorrow, bright and early."

After a quick hug, Glen sat back down. He chose a different seat, facing Rashid directly, so he could look over his shoulder at the woman who still showed no signs of wanting to leave. There were fewer customers in the bar than when they'd arrived. Those that remained seemed less raucous and more subdued.

"So, what now?" asked Rashid. He was eying his empty beer glass.

"I think I'm going to pay a visit to that lovely, lonely woman on the other side of the bar," said Glen. He didn't feel quite like his usual self, but maybe a quick flirtation followed—hopefully—by a quick seduction would be just the thing to help him forget about his recent error in judgment.

Rashid, lacking in subtlety as always, twisted around to follow Glen's gaze. He let out a whistle that caught the attention of half the bar.

"You idiot," hissed Glen under his breath, as the blonde woman raised her eyes and looked at Rashid with curious annoyance. "I honestly have no idea how you ever get laid."

Abashed, Rashid made his escape to the bar, promising to return with drinks if Glen wanted something. Glen waved him off with a smile, trying to smooth over his brief show of temper.

He waited to see if Rashid would return, but he soon spotted him chatting with two women who looked like they'd just had their conversation interrupted. One of them laughed, giving Glen hope that maybe his friend was making a positive impression for once. He stood and approached the solitary blonde's table. He didn't sit, waiting instead for her to acknowledge his presence.

"Hi," she said. Her voice was soft and lilting, with barely noticeable quaver brought on by alcohol or emotion. "I noticed you noticing me earlier. You aren't as subtle as you think you are."

"I'm not going to deny it. You're very attractive and I could tell there was some sort of drama going on. Did you get stood up?"

"Sort of. He did eventually text me to say he wouldn't be coming, but only after I'd already been waiting an hour."

"Did he have a good reason?"

"He didn't really give one, so I imagine not." She picked up her glass and swirled the amber liquid in it. "Why don't you sit down? You're making me nervous, looming over me like that."

He did as she'd asked, pulling his chair closer to hers. Up close, he could see that she was older than he'd imagined. The corners of her eyes were creased, as if she were a person who laughed often, even though she wasn't laughing tonight. She winked at him and he realized he'd been staring.

"Sorry."

"No problem. So, what's your name? I imagine it's something tall, dark and brooding. I'm Gertrude. Yes, for real. No, I don't know what my parents were thinking."

"Glen." He couldn't think of anything witty to say about her name. She'd obviously heard it all anyway.

"Most people end up calling me Trudy. One particularly annoying friend calls me Gertie, but I don't recommend you follow her example."

"Okay, Trudy it is." He flagged down a waitress and ordered a gin and tonic. Trudy made no comment but tilted her glass at the waitress and shrugged at Glen.

"So, I'm going to guess you wandered over here with supposed nonchalance in order to ask me why I'm looking so sad. Then you can be the good guy, swoop in and take me home. Right?"

Glen blinked. He honestly hadn't been thinking in such direct and cold terms, but that had been the general idea behind his approach.

"Um…"

"Save it. I don't want to hear either a lie or a flustered admission.

Both are equally uninteresting."

Glen decided to keep his mouth shut and was relieved when his drink arrived. He took a long, slow sip, searching for something smart to say.

"Let's just flip this whole thing on its head, shall we? You're a very good-looking guy, as I'm sure you know. Tall, well built. You seem like you can be charming, too, when someone isn't expertly shutting you down." Here, she paused to take a sip of her own drink and grin at him over the rim of the glass. "But I was watching you watching me and your attempt to seduce me seems half-hearted at best. I think something is bothering you. A lot. Am I right?"

His first instinct was to try to refute her claim, but it suddenly occurred to him that he had wanted to talk about Rebecca with Sarge and Rashid, only he'd been unable to. He didn't have anything to prove to Trudy, he didn't have any reputation to live up to. He could talk to her if it felt right. He sat in silence while Trudy waited for his answer.

"Yeah, you're right." "Want to talk about it?"

"Yes, I do." Glen took another long swallow of his drink and was surprised when one of the ice cubes clinked free and landed on the table. He'd downed the whole thing in only a few minutes.

"Well, Glen, talking is thirsty work. Get yourself another drink and tell me all about it."

Once he got started, he found Trudy easy to talk to. The story was simple, in essence, but he left out almost nothing, except for the most intimate details of the incredible sex he'd had with Rebecca. He made no attempt to hide his snooping or his cold treatment of Rebecca before unceremoniously dismissing her from his apartment.

"If I understand correctly, you allowed yourself to have feelings for this girl, perhaps for the first time ever, and when you saw that you might be about to get hurt, you decided to preemptively do the hurting?"

"I hadn't exactly thought of it that way, but yeah, I guess you're right."

Trudy abruptly downed the rest of her drink and picked up her purse.

"I'm getting out of here. Are you coming with me, or do you want to stay here and wait to see if one of those girls finally gets fed up and has sex with your friend just to shut him up?"

Glen could hardly have been more shocked if Trudy had announced she was headed off to join the circus and had invited him along.

"I can't tell if you're serious. And I'm a little afraid to try and guess."

Trudy stood, slinging her purse over her shoulder, and laughed. Another woman's laughter might have cruel or derisive in these circumstances, but she seemed legitimately delighted with his words and his hesitation.

"Oh, I'm serious. I think we could, maybe, do each other some good. And here's proof that I'm not kidding."

She circled the table and Glen noted how tiny she was. When she reached his side, she was only a few inches taller than he was sitting down and she hardly had to dip her head to kiss him. Their lips met softly and she darted her tongue out for only the tiniest fraction of a second. Before he could really get into the kiss, she pulled away.

"Coming?"

Glen nodded and stood, overwhelmed. He'd approached Trudy tonight with the idea of regaining his footing, of recreating the kinds of encounters and relationships that he'd been having with women for years. Instead, he'd found another who, like so many of the women he seemed to have met lately, had surprises in store for him and who wouldn't allow him to follow the script he'd been perfecting for so long.

He caught Rashid's eye and pointed towards the exit. Both men nodded and Rashid gave him a grin and an exaggerated wink that made the girls on either side of him roll their eyes. The one on his left, with long dark hair and almond-shaped eyes, gave Glen a searching look as he walked away.

It took Sam and Rebecca another hour to get back to the apartment. Sam balanced a bag of fries and chicken wings on top of a huge pizza box and held a bottle of white wine in her other hand as Rebecca unlocked the door and let them in. They were both glad to take refuge in the relative coolness inside.

Sam stepped in and hesitated in the impersonal room.

"Just drop everything on the coffee table. I'll go get us plates, napkins and glasses."

Rebecca ran to the kitchen, watching Sam out of the corner of her eye. The walk had been a lot of fun. Sam was easy to talk to and their conversation had very quickly slipped into comfortable banter and relaxed sharing. It was like talking to an old friend, someone she'd trusted and known for years. Except, of course, for the underlying sexual tension. She didn't know if Sam felt it, too, but it never seemed to go away. It was different from how she felt with men, subtler, but all the more exciting because of how new and strange it was.

She paused, feeling sheepish as she checked her reflection in the toaster, then gathered up everything they needed for their meal. In the living room, she found Sam parked on the couch, all the food already open.

"It smells amazing and I'm starving," said Rebecca.

She sat down, close enough to Sam for their elbows to bump awkwardly once or twice as they piled their plates with food. It was a greasy, cheesy mess and not what Rebecca was used to eating on a date, but it was delightful. They wolfed down the food in near silence until they'd finally satisfied the worst of their hunger.

Rebecca wiped her fingers on a napkin and sighed with satisfaction. "That was not a very lady-like display, but I can't say I regret any of it. How have I never been to this place before? It's fantastic."

Sam put her plate down and reached for the bottle of wine. "We ate so fast we didn't even stop to drink." She poured two glasses and handed one to Rebecca. The wine glinted beautifully in the glass, a pale straw gold with hints of green. "And, don't worry about being lady-like. I value other things in a woman."

"To not being ladylike," said Rebecca.

They clinked their glasses together and each took a sip.

"That's pretty good for something we basically grabbed randomly off the shelf because we were dying to get back here and eat," said Sam.

Rebecca didn't know if it was possible for the wine to have hit her already, but she felt warm and bold. She laid her hand softly on Sam's thigh, just above the knee.

"Yes, I was dying to get back home. The pizza was wonderful… but I'm still hungry."

Comprehension was slow to dawn in Sam's eyes. She gestured toward the ample leftovers, then stopped. She stared into Rebecca's eyes, searching for confirmation.

"I could go for some dessert," she said, her voice suddenly husky.

12

The walk through the parking lot was uneventful, but as soon as they reached Glen's car, Trudy pounced. He bent to meet her kisses, then lifted her, enjoying the way her full, round ass felt in his hands as he deposited her on the hood. He leaned forward as she wrapped her arms and legs around him, bracing himself against the warm car still radiating heat.

"Not that I'm complaining," he said during a lull in their kissing, "but wouldn't you like to go somewhere more comfortable?"

Trudy laughed and hooked her heels rather forcefully behind his knees, pulling him closer. "Like the back seat of your car?" she asked.

"Well, I meant my place. Or maybe yours. But whatever you want, really." He nuzzled at her neck, enjoying the way her long blond locks tumbled around them. He inhaled deeply, enthralled with her smell, suddenly wondering if she used the same hair products as Rebecca.

She giggled and squirmed as if he was tickling her and gently pushed him away. "Fine. Let's be adults about this and head back to your place."

Glen gave her one final slow, deep kiss and unlocked the car. He was almost ashamed to find his cock hard and pressing uncomfortably against his jeans. He took a deep breath as he dropped into the driver's seat, willing himself to concentrate on driving them safely to his apartment. Trudy gave a sly grin and raised an eyebrow as she buckled her seatbelt.

"Eyes on the road, buddy. There will be time enough for fooling around once we get where we're going."

He smiled, "What's your address?" - she just said go to his place...I'm confused.

"5323 Parkway Road, "she replied, smiling as Glen programmed the GPS.

He kept his eyes pointed straight ahead as he exited the parking lot but his mind wandered, first to Trudy, then to Rebecca. He wondered if her date had already started and if it was going well.

Surely she wouldn't spare him a thought, especially after he'd been so cold to her this morning. He sighed and tried to keep his thoughts on the road or on Trudy for the rest of the drive.

Putting her hand on Sam's thigh was the most daring act Rebecca was capable of at the moment. Despite the warm glow of arousal spreading between her legs, she felt frozen. She gazed into Sam's eyes, acutely aware of her all-too-feminine body inches away from her own. It occurred to her that she'd never touched another woman's breasts before and her hands suddenly ached for the sensation. She remained still, her breath coming in ragged gasps.

"Don't be nervous," whispered Sam, low and comforting. "Let's take this slow. And we can stop whenever you want or need to. There's no pressure."

Sam seemed to know that Rebecca wasn't ready to be touched. She allowed herself to recline on the couch, assuming a relaxed pose and a soft smile. Rebecca moved her hand slowly upwards, gliding over Sam's hip and stopping only when it rested under her left breast. Sam was wearing something like a sports bra under her plaid shirt and it pressed her breasts nearly flat. Despite this, Rebecca shivered as her fingers brushed over

Sam's chest and she wished she had unfettered access to her breasts.

Her desire must have been obvious because Sam put a hand over hers and said: "Would you like to see me?"

Mute, Rebecca nodded and watched, transfixed, as Sam slowly unbuttoned her shirt and removed it. She folded it and lay it over the back of the couch. Her skin was smooth and pale, as if she rarely wore anything but long sleeves, even in the sun. Feeling brave, Rebecca touched Sam's arm, her fingers playing all the way up to her the other woman's shoulder. Resting her hand on Sam's neck, she gently pulled Sam forward until their lips met.

The kiss was hardly less chaste than the one they'd shared on the street, but Rebecca's heart started to pound in her chest. She squeezed her thighs together, enjoying the sweet heat between her legs.

"Should I keep going?" asked Sam. Her voice was low, her lips soft against Rebecca's cheek.

Rebecca nodded again but didn't let go of Sam. She wanted

another kiss and she wasn't quite ready to let Sam pull back to see the flush spread across her cheeks. She parted her lips and gently pushed her tongue into Sam's mouth. The kiss lasted a long time. When they parted, both women were flushed and Rebecca was out of breath. She sat back and resumed watching Sam.

With a shyness Rebecca didn't expect, Sam slowly rolled her tight sports bra up over her head, exposing her small breasts. Rebecca stared, fascinated. Sam's nipples were pink and erect, protruding from her small, pale areolas. Rebecca reached out a tentative hand and brushed the tip of one finger over Sam's right nipple. She was gratified when Sam gasped. Still not quite believing what was happening, she cupped her hand over Sam's breast. The soft curve was almost enough to fill her palm and the silk of Sam's skin made her dizzy with desire.

Rebecca didn't pause, but followed her instincts. She dipped her head down and took Sam's other nipple into her mouth. For a moment she sucked softly, but when Sam moaned and arched her back, she flicked her tongue over the sensitive bit of flesh and even dared to nip at it with her teeth.

When Rebecca looked up, she found that Sam had tilted her head back and closed her eyes, lost in the sensation of Rebecca's mouth and hand on her breasts. Sam's lips were parted and she moaned and sighed with pleasure. Rebecca had never seen another woman this way, except in pornography. This was different, though, raw and real, not a performance to please the viewer.

She drew back, unsure what to do next, or if she wanted things to go further or revel in the present.

Sam opened her eyes and looked at Rebecca, her gaze searching. "That felt fantastic, but we can stop if you want or slow down...whatever you need."

Rebecca knew Sam was being earnest, but she could see the desire in her eyes and knew she wanted to keep going. Knowing Sam wanted her that way was enticing. She blushed with pleasure and looked at Sam from under lowered eyelashes.

Sam chuckled and raised her hand to tuck a strand of Rebecca's blond hair behind her ear. "You're cute, but you don't have to be so anxious. This isn't a test, you can't really make mistakes. Besides, I can teach you..."

They sat in silence, enjoying the physical contact and atmosphere of possibility for a while before Sam spoke again.

"Let me take the lead and you can follow. Just make sure to let me know if I go to fast or if you want to stop. Is that okay?"

Rebecca nodded and jumped as Sam stood and extended a hand to her. "Come on, let's head to the bedroom."

Trudy proved to be a very agreeable companion during Glen's drive home. It was only as they entered her tiny apartment that he remembered the mess he'd left at his own place after Rebecca's visit. He scanned Trudy's compact space, her hand in his as she led him to her room, and noticed an impression on her comforter. He smiled, imagining her seated there as she dressed for her day. As he and Trudy tumbled into it, he recalled the rumpled sheets in his own bed.

Trudy didn't seem to mind Glen's distraction as she expertly undid his belt and the fly on his jeans. He finished undressing while she did the same, pulling her simple shift dress over her head and dropping it on the floor. Her bra and panties soon followed and she kneeled on the edge of the bed, waiting impatiently for Glen. As soon as he'd removed his last piece of clothing, she pounced on him, neatly pinning him to the bed with her hands and knees and kissed him hard.

"I know you're thinking about her and, honestly, I don't care. I've got stuff on my mind, too." She paused to kiss him again, pressing her whole body against his and grinding her pussy against his already hard cock. "But I think we'll both enjoy this a lot more if we try to just focus on the moment."

Glen barked a short laugh and wrapped one arm around Trudy's waist. She was strong, but Glen's size was an advantage she couldn't easily overcome. He pulled her off him and flipped her over on to her back. She put up only a token resistance, giggling. She squirmed and laughed more as he pushed her thighs apart and buried his face between her legs. Her laughter quickly turned to sighing and she threaded her fingers through Glen's hair and made a fist.

Despite her words, Glen found his thoughts straying to Rebecca even as Trudy writhed beneath him. His cock was rock hard now, pressed against the bed, but he was content to focus his attention on making Trudy cum. He licked and nibbled at her clit, sometimes straying a little farther afield and kissing her inner thighs. She responded enthusiastically to everything he did, growing more and more wet. More quickly than he would have expected, she shuddered and clamped her thighs against the sides of his head, her hips bucking upwards.

"Oh, fuck," she cried.

When he was able to, Glen raised his head. "Should I keep going?"

"Oh, yes, please, don't you dare stop," panted Trudy.

Obediently, Glen bent his head again. This time, he slipped two fingers inside her tight, wet pussy. He loved how responsive she was, how enthusiastic, and how much pleasure she seemed to get from everything he did. Normally, he'd be thrilled with this unexpected turn of events and with what an active and carefree partner Trudy seemed to be. Instead, he could not stop comparing this encounter to the night before, to Rebecca. Trudy was no less attractive and Rebecca hadn't been any more enthusiastic, but something key was missing tonight.

Trudy shuddered to powerful orgasms at least twice more before she collapsed against the bed and released her hold on Glen's hair. She lay back, panting, and brushed a lock of sweaty hair off her forehead. She looked even lovelier than before, her skin flushed almost to glowing. Glen watched her squirm until she found a comfortable place for her head on the pillow before he lay down next to her. He pulled her warm, pliant body close and wrapped his arm around her. His cock was still hard and he knew that she could feel it pressed against her lower back.

They lay there for a while, neither of them moving, until Trudy's heart and breathing had slowed. Glen's erection had started to subside when she turned to him and put a warm hand on his cheek.

"That felt amazing. I'm completely willing to return the favor, but I'm sensing that maybe you don't want me to."

Glen shrugged as well as he could while lying on his side. "I'm guessing you're not the kind of woman who'll be upset if I tell you I'm not sure I'm up for it. Believe me, I'm surprised to be saying this, but I just can't seem to get Rebecca off my mind."

"You're right, I'm not offended. But I just want to make sure that I'm not leaving you hanging. If you want to cum, I'm happy to assist in any way you'd like."

Glen was silent for a moment, considering her words. "Let's just stay like this for a little while. I'm honestly not sure what I want."

"No problem. Heartache is confusing and distracting, believe me, I know."

Glen didn't respond, absorbed in his own thoughts. He wasn't sure if what he felt was heartache, but he knew he'd never experienced anything like it before. It didn't seem possible that he'd already fallen in love with Rebecca, but he felt like he'd lost something far more important than the chance to get laid. He had a beautiful woman in his bed, naked and willing, and she wasn't what he wanted. At least, this wasn't all he wanted, not anymore.

Finally, after Trudy had almost drifted off to sleep, Glen spoke. "Do you think there's any chance I haven't irrevocably fucked up my chances with her?"

Trudy yawned and stretched.

"The message you saw, it said she was agreeing to a date tonight, right?"

"Yes," answered Glen, forlorn.

"Haven't you ever done that before? I mean, go out with, and sleep with, two different girls two nights in a row? No offense, but you do kind of seem like the type."

"Of course I have," said Glen. "But that was different?"

Trudy scoffed and propped herself up on one elbow, rolling her head back to squint at Glen in the dark. "Wow. That's awfully hypocritical. What makes it so different when you do it?"

Glen opened his mouth to answer and realized how bad he was going to sound. "Well…I guess, to be honest, it's because I didn't care if I ever saw a woman more than once. And I never wanted to see a woman again if she cared about me sleeping around."

"At least you're honest," Trudy said. "So, what you're saying is that you were never looking for a relationship. You never wanted commitment or monogamy or any of that."

"Yeah, I suppose that's what I mean. I can't say I disagree with that unflattering summary at all."

"And now you are looking for something more than a one night stand." Trudy stopped and smiled ruefully. "Not with me, of course, but with Rebecca."

Glen rolled over on to his back and laid his forearm across his eyes. "I don't know! That sounds so momentous. I just like her. I like spending time with her, talking to her. But I also really liked fucking her. Is it so wrong or crazy that I want to spend more time with her and fuck her again?"

The sound of Trudy's laughter made him peek out from under his arm. "No, it's not wrong. It's also not so dramatic. That's what most people are after when they date and that's how many a long- term relationship start."

"So, what do I do?"

"You can't exactly go rushing over there to declare your love. She was on a date tonight. In fact, given how early it still is, if things went well she's likely still with the other guy."

"Girl," said Glen. "What?"

"I'm pretty sure the date is with a girl."

Trudy raised her eyebrows, "Really? What makes you say that?" "Well, the profile pic was either a short-haired woman or a twelve-year-old boy."

"That's an interesting wrinkle. This woman you're pining for isn't a lesbian, is she?"

Glen sighed heavily. "No, I don't think so. She didn't say anything at all about being into girls and she certainly seemed very enthusiastic about everything we were doing." He closed his eyes, briefly caught up in some intense memories from the night before. He felt his cock twitch and glanced quickly at Trudy to see if she'd noticed. She appeared lost in her own thoughts.

As she walked towards her bedroom, her hand in Sam's, Rebecca's gut twisted in the kind of nervousness and awkwardness she hadn't experienced since her teens. She had no idea what would happen next, but her lust and desire were much sharper than the urges of her youth. Calm confidence radiated from Sam, although she was obviously turned on, and it made a sharp contrast. Rebecca let out a long, slow breath, trying to ease her nerves.

Sam stopped at the foot of the bed and turned to look at Rebecca.

"It feels a bit like you're panicking and that's not at all what I want. I know you haven't said you want to stop, but I think maybe you do."

"I'm not panicking," said Rebecca, her voice almost a whisper. "I'm just nervous, really damn nervous. And unsure of what's expected of me."

"There are no rules and no expectations," said Sam softly.

Rebecca cast her eyes at the bed beyond Sam. It was pristine, the blankets laid out smooth and unwrinkled and the entire bed looked as big as a football field, somehow. On legs that felt shaky and uncertain, Rebecca walked to the left side of the bed and sat down. Her hands were on either side of her, fiddling with the coverlet and admiring its perfection.

"Do you want to lie down?" asked Sam.

Not trusting her voice, Rebecca nodded. She toed off her shoes and lifted her legs up onto the bed. More stiff than she would have liked, she let her head fall back against the pillows.

Sam went around to the other side of the bed and sat beside her. "What scares you most? Touching or being touched?"

The question surprised Rebecca and she gave it a few moments of thought before answering. "Touching, I think. It makes me feel so unsure of myself and I start to get convinced I'm going to do something ridiculously wrong."

Sam smiled in a way that let Rebecca know she was amused but not mocking. "Then let me touch you."

Rebecca felt a hot flash of desire at her words. "Yes, I'd like that.

Very much."

She imagined Sam would start with something overtly sexual, like cupping her breast or even thrusting her hand between her legs, but instead Sam laid two fingers gently on the side of Rebecca's jaw and slowly caressed downwards, over her neck and the part of her shoulder that was left exposed. Rebecca sighed with pleasure and relaxed down, her head to sinking into the pillow. Sam leaned forward and followed the same path with her lips, dusting Rebecca's skin with tiny kisses.

"That feels so nice," whispered Rebecca, turning her head to expose more of her skin and the underside of her jaw to Sam's ministrations.

Sam continued to kiss and caress her, sometimes darting out her tongue for a short lick. Rebecca fell into a kind of trance, passively enjoying everything that was happening. At first, she grew more and more relaxed. She closed her eyes and reacted only with a series of small, satisfied sighs. Gradually, she became aware of her arousal. Heat radiated up through her belly from her wet pussy. Her sighs were less satisfied and more filled with need. When Sam's fingers brushed her inner thigh, she parted her legs without thinking and raised her hips off the bed.

"Do you want more?" asked Sam. There was a husky edge of desire in her voice and it made Rebecca shiver.

Rebecca murmured her assent and spread her legs even wider. If not for her deep state of relaxation, she thought she might have grabbed Sam's hand and thrust it between her legs. Despite her obvious need, Sam continued slowly, stroking and teasing the skin of her inner thigh before gently running her fingers over Rebecca's panties. Rebecca trembled and arched her back, wanting more direct contact. Smoothly, Sam took advantage of her raised hips to hook her fingers under the waistband of Rebecca's panties and pulled them down as far as she could. Rebecca felt cool air against her hot, wet pussy and sighed eagerly.

"Oh, please...you don't need to go so slowly anymore. I want you to touch me, I promise." The words spilled out of Rebecca in a rush.

Sam laughed softly. "I know I don't, but I have to admit that I'm enjoying teasing you. You're getting so wet, so turned on, so needy. It's beautiful."

Rebecca made a small sound of frustration and defeat. With Glen she'd discovered her submissive side and she knew how enjoyable it was to put herself in someone else's hands. She'd let Sam have her way. The pleasure would be worth the wait.

Sam pushed up the stiff denim of Rebecca's skirt to create better access to the center of Rebecca's desire. She laid one hand on Rebecca's belly, not pressing, but resting, the weight alone enough to make the other woman squirm. With her other hand, she played with Rebecca's pussy, exploring the shape of her lips and the wonderful wetness she found there.

Rebecca ached for something more than these gentle touches, but willed herself to stay still and calm. She made an effort to control her breathing, which had grown shallow. Her hands, which had been resting, open, on the bed to either side of her, balled into fists and gripped the sheet.

The teasing and softness had gone on for so long that when Sam slipped a finger inside Rebecca it was a shock, though it was an intense and welcome one. Rebecca gasped loudly and her thighs trembled.

"Thank you, god. Thank you," she breathed.

In response, Sam laughed and started moving her hand. Her finger crooked upwards, searching, until Sam found the perfect spot to make Rebecca squirm and gasp. She moved her other hand down until her thumb rested just beside Rebecca's clit. This, too, caused a deep, needy moan.

"Do you need an orgasm, Rebecca?" asked Sam playfully.

"Oh, fuck, yes!" said Rebecca, surprising both of them with her loud enthusiasm. The both laughed for a brief instant, before the eroticism of the situation overtook them again.

"Lie back and try to stay relaxed. I'm going to do my absolute best to make you cum as hard as I possibly can."

Glen internally chastised himself for having such a one-track mind. Despite his inexplicable and unfamiliar feelings for Rebecca, his cock had taken fresh notice of the beautiful naked woman lying in bed with him. Trudy still appeared lost in her own thoughts until Glen snaked an arm around her and pulled her in close, pressing his erect cock into the small of her back. She turned her head to flash a cheeky grin over her shoulder.

"Done ruminating and feeling frisky?" she asked. "I guess you could say that."

"Then it's my turn," said Trudy, grinning even wider.

Without further preamble, she sat up and moved down. With one hand wrapped firmly around the base of his cock, she took the head into her mouth and started bobbing gently up and down. Glen couldn't tell what exactly she was doing with her tongue, but it felt incredible. His hand moved, unbidden, to tangle itself in her hair. He resisted the urge to exert pressure, to push her mouth further down on his cock and tried to rest his fingers on her head and enjoy the delicious friction of her lips and tongue.

She raised herself up and smiled at him again. "You can push down if you want. I don't mind if blowjobs get a little rough."

With a groan of pleasure, he pushed her head down. He was surprised at how easily she seemed to take the entire length of his huge cock. He felt the tip of it hit the back of her throat then keep going. It had to bend a little, but the pressure and friction more than compensated for any discomfort. He held her that way for a second, delighting in the convulsive feeling of her gagging, then released her.

She pulled her mouth away from him, one long string of saliva briefly linking his cock to her lips. She pulled in a gasping breath. "Wow. That was intense…Again?"

Glen nodded, but gestured for Trudy to lie down across the bed. He stood and pulled her gently by the shoulders until her head was hanging off the edge of the bed. She stared up at him, eyes widening in curiosity as he stroked his cock above her face.

"Ready?" he asked.

"Yes," she whispered. Already her hand was between her legs, one finger on either side of her clit.

She opened her mouth and tilted her head back as far as it would go. Glen put a hand on each of her breasts, squeezing them tightly enough to leave bruises. Slowly, he pushed his massive cock into her mouth and then down her throat. It was fascinating to watch her throat work as she gagged on him and moaned as her fingers moved between her legs. He pulled out and allowed her one gasping breath before thrusting forward again.

"Fuck," he said, through gritted teeth. "That feels fucking amazing."

He wanted to hold back and draw the pleasure out, but the sight of Trudy writhing beneath him and the incredible sensation of thrusting deep into her throat was overwhelming. He pulled out of her mouth one final time, allowing her a long breath and pushed his cock back into her, moaning.

"I'm going to cum," he said, teeth gritted. His fingers tightened on her breasts. This time, he'd definitely left bruises.

His cock pulsed in her throat and he shuddered as she convulsively swallowed every spurt of his seed. Just as he started to pull out, Trudy cried out, her voice muffled as she clamped her legs around her hand. He lay down on the bed next to her and stroked her sweaty skin as she trembled through the aftershocks of her orgasm.

"Wow," she said softly.

"Yeah. I'll say. Thank you. That was incredible."

Trudy nodded, seemingly beyond words for the moment. Rebecca closed her eyes and stopped wondering what exactly Sam was doing to her. She knew there was a wonderful pressure on her clit and that Sam had slipped a finger or two inside her, but beyond that, she could not quite form any solid idea of which parts of her were being touched and in what way. All she knew was that it felt good and that she wanted to simply abandon herself to the pleasure it brought her. She let go of everything, releasing her self- consciousness about her moans and the way she writhed on the bed. The sheet had pulled away from one corner of the mattress, but she couldn't bring herself to care.

As her orgasm grew closer, she found herself thinking less and less about Sam. Briefly, until the pleasure swept her away again, she felt guilty that her thoughts had turned almost entirely to Glen. With her eyes closed, it was easy to imagine he was the one kneeling next to her, his hands touching her in a surprisingly wonderful and delicate way. Sam made no move to break the spell. She was quiet except for her ragged breathing, which could have just as easily been Glen's.

Suddenly, Rebecca's moans quieted and she held her breath for a few seconds, poised on the precipice of her orgasm. When she went over the edge, she cried out and turned her face to the side, pressing her fevered cheek into the pillow.

Neither woman spoke for several long minutes. The only sound in the bedroom was their breathing, which slowed gradually. Rebecca knew she could easily succumb to sleep now, but tried to fight the temptation. She was dimly aware that Sam was still sitting next to her and her guilt had returned more strongly now. She opened her eyes.

Sam was looking at her almost sadly. "You were thinking about him, weren't you?"

Rebecca blushed and averted her eyes. "Yes. I'm sorry."

"It's ok. I knew this was a long shot. Maybe I should have asked you out sooner, before you spent a magical evening with him and started to fall in love."

The lamp on the bedside table wobbled and nearly fell as Rebecca bolted upright. "I'm not in love with him! He's an asshole."

Sam laughed. "So you say, but you can't get him off your mind. Maybe you aren't in love, but you're certainly on the edge of it. There's potential for it there and I get the feeling that you're going to end up exploring it—despite what happened this morning."

Suddenly conscious of herself, Rebecca pulled her skirt down over her thighs before drawing her knees up to her chest and wrapping her arms around them.

"I'm sorry I was distracted by thoughts of Glen, honestly. What you were doing felt so good and I should have been paying attention to you."

"I told you to relax. I wanted you to feel good." Sam shrugged. "Maybe it's not the best news for me, but at least you're being honest with me. And with yourself."

After an awkward silence, Rebecca unfolded herself and sat next to Sam in an attempt to shift the energy in the room.

Sam laid her hand on Rebecca's leg. I hope you wore sexier panties for Glen."

They laughed together, deflating the tension.

Rebecca eyes darted about the room, searching for her purse before remembering she'd dropped it on the kitchen counter. She smiled at Sam before standing to retrieve her phone from the bag. She scrolled through the notifications, mostly from the dating app.

"Ah…"

Sam's voice broke Rebecca's focus on the phone. She looked up to see Sam waiting by the door.

"I think I'm out of here now." She smirked, "Thanks, Becky.

And good luck—honestly."

Rebecca half-smiled and left the kitchen to meet her. "Thank you. And, I'm sorry."

Sam's smirk twisted, "Don't be." She leaned in and gave Rebecca a chaste kiss. "Bye, Vanilla Becky."

13

Rebecca opened her eyes to find it was 5:23 AM. She groaned, annoyed at waking so early on a day when she had the luxury of sleeping in. There was a pain in her chest, a simultaneous sinking and a burning, a feeling of loss. Sam had left politely the previous evening, but Rebecca could see the disappointment in her eyes. Unsurprisingly, no new message notifications awaited on her phone.

The sheets lay in a crumpled mess around her ankles and she still wore the skirt and t-shirt Sam had so deftly operated beneath. She'd fallen asleep staring at her phone screen like a nightlight in the dark, hoping for relief. She thought of reaching out to Glen, but froze every time she opened a blank text. She'd somehow expected things to be better when she awoke, but they were only more painful. Not only was she certain she had alienated Glen, but she was convinced she'd lost Sam, too. Her mother's nagging echoing in her head, Rebecca fought panic at the thought she might have run out of chances at love.

She felt guilty. Sam wanted her, wanted something from her, while Rebecca was only entertaining a curiosity. Before she agreed to meet Sam, she'd known in her deepest self that her feelings for Sam were limited, she couldn't give Sam what she truly wanted. Rebecca was growing all-too-familiar with this post-game analysis after a botched hook-up. Somehow, she either made receiving or creating pain predictable. This inevitability was precisely why, up until the last week, she had never been free with her body—and why she was so hesitant, despite the desire thrumming through her.

Maybe Glen wasn't right for her. Maybe he was. Rebecca had no clue, really. The truth of their dynamic lay in the future, well beyond the mess of feelings she harbored for him now. How could she make a decision, know anything, with all this want overcoming her? Her heart strained toward Glen, despite the sting, that much she knew. It was irresponsible, she thought to herself, to engage so much with Sam while she was feeling this.

She stopped herself, backpedaling from the machinations in her head and chest. Rebecca recognized the familiar trappings of her prudishness, the quickness with which she moralized her sexual actions and stopped herself from living, like she was the proper church girl her mother had tried to raise. But Rebecca had never really been that girl, despite her constant struggle. The confusion with Glen hurt, and she hated pulling away from Sam as the other woman was leaning in, but Rebecca resolved to push through the morass of discomfort and dissatisfaction. She deserved to fuck and feel just fine about it.

Rebecca opened her phone. A news alert about the handsome, single governor of California, a potential presidential candidate, popped up. She swiped it away, smirking at the irony: exactly like every other single woman in America, she had a helpless crush on the famous man. She opened her online dating app and although there was a plethora of messages from wanting young men, they did nothing to fill Rebecca's emptiness, only widening the cave inside of her instead. None of her new possibilities seemed to point toward anything meaningful—a string of probable one-night-stands in the making. She thought of Mike, who'd been so sweet and patient with her. She even thought about calling him, but she'd crossed a line with Glen and she didn't think she could ever come back.

With Glen, she'd bridged the gulf between fantasy— the kind of fantasy she'd buried inside for decades, unexplored—and reality, and found a level of pleasure she now worried she might be addicted to. What if Glen had filled her with his enormous cock and his complicated version of love and left her carved out like this on the other end? Her heart and body quaked both with regret and nostalgia for what had happened less than a day ago.

She longed for the days of Panopticon, for affection in the form of a fluffy, unspeaking, and nonsexual creature, benevolent in her innocent prancing, wanting nothing but physical space and a gentle touch. There was no intricate plot to Pan—a stark contrast to the mercurial emotional places that Glen and Rebecca had found together.

Rebecca slumped onto the couch, a spectator to her spiraling anxiety and confusion. Glen, huge and handsome, with a seemingly impenetrable heart, somehow absorbed and tossed aside all this sex and still managed to retain his charm. She hated his poise, even if his snooping on her phone meant she was wrong about his invincibility.

But the larger part of her believed Glen would move on easily. The image of a stranger's tangled blonde hair clinging to Glen's sweaty flesh brought bile to her throat.

Rebecca swallowed and inhaled deeply. If he had moved on, so would she.

She tapped on the dating app and scrolled through the sludge of unread messages, mostly variations of "hi" or overt sexual advances. A skinny, handsome user with glasses caught her eye. "DastardlyDave420's"status showed him as online, and his profile said he was a video producer.

His message asked if Rebecca was a robot designed to infiltrate his heart and turn it into a weapon. Rebecca giggled and, on impulse, replied yes. Dave was quick to respond.

DastardlyDave420: *Finally. I've been doing too much good. It's about time someone turned me into vehicle of capitalist means.*

MileHighBecky: You're kooky.
DastardlyDave420: *I was hoping you'd say that.*

Rebecca scanned back over Dave's photos as he typed. There was certain sarcasm in all of his poses, a clear refusal to take the endeavor of posting pictures of himself online sincerely. Rebecca usually didn't find this sort of detachment appealing, but it felt like exactly what she needed this morning.

MileHighBecky: *Why are you awake this early?*

DastardlyDave420: *I'm depraved.*

Rebecca read this message and felt a pang at the thought of Glen not even five minutes into her conversation with Dave, that tall jerk was back in her head, invading. Whatever she did romantically or sexually, whomever she did it with, she suspected she would transpose on it—on them—the twisted depths she had shared with Glen.

MileHighBecky: *Tell me—what's the most depraved thing you've done recently?*

Glen spent a restless night at Trudy's. Despite the tremendous satisfaction she'd given him—he seriously wondered if she had performed the absolute best blowjob he's ever received. His relaxed body still burned with regret for how he'd ended things with

Rebecca. Trudy nuzzled into him in her sleep as he stared at the ceiling, aware of how much of a cliché he was, caught in his feelings. He was the picture of forlorn, the sad sight of heartbreak he'd always vowed he'd never be.

Perhaps this state was merely a barrier he had to break through. Glen felt in himself a push-pull between how he had been and how he might be—a defining, adult test.

As hints of the sun peeked through Trudy's blinds, she stirred against him. Coming into consciousness, she started to dig her nose into his pecs, then lick him. With a sexy, groggy voice, she asked if he'd slept well.

"No, I was too pleased to sleep," he said in half-truth. "And with what you're doing right now," he said as she nibbled on his nipples, "I'm beginning to wonder if I'll ever sleep again."

"I'm glad you appreciate my art," Trudy said, straddling him and running his cock between her thighs as it hardened. Glen thrust up against Trudy's body, pressing down on her shoulders. The head of his penis ran along her stomach and she guided it with her hands up toward her breasts. "Good morning," she said. Glen laughed as his member slid between her breasts and she pressed them together to create extra pressure.

"Oh my god," Glen said. "Oh my god." He grabbed Trudy by her blonde hair, nearly lifting her small frame up as he throbbed with pleasure.

Trudy pressed her thumbs into Glen's temples and looked into his eyes. "I want to do something to you that you might not like," she said, full of conviction. She put her arms around his shoulders and turned him so he was on top of her, demonstrating such surprising strength that Glen acquiesced in his state of foggy bliss.

Although he straddled Trudy's tiny body, Glen felt almost no power at all, nor did he want to. He was happy to be in the hands of a master, ready to see what she had in store for him next. Even Briana, who had owned and rearranged his desires just days ago, exhibited a certain anxiety in her sexuality and power games. The seasoned Trudy seemed completely devoid of self-consciousness. Glen wondered if he could ever fuck a younger woman again, or if he was now exclusively in the land of veterans. Trudy positively stopped time with her confident carnal aggression.

Coy, Trudy asked Glen if he was ready, but didn't wait for his answer. Her small, delicate hands crept down his back before suddenly diving between his ass cheeks. Glen shrieked, his body instinctively convulsing as Trudy manipulated erogenous zones he didn't know he had. He slapped his palms against her headboard while she tickled his stomach with baby kisses, twisting her fingers slowly in his rectum. He found himself laughing, almost uncontrollably, and Trudy chuckled too as she continued her shocking performance on him.

DastardlyDave420: *The most depraved thing I've done recently? Internet dating.*

MileHighBecky: *Tsk tsk. I feel you're hiding something with that reply.*

DastardlyDave420: *Am I hiding something, or are you just eager to make a confession.*

MileHighBecky: *Maybe I am. Maybe not. It's been an unusual week, that much is for sure.*

DastardlyDave420: *Unusual how?*

Rebecca bit her lip in the sort of blatant sexual overture she reserved for moments when a man—Dave or otherwise—could see her. Internet dating always brought this behavior out in her, the constant performance, especially when she was logged into the app. She knew hardly anything about Dave, but the idea of seeing him right now, of seizing this weird moment of slumber time in which both of them were strangely awake and looking for love, was distinctly erotic.

MileHighBecky: *I can't explain...words don't really do justice. I'd have to show you...*

DastardlyDave420: *Show me how?*

MileHighBecky: *With my body. I've been learning new tricks and I'm eager to practice.*

DastardlyDave420: *Show and tell.*

MileHighBecky: *Yes, show and tell. I like that.*

DastardlyDave420: *Show and tell where?*

MileHighBecky: *Come over now or risk me putting my chastity belt back on and locking it forever.*

Rebecca sent him her address and logged off. She rolled over onto her back and pressed her phone against her chest, her heart beating in excited panic against it. Glen was not exactly an afterthought now, and neither was Sam—but both of them felt like pains and confusions she could easily put on a shelf inside of her, in a catalog, a library of loves.

She enjoyed this feeling of accumulation, of poking out into the world and taking feelings, of collecting experience so easily. She'd had the body, the face, the charm to do this all along, but never thought to weaponize herself. So much pent up in her now rushed to life, roaring to the surface of the breathing, touching, cumming world, and it made her blood run faster in anticipation of more.

As Glen lay on Trudy's bed trembling in newly discovered delight, Trudy went to her dresser. "I don't know how much further you're willing to take this," she said, "but I have a toy that I'd like you to at least meet."

"I can't imagine what else there is," Glen said with a laugh. When Trudy brought him to orgasms with her hands in his ass, he could feel his eyes bulging and sweat dripping. Now was the cool- down after a fire. As much as Briana had tortured and manipulated in the name of a coming aching pleasure, Trudy had shown him yet another level of acquiescence, and for the first time, he had enjoyed a profound sexual encounter without use of the engorged penis women had so enjoyed. It was strange to look down and realize he'd come to release without it.

As Glen turned over onto his back, Trudy leapt onto the bed. She drummed playfully on Glen's back as the mattress bounced. Glen couldn't help but giggle as Trudy treated him like an oversized instrument. She awoke something childlike in him; with her, he felt like everything was, really, rather silly. The weight he'd felt with Rebecca or Elena disappeared with Trudy. He didn't know if this state could last, or if he'd even see Trudy again, but he'd never felt lighter in his entire adult life.

Then he felt something else plop onto his back. It ran perpendicular along the notches of his spine and felt rubbery and large and rather long. "What is that," he asked. "You just happy to see me?"

"I think you know what it is," Trudy said coyly. "But I'm wondering if you've ever played with one before."

"Well, I've certainly heard about them, if it is what I think it is," Glen said with a laugh. "I'm just not sure how we'd use it, though," he said.

He grabbed the dildo to examine it, finding it was actually a bright green strapon attached to leather underwear. "Trudy," he said. "I don't know if I'm ready to graduate to this just yet, or if I ever want to." His voice didn't have as much fun in it, and he looked down at the tool with mixed skepticism and fear. "Have you...have you used this with guys before, and do they like it?"

"All the time," she said. "And honestly, most guys love to be pegged. They might not like to talk about it, especially not around other guys, but I can make you feel things you've never imagined. Whatever pleasure you got from my hands, artful as those are, this is a million times more intense. It might hurt, at first, but then you're in ecstasy."

"What do you get out of it, though? It's not even your body, really, that's doing the work or feeling me." He stalled, trying to work out where he drew the line in his sexual experience and a little afraid it wasn't where he'd always thought.

"Oh, but it is. It's me heaving my weight against yours, working the angles. Believe it or not, Glen," Trudy said with a wink, straddling him and pinching his earlobe between two fingers as she kissed his left shoulder, "it's actually a lot more fulfilling for me than giving a blow job."

"Well," Glen chuckled, "that's your best argument yet. Because in that department, you're most certainly a shining star."

Glen grabbed Trudy by her plush behind, squeezing hard and pulling her body into his chest. She nuzzled between his pecs, her long locks mingling with his chest hair, and he stroked her head to soothe his own fears. "I don't know," he said. "Something about that thing scares me. I trust you, but it worries me. I don't know why."

"It's because men are taught to like a certain sort of something," Trudy said gently. "They're supposed to be in control. But most of them haven't stepped back enough of a second to know how good it might feel to let the lady to do the walking, and take you for a different kind of ride. For *you* to be the one whose body is invaded and penetrated. I know that's scary, but isn't everything great always scary when you try it out the first time?"

The knock at Rebecca's door was soft, but repeated three times in a melody somehow sarcastic. Dave. She'd never met him, but after their short exchange of spunky messages, he felt familiar—like an old friend, a friend she wanted to fuck. She jumped up from bed in her underwear—it had never even occurred to her to change into anything else. She skipped to the door, a bit giddy and laughing at herself. When she opened the door to Dave, whose eyes were bulged at the sight of her, she laughed even harder.

In fact, suddenly Rebecca could do nothing but laugh. She stumbled to the couch in hysterics as Dave closed the door and followed. He was wearing a barely buttoned pale blue Oxford with khaki shorts and sneakers. He was unshaven and his curly hair unkempt.

"You're quite the rascal," he said as he sidled up beside her. "Pulling me over here only to collapse in laughter at me."

"Oh it's not you! I just can't believe what I'm doing," she said, her amusement with herself subsiding. "I'm never like this. I never have been. I'm really going crazy or something, I think. But I like it." Rebecca placed her hand on Dave's exposed chest as she spoke, slipping her other hand behind his neck. After Glen's impressive size and Sam's lust for her, she felt so much more in control. She'd almost never made first moves before, but now she knew what she wanted. She was hungry and it was so easy to take the prey before her.

"I feel violated," Dave said, even as he unbuttoned his shirt with a grin. Rebecca slid her hands around his and sat on his thighs, helping with the buttons. He put his free hands to work under her bra, his mouth finding her nipples. She held tight to his head, almost maternal in the act, and she began to thrust against his midsection friskily. He was absolutely her toy in this moment, and

Dave didn't seem to mind being used.

Trudy pummeled Glen from behind. Bent over the bed and screaming in the discovery of pure new ecstasy he'd given up control and lost himself in the pleasure.

It had taken him hardly any time at all to get over the stigma of being penetrated, finding new pressure points within the full and crazy range of the sensual body. Once Glen stopped caring about being dominated, he accessed a waterfall of release, a ceaseless rushing of blood to places untouched, and he shouted for more. At first, the dildo felt alien, inhuman, but it quickly evolved into an extension of Trudy's will, of her love in this uncanny moment of learning and change.

Soon, he couldn't feel the specific object at all, just the heft of her, so small but bursting through with the weight of confidence and knowledge. It was the gravity of her desire and expertise pressing him into the bed and causing an extremely strange new sense of his body in Glen. His eyes rolled back as enjoyment washed over him, his ass expanding into another zone of sensual deployment. He tried to restrain his erect penis, pressed between his stomach and the mattress, from explosion all the while, but he could also feel precum leaking out of him much faster than he was used to, as well as a series of what he imagined were dry orgasms. There was a first for everything, and Trudy seemed bent on retrieving every sexual first still remaining in Glen.

Trudy slowed, digging in with her strap-on and pushing deep into Glen firmly as she nuzzled him from behind, holding onto his shoulders and softly kissing the nape of his neck. He could feel her form spooning him, every inch of her pressed against him. Her nipples against his back make him coo. Their mixed sweat made their friction slippery. "I think you might slide right off of me," Glen said through his panting.

Trudy laughed and pulled out of him, removing her

strap-on before sitting atop Glen's back like he were another piece of furniture in the room. "If you turn over like a big massive pancake," she said, "I'll sit down right on your dick and finish you in a familiar way. But you have to get out from under me while I'm pinning you like this first, and you know how big I am. You just felt my size for a while, didn't you?"

Rebecca laid her head against the fur of Dave's slight chest. Post-coital and underwhelmed, physically, by the encounter—Dave had not the heft of Glen, nor his force, nor Sam's mastery of female anatomy—she was nonetheless content. After the emotional tornado of Glen, she felt an old need to be near someone she could trust, an impulse she was beginning to wonder about. Dave had no reason to trust her, to trust her ability to love him, or to even want to see him again, but recent experiences had taught her that she could impose any kind of terms upon him.

Then as Dave ran his fingers through her hair while she used him as a pillow, he began an unexpected line of inquiry. "Flight attendant, huh?" he said. "What's that like? How much do you work?"

"I've had a lot of days off recently but only because I have to work for ten days straight soon. Starting tomorrow, actually. I haven't really thought about that recently. My time hasn't been... relaxing, exactly. A lot's been going on."

"What kind of stuff's been going on? Am I not the only man you've recently known."

Rebecca chuckled a little at Dave's phrasing, but also caught a bit of unearned, self-aggrandizing in his voice. He wasn't anywhere near as cocky as Glen, but he was still a little cocky. Of course, with Glen, the big difference was that he performed so well he almost earned himself the right to be a jerk.

"You're not wrong," Rebecca replied, hesitant. "I've

MARLEY

been doing a lot more dating than usual. Dating, if that's what you want to call it, anyway. Is this a date, do you think?"

"Do you not remember when I took you to the ballroom in my tuxedo, and showered you in roses, tipping my top hat to you, then escorting you home in a chariot, officially making it a date?"

Rebecca laughed with her whole body. "No, no, I suppose I don't remember that. Shows how good my head's been lately. Sorry. Do I seem distracted or out of it? I don't mean to be."

"It's fine. Honestly, if you're interested in honesty or full disclosure anyway, and I'm going to tell you this either way because it feels bad not to, I'm married. I mean, I'm separated. We're estranged. We don't talk. Only through our lawyers, anyway. We're getting divorced. But if you're worried about being distracted, don't be, is what I'm saying."

"Well," Rebecca replied, pulling back, but still using Dave to lean on, "I certainly haven't been *divorced* before or recently. I'm sorry to hear that, it sounds like a drag."

"It is a drag, but, really, I'm dragging my ass out of a painful purgatory is what I'm doing. It's necessary, at the end of it. And things like this make the process so much more bearable. So thank you, Rebecca. MileHighBecky. Have you ever joined the mile high club, by the way? I'm sorry, people must ask you that all the time. Especially on that lecherous dating app. You don't have to answer that."

"No, no, it's fine," Rebecca said. She planted her chin in the middle of his chest and looked up at his face. Dave looked tired with life in a way that was familiar to her.

"I haven't been part of the mile high club, no. I think that would be a bad professional move. And really this has been just about the friskiest week of my life. I don't usually do the whole sexual exploration thing. It's a brand new MileHighBecky over here. Shooting out into the world!" Rebecca was surprised to hear herself speak so sarcastically; maybe Dave was rubbing off on her. "Maybe I will join that sordid club, though, after all."

"Well, as a member myself, let me tell you that it's not as glamorous as it sounds."

"Oh? You've been to the club before?"

"With my, you know, wifey-ghost. Boo!" Dave said loudly, causing Rebecca to jump up off of him in a moment of actual fright.

"David," she said, laughing as she came down from the scare. "Don't startle me like that! Dastardly, dastardly David. 420."

"I'm just preparing you for the nerves it will take for you to join the mile high club."

"Never!" Rebecca said, slapping his mid-section teasingly. "Never!"

Rebecca watched Dave laugh in the moment, enjoying the fast charm they shared, but then his expression changed. Unsettled by the quick shift, she asked him what had happened.

"Sorry," Dave said. "I don't want to get heavy. Don't worry about it."

"Well, now you have to tell me, because I *am* worried about it." "Okay. Okay. I'll tell you. You're so insistent. You're killing me right now, but surely I will tell you, Rebecca. It's about the past. Ghosts."

"What kind of ghosts?"

"Well, you know—just right now, the two of us laughing, I was reminded of my ex-wife. How silly it is to be divorced."

"It's okay," Rebecca said tenderly. "You don't have to feel silly."

"It's weird, but it was just a similar laugh to hers. Otherwise you're not like her. Not at all. I wouldn't be into you if you were. And I am very into you. But that laugh hit a chord in me."

"I'm sorry," Rebecca said.

"No, no, don't apologize. It's not your fault. You're great. I'm just still getting used to things. There's still spaces in my apartment where her things used to be. I feel haunted by all those empty spots. I need to get new things. Another cocktail cart, a different couch, or maybe I even need to move. It feels so nice to be here. I was so glad when you asked me over. I needed to get out of my spot and stop feeling that emptiness. I'm trying to fill myself with new things and I think I really like you."

"I like you too," said Rebecca. She smiled wide and honest, although she was taken aback. Dave had been so wry about everything, but now he punched through that sardonic wall with a fist of raw emotion. He'd been quick to put his defenses down, unlike Glen who—even after that most transcendent sex—kept his walls up. "I hope I see you again."

"I hope I see you again too," Dave said clutching her.

Glen held Trudy, post-orgasm, as she melted into him and faded into a morning nap. He wanted to join her in his slumber, but even after all that exercise and new experience—he felt sore all over— Glen couldn't get his mind to settle down. His neurons bounced everywhere and urged him to reconsider everything. He missed Rebecca, sure, but he missed Trudy, too, even as she was with him. All the satisfaction of sex was taking him further from people, he realized—not closer.

Playing with Trudy's hair splayed on his chest, he

thought about the man she mentioned while they were still at the bar. The man who'd hurt or confused her such that she was trying to avoid dealing with it by taking Glen home. Meanwhile, he was avoiding dealing with the caves Rebecca had dug into his emotional core, settling into them like a wraith. It now felt both like she'd shared the most impactful moment of his life but also that it had not happened at all. He recalled her adorable struggling face as her pleasured her while she played Katamari Damacy and tried to restrain herself, but the memory was hazy in Glen's head, like a movie he'd seen as a child rather than an actual event only two days earlier.

Glen's dick was sore, and so was his ass. As much as he'd had his way with women over the years, made a playground for his desires out of how much they wanted his size and poise and comfort in forcefully pleasing them, he had never had a week quite like this. This much release brought relief, but a gnawing, too. The more women he had, the sooner they were gone from him after the act. Here was Trudy, still on his body, and he felt like she was already a million light years away, some imaginary substance found only in deep space. With Rebecca he felt his soul tethered to hers, but that feeling had already faded, trampled in the mere 24 hours he'd needed to take hold and boldly ruin the romance.

Glen reached for his phone on Trudy's nightstand, careful not to wake her while he acted as her pillow. He texted Rashid: "How was your night, man? I had a weird one, and could definitely go for a friend to talk some things over with right now…"

As Glen put his phone back down to give Rashid time to respond, he began to fantasize about what his life would be like if he didn't make chasing women a full-time job. He spent more time and energy on getting laid, he realized, than he ever had on vocation or ambition. He was good at it, at least—there was no denying he could field the desires of many women. He knew he could make them both happy and eager for more. Yet he could still move deftly through social networks, wetting his veritable beak without getting snagged into something serious or burning too many bridges. There was a skill to that, to be sure. But what, at the end of it, had any of it amounted to? What did he have to show for it?

Glen used to dream about the FBI, about the military, about being an athlete or a protector. About using his unusually impressive frame toward a more socially relevant end. Somewhere along the way, though, sex became the drug he couldn't get enough of. Women clung to him at parties when he wasn't even thinking about them, and it warmed him every time. Without considering whether he wanted to, he found himself making moves. It was like he had no say in the matter. Not that Glen minded; for the longest time, it was all he wanted, all he needed or cared about, to continue stacking his résumé in the bedroom. But now that he held such outstanding credentials between the sheets, he couldn't think of anywhere they would take him aside from the arms of more women.

Trudy had broken him, in a way. A lot of women could have, but she was the one who'd done it. He'd been ready for breaking. But her sexual adventure took him past a line he'd long been fast approaching. He didn't know what the alternative was to living like this, didn't know how to take a different turn and become someone else with a more fulfilling path, but he knew he wanted these desires sucked out of him for a while, vacuumed out of his insides. He wanted to detoxify from love and its lesser forms. He wanted to be alone, a monolith, for his stature to be a monument of indeterminate value for a while. He wanted to do something new with his body. Glen couldn't wait for Trudy to wake, to put his clothes on and walk out her door toward something else. Whatever that something might be.

His phone vibrated. Rashid. "Bro," it read, "You're not going to believe how things went for me last night. And how I feel about it. We should definitely meet up later. I got a LOT of stories to tell…"

As Rebecca put her flight attendant outfit on for the first time in nearly week, she knew she'd see him again soon, in Chicago. Dave was going there for work and she was working a connecting flight as part of her many long, upcoming shifts, and the two had agreed to meet. Dave made plenty of jokes about making love to her in the airplane's bathroom, but she deflected each of them playfully. The thought fermented in her after he left, though, until it started to seem more possible to her. It started to seem like something she wanted to do.

Rebecca had never taken any risks while on the job. If she was honest, she hadn't taken many risks at all. Not until this past week.

Not until she overheard Glen in the bathroom, wrecking a young eager woman into ecstasy. A fever had come over her. She'd thought for some days that the fever came from Glen, and maybe it did. But more importantly, he was the carrier and he'd infected her. Now she wanted a deeper range of feeling, to be plied and rearranged and manipulated, loved and touched and ignored, and generally thrown into the thresher of chaotic human emotion. She wanted to be a mess the way other people were a mess, to move within the soap opera of her species' sexuality.

She fastened her neckerchief and pulled at her skirt, feeling its tautness against her tights as she prepared to leave for the day. Today, more than usual, she liked the way this outfit played into clichés of what men want. Harassment, bothersome flirtation, general disrespect—males had always given her attention when she dressed how she had to dress for her career. She hated it. Now she thrummed with new power to filter out the toxic parts of this energy, localize the waves of infatuation she wanted, and turn them into delight. Glen had given her the road map and she was ready to embark on her new adventure.

Glen sat alone in his car in an empty parking lot. He had driven straight from Trudy's in a blankness he'd never felt before. The blankness was calm. The horny energy that had wiled him for as long as he could remember subdued. He didn't know what he wanted next, how to be a different Glen now and later, but he sensed that wasn't the important part right now. With his shirt lazily buttoned and his bare feet on the pedals, he could feel his car as an object and breathe in the air from the open window in a way that felt elemental. He felt closer to his environment than ever before, less distracted, more present and ready for anything. The hunting urges engrained deep into his soul, the source of his sex-obsession, already faded into the past. He longed mildly for a cigarette, though he didn't smoke. Or even a glass of water. Or a bagel. Anything to consume and make him feel his body working toward its existence, pumping blood and digesting and vibrating in recognition of life. He felt he could shout in glee, in acceptance of a life less yearning and chasing.

"Thank you!!!!!!" He barked from his window. He felt detached from the things, the strings and the interpersonal spider webs, that had held him into a place of always needing some salacious sort of approval. He honked his horn repeatedly, laughing hysterically with relief. He unbuckled his seatbelt and opened his door, running childlike to the bank of nearby trees and scrambling up the nearest. His body, he realized as he climbed, was capable of almost anything. He felt the heft of his massive thighs as he scaled, the weight and lift of his arms hoisting his huge skeleton and shooting his body toward the sky. The air was thick with the dewy green spice of the leaves around him. He could feel their scents flowing through him, seeping into his bloodstream.

His elbow scraping against a branch near the tree's zenith as he got to that rare air. A small drop of blood fell from him and he laughed. Here he was running and climbing over the earth like an unbridled boy, bursting at the seams with a joy he hadn't known for some time. He felt free of the need to wink or prove himself to women or men or to anyone. He was driven by the urge to explore and build something. From his perch at the top of the tree, he looked over the undeveloped space surrounding this parking lot and saw possibility. He also saw a runway to sprint through. Glen wanted to *exert* himself endlessly, to be a kinetic crazy lover of the world as it was and had been. To feel his feet naked against the ground and for the turf to season him further.

Glen jumped to a lower branch, letting his body fall far beneath it before snatching its width with his massive hands, feeling the wood resist as his weight came down on it. It almost tore off from the trunk, but as he swung back and forth, safe, his feet barely above the ground, his hands chafed and bleeding, he laughed ecstatically. He could have fallen far enough and fast enough to break his legs. But these were the sorts of chances he wanted to take now: the kind that could hurt him, that could steal from him his movement, his freedom.

Using this physical frame, his ultimate tool, for sexual love had run its course for Glen. He let go of the branch and laughed while he fell several feet onto his still-sore ass. He wouldn't be a monk, a chaste denier of carnal delights, but sex was the furthest thing from his mind. It was like he had come enough, in enough different and aching ways, to have been cleansed of those desires for now. He wanted to direct his feet onto the path of humanity in a more memorable way. He wanted to swat at the agents of chaos and hate and love and life all around him with greater authority.

Rebecca greeted Dave like any other passenger. She tried to, anyway, but there was a hint of sarcasm in her tone as she said, "Thank you for flying with us." The kind of kidding she was learning from him was creeping into her voice, her job. Dave looked in her eyes and glanced around the plane to see if anyone was looking before sneaking a quick tug of her kerchief and a wink when he was sure no one could see. Rebecca batted his hand away and shooed him along.

Sitting in the jump seat, Rebecca tried to keep her face straight while Dave shot her a series of cheeky, furtive glances during takeoff. He winked, licked his lips, put the back of his hand to his forehead as though he were sweating uncontrollably. Rebecca's satisfaction, despite her stifled laughter, was the knowledge that the joke Dave was making was an expression of the truth. Though she knew it to be retrogressive and decidedly non-feminist, she liked how the taut skirt and vest made her appear to men. She reveled in the power the sexualized cliché of her profession gave her over the opposite sex. In Dave's funny face was the confirmation of the force she always held in her stride up and down these aisles, the power to melt male passengers.

But Dave's comic confirmation wasn't enough. Rebecca wanted more. She wanted to lean into the thrust, the lustful spirit of seduction she felt raging within her. Dave, like no one she had met, had a way of converting humor into arousal. He wasn't especially handsome, not unattractive, but she wasn't exactly in what most would consider to be his league. Rebecca knew, but she didn't care. Glen had been the most beautiful, ripped piece of male ass she'd ever had and maybe even ever seen, but he'd led her to a place of staggering self-destruction and doubt. With

Dave, she felt in control, even as he coaxed her into actions she initially was resistant to. She held the metaphorical ace in her back pocket, snug against the butt she knew men fantasize about as she served them alcohol and pretzels miles above the earth.

After she served Dave his orange juice and vodka, he raised a cheers to the air in front of her. She caught herself giggling and tapping her ass into the drink cart suggestively. She had hoped that no one else had seen, especially her co-workers, but her disregard for restrictions grew daily. For the first time on the job, for the first time so high into the sky, she felt a sort of ownership over the clouds, a license to do with this rarefied space what she wanted. She desired to direct this cute, wise-ass man into a scene in which he lifted her and tossed her against the cart, ramming himself into her and pushing its wheels all the way down the aisle for all to watch. Physically he couldn't do for her what Glen could, but Dave brought different types of possibility to ordinary places...

After stowing the cart and attending to other passengers, Rebecca approached Dave. Committed to staying totally within her role, to playing her part with utter precision, she kept her voice level. "Sir," she said, leaning over his seat, her ass in the aisle and her breasts subtly grazing his shoulder, "I've got to ask you to help me with an issue in the back of the carriage. I'm afraid it's a two-person job and that the rest of the staff is occupied, and you appear to me more able than anyone else on here." There was not even a hint of irony in her voice and performance, not a single lilt of conspiracy. It was flawless, an award-worthy performance.

She pulled away and walked with an arrogant, smirking strut toward the back of the vehicle, her heels tapping a harmony for Dave's suddenly racing heart as he grew hard. She knew he would try to play coy and follow as slowly as he could, sure of himself and his motions, but that wouldn't last. She'd shaped her voice into a drill, finding the screws that held his hormones and unscrewing them, loosening him into malleable dough.

Rebecca stepped into the bathroom and waited less than ten- seconds before she felt Dave press against her from behind, his bulge smashing into her ass as he clasped her shoulders and shut the door with his foot. She didn't need to look back, didn't need to wonder— she knew who he was at that moment because she'd sent forth the siren call to make him hers, a tool for her use.

He snatched her kerchief, untied into it a pull, and turned her around, setting her on the minuscule sink bar and submerging his face into hers. The motion slammed the back of her head against the mirror. She felt it give a little and wished he had done it harder, that they'd shattered the thing and would fuck amidst broken glass. It didn't matter if there was blood, it didn't matter if there was danger; her skin, her physical self, was merely a convenient container for the unstoppable urges consuming her, urges more powerful than the gravity fighting to pull down the plane around them. Rebecca was an alien to anything but the love for lust coursing through her. If they were loud and heard, then she was fired for fucking on the job. It didn't matter.

Dave lifted her skirt and pulled down her tights with an urgency suggesting they were not in the plane, but falling out of it, racing toward death with mere moments left for insertion before they were broken bones and goo on the surface of the earth. He shoved himself into her before he could get her pants off. They were at each other's faces and covered their mutual cheeks with saliva, sloppily slamming against the mirror again and again.

They came together, almost immediately. Rebecca held his head in a state of delirious relief. She felt a sense of closure then, closing a sinkhole of wanting that had opened within her when, just two weeks ago, she'd heard those horrible moans from outside of the bathroom, those shrills of ecstasy Glen had treated his instant friend to in the airport lavatory. How could that Rebecca, the one who heard what she longed for and considered it repulsive, possibly be the same person she was now? Dave's seed had shot all over her thighs and dripped into the sink, but she felt open to a universe of new personhood, where she could scheme anything with the architecture of her physique. She was flying high and not sick of ascending.

MARLEY

14

Glen reveled in his newfound ease as he turned into the café parking lot. Rashid's texts, full of cryptic confusion and seemingly loaded with meaning, told Glen he'd need to be the soft half of this conversation. Glen couldn't imagine what had happened with Rashid and the two women after he'd left the bar. His curiosity was piqued, but not in the old salacious, gossipy way. Glen didn't really want to know the sordid details of any potentially sexual episodes, but he was concerned for Rashid. He hoped the anxiety in those texts was impatience to share, rather than anything worrisome.

As he meandered from his car to the café, he heard Rashid shouting his name. Glen stopped and turned to find his friend still sitting in his car. Rashid beckoned for Glen to join him.

Glen slid into the passenger seat, "Hey man. You okay?"

Rashid nodded without meeting Glen's eyes. He was staring dead-eyed at nothing, fingers twitching on the wheel. Glen had no idea what to expect, so he waited.

"I don't know what to say," Rashid mumbled, his voice apologetic.

Glen realized Rashid wasn't twitching—he was trembling.

He forced the words out, like existential chores completed with reluctance and fear. "I just don't know, It got weird, I can tell you that much....really weird...wild...after you left last night...I didn't know why it got that way....like, it was everything I thought I always wanted and then it was all sorts of

219

things I didn't know I wanted, but that I definitely do want, I mean, I think I do anyway... I'm not sure who I am Glen...I hope I'm not being too weird...I hope I'm not freaking you out man."

"No, no. Nah. I mean...I don't know what you're about to tell me—I hope you didn't, you know, kill somebody or contract a fatal disease—but it's probably not going to freak me out." Glen chose confident words, but didn't feel confident. His body, relaxed after the release of Trudy's stunning touch, started to seize. But he knew he had to fake poise and assurance for his friend, to pull him through—whatever was happening with Rashid. "I'm not in anything like the same place that I was 24 hours ago, either, man. So don't worry man. Tell me whatever you've got to tell me. I'm listening and you know I don't judge. You wouldn't believe what I did first thing this morning, myself, but I don't want to talk about that right now. I want to talk about you."

Rashid gripped the steering wheel and swallowed hard, "Thanks, thanks man...I appreciate it. I don't wanna say it...but I know I gotta say it. If I can't tell you, I can't tell anyone...I mean, it's not like I can't even tell my parents. They're so traditional I can't talk to them anymore. When I do I'm just lying, I pretend I'm normal and like nothing's wrong...but, I'm not normal. Or...I don't know what it is. I might be...I might be gay. I guess I should just come out with that. Or a woman. Or maybe both." He shrugged, "Maybe I'm gay and a woman, I don't know, I don't have the right words, just, like... I'm definitely not the guy I pretend to be, you know, the guy everyone thinks I am. That much I know for sure."

"How long have you known?" Glen asked in the slowest, lowest tone he could muster. He didn't want any of his words to come out harsh. Rashid's revelation shocked him. Glen wasn't prepared for this re-jiggering of the person he knew. He wished Rashid wasn't sitting next to him right now. He couldn't show Rashid what he was feeling—he had to show support. He struggled to absorb the blow of emotional new information before he spoke again. "And like…what does this have to do with last night?"

"Well I think I told you, at the bar before you left when I was hanging out with those two girls—Addison had already gone, so there I was with them. Sorry, that didn't really make a lot of sense. But, remember when I told you I'd been using the dating app and swiping right a lot. There was more to that story. I just couldn't get into it then. Or didn't want to. I don't know. But I wasn't just swiping on girls. And…I met a guy. Not somebody I'm still seeing or even saw again. It was a one-time thing with him. But I met him. And he took me home. And I liked it."

Rashid paused. "I actually liked it a lot. I felt bad about it, guilty, you know. I kept it hidden from everybody. But I don't feel as bad lately. It's hard, this is hard, but like—I gotta do it and I know I gotta do it. I have to tell you. Because it happened and I keep thinking about the guy, it's probably not gonna go away. I kept telling myself it was a phase. That, and then maybe thinking I'm more of a lady than a man thing…but that's a whole other story, I don't think you wanna hear that one. Just the guy thing for now, gay, whatever. I don't know. I'm sorry, I'm rambling."

"So you met a guy. How'd that happen? You guys just hit it off sending messages?"

"Yeah. I matched with him, on the app." Rashid sat back and dropped his hands into his lap, the words tumbling out now. He'd broken through something inside. "And he started talking. It was like he had done it before—started talking to a straight guy but knowing he had something else going on. His first message said 'I know why I'm here, but do you?' I told him that I really didn't know, how I'd been swiping right on everybody and just seeing what happens. It just kind of kept happening from there, the messaging. He was funny, man. We kept talking for like a week, and honestly I really started to look forward to hearing from him, and seeing what he had to say.

Even about the stupid things, the little things like 'how was your day.' Like a good friend, but, more?"

"That's cool, man." Listening to Rashid, so eager he tripped over words, Glen felt compelled to tell some truth too. "To tell it to you honestly, I've never really had a relationship like that with a woman. It's always been a game that I'm winning. I don't think I can keep on playing it for now." Changes for me, too."

"Didn't you go home with that lady last night? She seemed completely into it. I mean, the ladies always are, with you." Rashid finally looked at Glen as he laughed, settling into his seat as they returned to a more familiar conversation: Glen scoring, Rashid collecting the details the day after. "One of my new friends from last night, Tiffany, was asking about you after you left. I could give you her number."

"Tiffany, huh?" Glen felt a pang of the self he'd been, the one who needed to know how desired he was, to plow his mating victory into smaller female bodies. But he was getting a hold on that spirit now, putting it into penalty. "No, no. Don't do that. She was hot, for sure, but not for now. I'm doing things different. And yeah, I went home with that lady last night, Trudy. But I can't describe howthings happened. Not just yet anyway. Tell me more how it went with you. With Tiffany and whoever the other lady was. And this guy you met on the dating app."

Rashid smiled, "Mitchell. His name is Mitchell. I told Tiffany about him, and the other girl, Greta. They took me back to their place like I was a puppy who needed a home. They live together, and they seemed like they'd definitely done this sort of thing before. I sat between on them on the couch and we were joking around and it wasn't long before they were both straddling me and making out with each other."

"That sounds awesome," Glen said, chuckling in spite of his new lease on life. He couldn't help it, amused at the thought of his friend being used as an aphrodisiac for two beautiful women.

"For a second it was kind of like I was furniture. Just sitting there, part of the couch. I kind of liked it that way but then I got curious and they started taking off my pants, and then taking off their pants. Everybody was game for everything. And I mean, like I said, I'm not really sure what I 'am,' because these were ladies and even though it wasn't quite like my amazing experience with Mitchell, I was definitely liking it. I was liking it in a friendly way, like I thought I could just live with these ladies and laugh with them and be their third wheel forever, but my dick was getting up too. No mistake. Tiffany started to ride me for a while and Greta was grinding on me from behind. They were making out again, over me. To be real about it? I couldn't stop laughing. The whole thing was surreal. I didn't know my life was going to turn into a movie like that."

"Tell me about it," Glen said, smirking at the image Rashid had just painted, but also in remembrance of how Trudy had transformed him that morning.

"I didn't finish though, not even close. We all kind of started laughing too much and rolling over off the couch together naked, and then it was more of a naked slumber party - like we're in one big kiddish pile, ready to tell secrets. I loved it. I wanted it to go on forever. They told me they'd done this thing before, lots of times, and when I asked if they were in love with each other they said they didn't know but then they kept on kissing on and off. I told them about Mitchell, about how he held me after we fucked, although I think it was love-making, if I'm honest, and told me the story of knowing he was gay when he was 11 and found himself in the company of older men. I told them about the boobs I have, the prosthetic things I keep in a locker bag in my trunk and sometimes wear with tights and a bra when I want to drive around to feel more like myself, more like the lady at play inside of my heart."

"That's awesome, man," Glen said and meant it. He wasn't sure if, even a week ago, he would have so readily approved. "I can't say I understand it, but I don't think I understand myself all that well either. I mean, do you want to be a lady more often? Like full time, kind of thing? Switch over? I don't know the language. I don't know how it works."

"I don't know. I don't think so. Not now. I'm not ready to explain myself to too many people. I told Tiffany and Greta and now I'm telling you. That's as far as I've gotten. And I only do it in my bedroom or when I'm in my car alone, just kind of riding around as myself as a lady."

Glen raised his eyebrows. "Think you'll tell Addison?"

"Naw, I mean, not anytime soon. I don't think he'd react as well as you are. I'm surprised you're taking it this well, that you're this open about it, to be honest. No offense. It's just that the way we are about girls, the way we always talk about them, it's kind of a lot different from what I really have going on in me."

"I think it's the same for me, man. I don't know if anyone actually means it when they brag about sex. Something happened to me recently. I was just getting laid so much," Glen said with a laugh, "I was so busy proving how bad women want my cock that I almost...got sick of it? Not exactly that, but something like that. It's hard to explain. My wants just changed very suddenly. Not that I know what they are. I know I want to run and leap and be an athlete of some kind. Use this body for something different. I can't say what."

"We should send all the women we don't want to Addison."

"He wouldn't know what to do with them," Glen said, slapping Rashid on the arm. "Listen, if you ever want to do your thing as a lady, out in the streets or at a bar at whatever, not just alone and cruising through the city, I'm down to be your wingman. Lord knows you've been there as mine."

"I'll only do it if you dress up as a woman too," Rashid joked.

Glen pictured it: the two of them in heels, arms hooked around each other, wigs and dresses and lipstick. Maybe, Glen thought, he would do it with his friend for Halloween, as a gateway into his new self—if that was what Rashid wanted. Like a butterfly flapping its wings in his chest, this sort of consideration was a new sensation for Glen, a new way of seeing the world: a series of the needs of others, a vast and intricate, interlocking series of emotions that he could help guide to grace.

"What's a woman anyway," Glen said. "What's a man?"

Rashid smiled and patted Glen on the shoulder. "Thanks man, I feel better now," he said. "Let's get the hell out of this car. I need coffee."

Glen and Rashid shoved each other jokingly as they crossed the sun-scorched parking lot to the cafe. But Glen's happily pumping heart skipped a beat when they walked through the doors and he saw, sitting with a man who didn't look too unlike him, Elena. She of the scars above her heart, so brave to show them to him, so beautiful— not in spite of them, but because of how she carried them, how forward she was about her hurt in that one ecstatic moment with him. As his own pain over that fleeting second of sexuality confirmed his ability to feel, his ache to bridge hurt into bliss, emanated through his chest. In that moment, Glen understood that the tornado, the orgasmic whirlwind of women he had thrown himself into were but one big distraction from another failure of love. Elena was sitting with another man in front of him, and it was an insult to his soul.

He grabbed Rashid's elbow to stop him. "We've got to get out of here," he whispered. He didn't think she had seen him yet. "There's someone here. I can't see her. We've got to leave."

Rashid put his hand on Glen's shoulder and stepped back out the door. They made it to the curb and Glen dropped down to sit on the concrete, his head between his knees, hands over the back of his head, like a turtle retreating into the safety of its shell.

"Man, what was that?" Rashid said, looking over his shoulder into the windows. "Who was that?" Rebecca? That hot little flight attendant, is that who was in there? I've never seen you get messed up like this over a girl, any girl."

Glen spoke to the ground, "It was Elena. I know I told you about her before. But I don't even know if it's her. I mean, that was definitely her in there, but I don't know if that's what's throwing me for a loop right now. I feel like there's a bigger, unspecific change that's happening in me. I don't know what it is. I'm not the same."

He paused to breath, forcing himself to sit up. "That was painful, seeing her, but it's also suddenly painful to think about women and sex and love at all, in any way, and extremely freeing to imagine a life that's past that stuff. At least for now, it is. Times are always changing. But right now, Rashid, I want to be something else, someone else. Some kind of hero or warrior. A man of a greater cause, for the people, for the culture, for society or the world or whatever. I want to be a tool for good I guess. Does that sound lame?"

"Not lame, awesome. But what are you talking about? Joining the military? The Peace Corps? Being some kind of coach or a teacher?"

"I don't know," Glen said, shaking his head and fighting the urge to fold into a turtle again. "I don't know. But we've gotta get out of this parking lot before Elena comes walking out. I can't handle her right now."

Glen worked the next night. He'd driven around until he found himself at the gym after his episode with Rashid outside the cafe, but didn't stay long. Exercising within walls was no longer enough. He needed to make his path over the earth, untethered by buildings or equipment or the glares of other people. He'd devoted hours to the gym to attract the gaze of women, to impress them with how he'd sculpting himself. Now he wanted something more solitary.

He didn't want people to see him here at the airport, anymore, either. The relative invisibility of his job, despite his size and sex appeal, no longer appealed. He spent his break sitting in the terminal, observing, noting the varied purpose in the steps of people rushing around him. He imagined how they moved to or away from home with a kind of love he didn't have. A singular tie to vocation or hobby or artistic passion— whatever the reason they left wherever they had been—that he now envied. Glen wanted his calling, his purpose to hold weight beyond the world he was born in and lived in. He ached to break through the borders of his life as he knew it.

He watched lovers finding each other again, dropping their bags to hug and kiss. Glen admired those people, but cared less about them than those individuals with briefcases and outsized backpacks, big portfolios for their paintings, and those chattering away on important phone calls, leaning into their business as they moved. What could Glen be in the world, how could he put his hands to the gears of society? He thought of the hours he'd just spent lugging passenger cargo around, charming all the while. He was good at his job, but his gut sunk at the thought of all the people on the rungs above him in his company.

That was when he saw Rebecca on the other side of the terminal, on her way to a flight. The sight of Elena had crushed him, but seeing Rebecca was like looking into a peaceful snow-globe. Though it had been only days since he and she had changed each other with the force of mutual passions, the vision of her had already faded to sepia-tone in his head, a snapshot memory as he moved toward a different life. It might as well have been the 1940's when they met and splashed about in the ocean of feeling. As she disappeared through security, a finality settled over him, a sense that he'd never see her again and that this would be okay, or more than okay, or something he was so completely ambivalent about that he needn't in any way qualify it. Glen was going to write his résumé and send it everywhere, swipe right on the world, like Rashid, and learn who he was based on who responded.

When he returned from his break, he put in his two weeks' notice.

Having told Glen about who he sometimes was when no one was watching, Rashid felt fresh license to explore his split-gendered self. As he pushed his heel to the pedal, his breasts strapped on and his dress hugging his body, he applied lipstick with his free hand. It was beyond late at night, but he drove toward the coast, fixated on the idea of kicking off the heels and running along the shoreline like it were the marathon of all earthly meaning, his wig flying into the wind behind him. He'd desired to dress this way and be someone else for so long, and had always imagined himself this way, in that setting, like a scene from a film.

The first time Rashid had seen this in himself was in high school, when he ended up stuck in the women's locker room. Bigger boys who'd decided the meek and skinny Rashid, who never spoke to anyone, should be their "scout" in the women's locker room after soccer practice and had thrown him in. Moments before the girls came back from their sweat and play in the school's fields, Rashid had been shoved into a locker and heard the locked click shut. He'd been instructed to scope the dimensions of the girls' bodies and report back to his boy masters about them.

Instead, Rashid's attention was drawn to the gentleness he saw. How kind and intimate, understanding and inherently allied these women could be with each other—when they weren't competing and thrusting their sex into the hormone-filled air of the hallways. He watched two friends help each other with their breasts, propping them up for extra definition beneath their push-up bras, strapping them on for each other and applying makeup on their respective faces. This, Rashid felt, the club he wished to belong to, not the one full of men he'd been forced into by the simple fact of the genitalia he'd been born with. Although it did arouse him to see these women vulnerable, nearly and entirely nude, what inspired him was their warmth, their ability to trust each other with the ever-loaded tasks of self-presentation. It made complete sense to him, in this moment, why men had always been less well-dressed, not so clean, and otherwise sloppy, everywhere he had ever seen them next to women.

Rashid had stayed in that locker for the whole of the afternoon, waiting for someone who wasn't a student. He didn't want to alarm any of the girls, knowing they might think he had invaded their privacy. If he was to belong in their club one day, the club of women as he envisioned it then, he didn't want to break their trust before his bid for inclusion had even begun.

Finally, a janitor came to mop up the floors trod by those delicate bodies like the one he wanted. Rashid banged on the locker door and the janitor let him out. He was covered in sweat and sore in all his bones from that cramped position. He fell to his knees and dry-heaved before rolling over onto his back to breathe frighteningly fast for a moment. But then he started to laugh. That horrible little locker had been his cocoon. Inside it he'd found there were spirits more like the one inside him in the world, so he'd emerged someone new.

On his way to the beach well over a decade later, he had only just begun to share that self with anyone else, though it had long been blossoming away from the public eye. Rashid had considered some alternate names for himself, if he were ever to bring the woman he was into the world full-time, but hadn't settled on one. For now, he was still Rashid, and he was still a he, but he didn't dismiss the idea of never being that again. And this was why he hadn't seen Mitchell again, either: he didn't want to tell him who he was, how he'd gotten there. No, he wanted their love to remain pure and untested in his memory. When he knew how to be who he wanted to be out on the streets, not just in his car and not just for one cinematic moment on the beach, that's when he would find someone to tell everything to and, perhaps, make love to them, too.

As Rashid pulled into the parking lot before the sand, he felt his heart roll around his ribcage taking horrible, nervous laps. The prospect of actually being this person outside of the safety of his apartment or vehicle, even for an audience of no one—he saw not a soul at this shore—had Rashid ready to puke. He thought of the women in the locker room helping each other and of Tiffany and Greta too, imagining all four of them, Glen carrying him like a winning quarterback to the water in his dress. They were the people, whether they knew it or not, to push his fictional movie moment into an image he might actually, for a few brief moments, live. But the emotional distance between being a woman in his car and being a woman at the edge of the ocean was longer than he'd anticipated. Could he ever exit his driver's seat the way he shot out of that locker, gooey with relief, like a new creature torn from one of the earth's more secret and precious wombs?

He started by opening the door. Rashid swung his legs with the heels on his feet out, sitting sideways in the low fluorescent light. Sometimes he wore tights, but not on a sweltering night like tonight. Tonight he would be a free girl and he would feel the relief of the breeze flowing up his skirt. He would throw the heels like a pasteboard hat at graduation when he took them off, launch them into the constellations. That's how it would go, and he would do it with the joy of Mary Tyler Moore tossing her hat before the freeze frame paused its battle with gravity.

But first, of course, he had to exit private doors in this ensemble, to crash into that negative space of his gender with confidence or perhaps without it. He had to step over that line one way or the other and—even inches away—he still didn't know if he could.

Then his id overtook him. Whatever woman he harbored inside, she snatched control of that moment, suddenly and irrevocably. Rashid stood with gusto and stepped onto the pavement. He twirled. He stomped one of his heels in delight, giggling.

"I have to text Glen," he said aloud to himself, almost delirious with the novelty of it all. "I'm outside," he typed. He felt all inhibitions fall away, like a teenager after he'd taken his first ever shot of vodka. His vision of running on the beach didn't matter anymore. He'd thought enacting the fantasy was the light at the end of the tunnel, but now that he was out of the tunnel and in light, all he wanted to do was dance within its glow.

"You have to see this," he texted Glen, and told him where he was.

Glen said he didn't know what Rashid meant, but that he would be there as soon as he could.

Glen was worried for his friend. He knew Rashid was becoming something different and better, more free, but he also knew the world didn't always want people to be different—or free. As he drove to meet him, Glen was acutely aware of this limitation because of the day he'd had at work, asking around about pilot school. Smugness, condescension, and dismissal had met his requests for information. Glen didn't want to be a pilot, per se, but he didn't know what he did want to be either.

Metamorphosis of any kind pisses people off, Glen thought, and Rashid was trying to change his gender, find a new one, maybe, and he didn't want to find his friend pulverized in a wig in a parking lot, gasping for help because some unthinking, unimaginative moron had made hay with his face for daring to be a different kind of citizen.

Glen sped down the highway, far faster than he normally dared. There was no hint in Rashid's messages that this was an emergency, but it felt like one in his heart. In need of meaning, in need of a mission, Glen had decided if there were ever a chance Rashid was in trouble, he would be his unstoppable savior. He imagined an army of miserable dip shits rushing a dress-clad Rashid as Glen swatted them away, grabbing one to use as a broom, like a cartoon, sweeping away the rest of them as they charged.

He was thoroughly engaged in the fantasy when he saw the red and blue lights flash in his rearview mirror. "Fuck!" Glen slowed down and pulled over, whacking his hands against his wheel in frustration. "God dammit!"

Just as the officer arrived at his window, Glen forced himself to calm down and composed himself. He rolled down the window to hear the officer's surprisingly amiable tone tell him that he "shouldn't be in such a rush." Glen's panic abated.

"I'm sorry, I'm sorry, I'm just worried about a friend," he said. The officer was tall. Glen didn't meet many men of his stature, so when he did, he felt he could relate to them. "I shouldn't have been driving that fast, I know. I just want to make sure he's okay."

"Well," the officer said, "if it's any kind of physical danger he's in, that's my job to take care of, not yours. That's what I've got those lights and that siren for."

"No, no, it's more of emotional thing. And I don't even know if anything's wrong. It probably isn't. He's just in a confusing time and I'm worried about him. Probably that's misplaced and it's really me who needs to be worried about. Either way I shouldn't drive like that. If you give me a ticket I'll pay it and I'll promise to find a better way to worry. Without breaking the law, you know."

"You're okay. Trust me, you're not the first person to drive fast on these roads, and you're not even close to some of the stupid speeds I see pretty much every time I'm patrolling over here. And your attitude's a lot better. Just don't let it happen again, big guy," the officer said in a familiar tone. "Now go check on your friend. At a reasonable speed."

Glen smiled and thanked him, pulling away as the officer retreated to his car. He'd always instinctively disliked police, but the interaction made him wonder. Maybe he could be a cop and make a difference as one of those rare nice guys, shake up expectations for people under duress and help them when they expected to be rankled and bothered. The idea was appealing.

Coasting into the parking lot, Glen realized he was meeting Rashid in "Cap Hill", a well known LGBTQ community, where picking up trans women was common, Glen was stunned, despite what he expected to see. Rashid wore a wig, a dress, and heels. His phone, out of sight, blasted 70s disco music as he danced. Glen was okay with all of this in principle, but actually seeing his friend this way was destabilizing like an intense vertigo. He had to stop his car to watch from a distance, like he was a specimen. His gut twisted, reminding Glen this was the same way he had watched Rebecca walk off into the terminal instead of chasing after her.

Glen felt like he'd been kicked in the chest, but the relief of tears came in waves. Though the change was immense and shocking, he was proud of Rashid. Glen didn't want to be a woman, but he envied his friend for embracing his new identity. He parked and started to walk toward Rashid. Despite his pride, he was tepid, hesitant, unsure how to react to this version of his friend.

Before he made it to Rashid, a Jeep pulled in and two men got out. Wearing flip-flops and tank tops and jewelry that looked like it weighed a lot, they paced toward Rashid with menace in their step, so Glen started sprinting. Before he got there and swung his balled fist, though, he saw the men were flirting.

"Girl," one of them said, "Whatcha doing out here alone, without us?"

Glen stopped his sprint and panted in the dark, curious how this strange encounter would play out. It occurred to Glen that they were far enough away not to recognize Rashid was trans. A surge of protective force pumped through his heart and spread through his body as he strode toward the trio, afraid the guys might turn violent when they realized.

No sooner had he moved than the men saw him. "Hey," one of them slurred in a shout, clearly intoxicated. "Go find your own gal. This seat's taken, man. We been here, you queer!"

Seeing Glen, Rashid stepped out of one of his heels and faked throwing it at the men, who were drunk enough to fall backwards at the feint. Glen rushed the area and chased them away.

"Ya fuckin faggots!!" one of them screamed as they disappeared into their car in the distance, peeling away in a perhaps fatal streak of inebriated fear.

Rashid removed his other heel and sat on the pavement under the glow of the light, pulling off his wig before he looked up at Glen, his face glum.

"Rashid," Glen said, "I'm sorry. I didn't mean to...well, I don't even know what just happened, but I'm sorry."

"It's fine," Rashid said, dejected but smirking. "Those guys were terrible. There's no way I would've wanted them around, for any reason. Please."

"So," Glen said after a pause. "This is you in a dress, huh." He laughed. "Looking good, buddy. I'm all for it."

"Thank you. But I think I'm ready to change back into my usual clothes, for now. This was fun. I just need more time to think about how people are going to treat me out in the streets."

"Either way," Glen said, sitting onto the pavement next to Rashid. "You'll be my friend."

Rashid lay in bed, fingers quivering over his phone. He reread Mitchell's contact information again. Though he never pulled the trigger, he'd come close several times every week in the two months had passed since their tryst. Mitchell hadn't texted him, either. There was no fight at the end of their last encounter, no drama—it had been nothing short of completely sweet and assuring and understanding and devastatingly romantic, in fact.

But as time passed after the love they'd shared, it hardened in his. It condensed into a prickly hot ball rolling around in his guts as he agonized over how his parents, his friends, his co-workers—even strangers, would perceive him if they knew how his love was. It was even harder to admit that love, somehow, than to want to be a woman. In that role he could be someone else, hide who he used to be. As a gay man with Mitchell, lovely soft Mitchell, he would be every part of himself in a way the world had a history of assaulting.

What would he even say? He wondered first of all whether this long silence between them had offended Mitchell, even though he hadn't reached out either. Whether Mitchell had moved on or was used to this sort of thing—men finding their love with him, then running away afterward. Maybe Mitchell had unearthed the buried impulses of dozens of other closeted men since Rashid had seen him.

There was a knowingness, after all, to how Mitchell had entered him. His hand steady, showing Rashid how this was done, how to partake in this forbidden fruit with pleasure, not dread or fear.

"Hi," Rashid typed into the draft text. "Hi, I hope you're well. I'm really sorry I haven't texted you. Things are crazy and as I hinted to you, I'm not used to this sort of thing. I've been hiding for all of my life and you helped me not do that, but then I got scared again. I hope we can talk again," he wrote even as he thought, "I hope I can see you again." He wasn't ready for that, yet. He wasn't even ready to press send on this message, actually.

Rashid dropped his phone on the sheets. He stared at the dress he'd worn the night before, draped over the chair near the foot of his bed, red with a yellow flower print. He didn't want to wear it again, not right now. He didn't know when he would want to again— certainly not out in public. Breaking free from the rigid frame of his gender was something he'd explored so far before, not like he'd done in that parking lot by the ocean, and that night had left him exhausted. He knew, though, regardless of what happened now or later, he'd feel less tethered to the ways of being a man he'd once felt were obligatory.

His life felt less burdened. He fished his phone out of the bedding, and sent a group text to Tiffany and Greta. "We should hang out again, guys. No funny business if you don't want. I just want to catch up…"

Rashid sent it. After the paralysis over contacting Mitchell, this felt like a positive act of rebellion. Reaching out, it turned out was possible.

Tiffany messaged him back right away. "Oh my god, Rashid," she said. "Yes, yes, yes. We should all go dancing..."

Under the multi-colored flashing lights, enveloped within the sonic wash of the bass and synthesizers, punishing their skulls, Rashid was covered in sweat from dancing with Greta and Tiffany. They'd barely spoken before skipping inside to the bar—Greta knew somebody at the door, so they skipped the anxious line filling up outside—and downed shot upon shot. Rashid had taken the shortcut to inebriation before, chugging and taking shots with Glen and Addison, but he'd never done it as a prelude to dance. Usually, this led only to a lot of idle chatter and displays of manliness by way of sport. Glen had once smashed a watermelon with a baseball bat after Addison tossed it up for him. But none of those drunken nights felt as celebratory and freeing as this night. He'd texted Glen to say he was coming here, but doubted he'd show up to a packed dance club on a Thursday night—especially given Rashid's recent confession.

The trio hung their arms around each other as a ballad came on, swaying back and forth and looking into each others' eyes playfully before Tiffany started coyly pointing around the room at various guys, her face wondering if Rashid was into any of them.

He mouthed his appraisals of several—"too tall," "not tall enough," "doesn't look gay," "too gay for me," "wouldn't understand me," "way too hot for me," "not nearly hot enough for me"—and had the two of them laughing until they were in pain before Tiffany pointed at Mitchell.

Rashid froze. His face blanked. He spun and walked toward the exit as quickly as he could, before Mitchell could see him. Tiffany and Greta followed him out into the alley.

"That's him," he said, after the three of them sank to the ground, their backs against the brick wall, heads knee-level with the people smoking cigarettes and holding similar discussions about difficult love. "That's Mitchell. I told you guys, we haven't talked, not since that night, and it scares the life out of me to see him. I don't think I can go back in there."

"You have to talk to him," Greta said, putting her hand on his thigh for comfort. "Not only because it's killing you but also, and I don't say this lightly, because he is pretty as all ever living hell. I don't want you to regret letting a man so fine fade away, Rashid. Many straight women would be upset at you for stumbling into such a catch on your first lap around with men, because they sure as hell don't all look like that."

Rashid smiled and put his hand on top of Greta's hand. On his other side, Tiffany put her arm around his shoulders. Rashid laughed and rested his head on her draping his feet across Greta's lap.

This—or something—triggered one of the men smoking. "What the hell is wrong with you women," he said. He was large and wearing a pink-striped polo, hair gelled into submission, and clearly intoxicated. "Giving all that mother-loving or whatever it is to a brown man. He better be gay or retarded or something. If y'all are fuckin him I can't stand by that. My country can't live with it."

"Wow," Tiffany said, "I always thought that some guys wore pink to pretend to be more tolerant than they are, but now I know for sure."

"I don't give a lord's fuck about tolerance," he roared. "Some things are an aberration of nature and you're coddling one right now. He's probably been thinkin' about bombing this place since the moment he woke up."

Rashid's eyes tightened into angry slits as the man bumbled on in his anger, but he wasn't about to get up and do anything. Floating amidst his thoughts and paralyzing him, still, was the vision of Mitchell that had just appeared before him in real, neon-lit space.

Greta spit into the man's face. Her aim and force were excellent and she caught him right in one eye. He fell backward screaming and clutching his face. Strangers started to notice what was happening, laughing at this slapstick.

"You bitch!" the man yelled. Then he wiped off his eye, ripped off his shirt, ran to Rashid and kicked him in the chest.

His wind left him and his vision blurred as the mammoth shoe caught him square in his sternum. Rashid felt the acute limits of his mortality as the beast wound up his foot to deliver another blow. Just as he swung, an even larger person cut through the crowd like a superhero bullet, tackling the topless specimen of rage like a cannonball. Rashid passed out before he could see who it was.

He awoke in a hospital bed. No one was hovered over his face like in the movies. But through the door, he could see an unusual collection of people who loved him in the hall: Tiffany and Greta, Glen, and somehow Mitchell. Mitchell. How?

The nerves he'd felt upon seeing Mitchell in the club were gone, now. Rashid was getting his body back, the sensation of touch coursing through him. He wondered how long he'd been here.

"Hey," he said in a low shout.

All four faces turned and scurried to his side. Mitchell, who'd remained silent as the other three spoke and recreated the night's events, approached slowest and with the most trepidation.

Tiffany told Rashid it was Glen who'd speared the bigoted idiot. The idiot had also been arrested shortly afterward. Rashid had been in this bed for under an hour and the doctors said he was likely fine - he appeared to be sleeping as much from exhaustion as from a slight concussion, suffered when his head hit the wall. He wasn't supposed to drive for a few days, but they expected he'd be back to normal after that.

"And Mitchell," Greta said. "We went back for Mitchell."

As he heard his name, Rashid's undefined friend stepped to his side. Artfully bald, wearing a black blazer and black jeans with black boots and white shirt, Mitchell emanated sartorial choices. The elegance in his form made women coo, even if he wanted nothing to do with them in the bedroom.

"Hi," Mitchell said. The rest of them walked slowly backward, leaving them alone. "How are you?"

"Well," Rashid said. "I know I've just had my stomach kicked so hard that they put me on a stretcher, but all things considered? I'm feeling pretty great." He could feel the most ridiculous smile colonizing his face.

"I'm glad to hear that," Mitchell said. "And I'm feeling great too. I didn't think I'd see you again, and certainly not under these circumstances, but I'll take it, weird or not."

"You'll have to take me winded and concussed and with cream," Rashid said, pointing at his friends outside in the hallway.

Mitchell bellowed a deep-chested laugh. "I like it with cream. I like it all kinds of ways if you're at the center of things."

"I didn't think I'd see you either," Rashid said with relief. "But here you are. I wanted to. I just didn't know what to say. It's a lot, it's all been a lot, and there's so much you don't know. So much that I don't know. Maybe I shouldn't even be saying any of this right now because apparently I'm not smart enough to start driving again just yet. But it's a lot and if you're going to be around I want you to know that and I want to tell you all about it."

"I want to know about it, too, and trust me: there's plenty on this side that I'm hoping doesn't scare you away, either. It's not like I came out of my momma this way. There's a lot of shit I don't spill to just anyone. But we're in a hospital together now."

"Mitchell," Rashid said, pre-giggling with the joke he was about to deliver. "You're the father."

Mitchell laughed even deeper this time, an earthquake of joy.

Greta peeked into the room. "I hope these jokes aren't about me," she said.

"All about you," Mitchell said with the hesitation of a lover meeting friends. Rashid heard the intent in his lilt and liked it. He liked that, without effort and without design, he and Mitchell gravitated toward coupling so long as they were brave enough to be near each other. If he was ever in a hospital bed again, he wanted Mitchell nearby.

MARLEY

EPILOGUE

ONE YEAR LATER

Rebecca had never been this nervous about her job before. Not even when she was seeing that weirdo Dave, who had somehow gotten her to agree to fuck him in an airplane lavatory. Whatever happened to Dave? She didn't want to know. He was just another face in the cave of her past, full of ghosts. Thinking about him reminded her of what she was always somehow reminded of: she was perpetually single, resistant to the ties that could in any way bind a man and a woman for more than one night. Or a woman and a woman, for that matter, or even a woman and a cat. Her mother had texted a picture of Panopticon that morning, with the message "you'll be great!"

She was attending a flight that, for reasons involving photo ops and campaign emotion and the like, would be hosting the governor of California, who also happened to be one of the lead candidates for president. Rebecca didn't follow the news, but everyone knew who he was; he was so much more handsome than anyone was used to politicians being. He had the face of a movie star, like an actor playing a politician. She would be shocked if she ever met a woman who didn't think this, who wouldn't throw caution to the wind for a chance with this man.

Rebecca had certainly pictured it herself, this opportunity looming. As soon as she'd learned she'd work this flight with the man they called "The Prince William of America," she'd seen the opportunity to win over the most prominent presidential candidate to ever be without a wife. Rebecca and John, John Milford, the man whose face filled the cover of last month's TIME with the title "HOT GOVERNOR. HOT PRESIDENT?"

Rebecca had stared at that photo for what felt like an hour yesterday. She could feel the perfect crease of his dimpled smile reaching into her consciousness, embedding itself there. She dreamed about him that night. In the dream, she leaned over him in his seat the way she'd once leaned over Dave, and he looked up and said, "This is first lady material." It was a terrible line, and surely the governor wouldn't actually use such a flimsy line outside of her dreams—his speeches were always profound—but in Rebecca's subconscious, these were the words she most wanted to hear from him.

Then, amidst the fumes of her imaginative sleep, she found herself in the governor's mansion. She sat on John's lap on a balcony in Sacramento, her skin breathing the morning's post-orgasmic air through the thin impossibly creamy silk of her robe. As he held her, she felt a state of utter, unquestionable security.

"You are the one I'll take to the White House," he said. He reached for a piece of toast slathered in a special marmalade he'd had made especially for her—it was too delicious to exist in the real world.

Rebecca blinked awake, but only for a minute before falling back into her dreams. Now she was in Washington, the paparazzi clamoring for her as she got out of a secret service car, surrounded by bodyguards as she entered the White House gates.

Inside, in the oval office, John slowly undressed her after delegates left, mumbling in non-words about national security and the state of the economy. Everything sloughed off her body like a tree shedding its leaves in autumn, and as she sat on the famous couch in front of his desk, he dropped to his knees and suckled her breasts. She took her time undoing his tie, letting him taste everything before she tasted him in this historic space. Eventually, he became enraged with lust, standing and lifting her by tiny armpits and carrying her across the room to set her on the desk. He pulled his pants down gracelessly, thrusting into her with primal urgency. Documents determining the fate of the nation flew from the surface, secondary to the president's unquenchable love for her.

When Rebecca woke, her thighs were soaked. She was numb with pleasurable relief, but as she showered, her nerves slowly rose. By the time her mother texted the picture of Pan to her, she could hardly walk across the room without feeling the need to dry-heave with angst. The future president would never want her, she told herself. She was just a silly little flight attendant, chronically incapable of love or commitment.

In the car it was even worse, and at the airport—where she arrived two hours earlier than she normally would—it was worse yet. A second person appeared to be controlling her to ensure that she survived the usually routine processes of the day. The self she was familiar with, the person she lived as every day, was completely bewildered and incapable of any of this, stuck in her dreams and crushed by the gap between fantasy and reality. Likely, she'd say hi to the governor and he wouldn't even look up long enough to notice her. Likely, she'd be alone forever.

Time passed impossibly fast as Rebecca stared at the terminal ground in a state of scared despair, gently sipping a coffee, but consuming less than half of it. When her phone's alarm told her it was time to start her shift, she set the room-temperature cup on the small table beside her chair and snapped out of her haze, scurrying down the terminal.

At the gate, Rebecca met the stern gaze of her supervising flight manager, who seemed even tenser than she did. Her manager's eyes were harsh and cold, directly at odds with the romantic flights of fancy soaring within Rebecca. No, her superior's eyes said, you will not be in love with the new president. You will speak when spoken to, you will be a prop and a tool and you will move only as I see fit for you to move. Rebecca lowered her head as she walked in double time toward her crew, hoping her thoughts weren't obvious from the outside.

The nervous paralysis made it difficult for Rebecca to focus on what her boss was saying. Words like "professional" and "opportunity" and "perfection" stood out like sculptures in the blur of language washing over her, sculptures leaning over her, imposing. She was now afraid to even speak to the governor, to look in his eyes or be near him—she feared she might lose her job, or even worse, risk mortal embarrassment, the kind of stain on her psyche that would haunt her forever.

Her manager led them onboard to discuss which seat the governor would take, which words to use in addressing him, and how staff was to comport themselves at all times, since every moment was likely to be photographed and disseminated everywhere online. John Milford was, perhaps, the most famous politician in America at the moment. Rebecca thought of what it would be like if an image of her, with him—at his side like any other citizen; smiling for a photo-op; in the background as an anonymous blur; floating at the picture's periphery, only the silhouette of her curves visible to the thirsty eyes of social media—was all over the web.

What would it be like to be a celebrity? She wasn't going to marry John Milford. Probably not, despite her heart's hopes. But she could still stand within his halo long enough for fifteen-minutes of fame. The idea terrified and thrilled her.

"Rebecca," her boss said.

She'd been staring into the seat that governor would take, imagining her hands against its leather as he thrust into her hard enough to shoot her into the cabin's ceiling.

"Are you ready for this, or do we need to find someone else to take your place today?" He raised his eyebrows as he spoke.

"Yes, no," she said, feeling a drip of sweat roll down her armpit. "I'm sorry. It's just a lot. But I've got it. I'll be my charming, most effective, best self. Professional and prompt. You don't need to worry about me."

"I am worried. About everything. Today is our most important day. Just pay attention and look prepared and make me worry a little less, please." He turned back to the cabin door.

"Okay, okay," Rebecca said. Her heart bounced in her chest like a rubber bullet in an empty warehouse. She pictured it damaging her ribs, cracking them further with each worrisome pump. There were only 20 minutes left until the governor would arrive at their gate.

As Rebecca followed her boss and her crew back out of the chute and back to the gate, she heard a journalist speaking into a microphone in front of a camera, clearly poised to make something of the spectacle heading their way. "Governor Milford has been traveling the nation, breaking even more hearts with his ascendant bachelor handsomeness. The presidential candidate who many are saying is a game-changer takes off from California again today, and we're on the scene to see him off."

Then Rebecca heard the clamoring. The wide terminal hallways felt narrow as people rushed to witness the scene approaching: Milford was near.

Lighting shot through Rebecca as she stiffened her posture in anticipation. Suits emerged from the crowd, black, uniform, over crisp white button-downs with black ties. Then she was struck with something infinitely more powerful, even more electric, as several large men cleared the crowd for the man who could be the future president. Above one suit, a familiar face came into focus.

Rebecca's knees went weak and nearly buckled. She was numb. Her armpits were damp with sweat. She hoped it wasn't showing through, but she wouldn't dare look down at them, not with this reunion one terrible moment away. John Milford was who, again? He was nothing against the man who'd hit her hard enough to inspire her to find more freedom in the world, the one she'd tried to forget with a cavalcade of men. Was he single? Would he talk to her? How had things faded away so swiftly with him? Did she look good? Would he recognize her? Had the love she felt mattered at all, or was he merely a notch in her belt? She'd been sure she had dinged his soul and ego in their passionate jousting, but now it felt impossible she had ever been relevant to him. If she ran, right now, would she be able to do it quickly and unsuspected enough for no one to see her?

As these questions raced through Rebecca, the suit walked past her onto the boarding ramp raising his sunglasses to look right into her with a wink.

Lecherous beast! He hadn't changed at all.

Rebecca remembered how much she had hated him before she loved him, how it had killed her how close those two clashing emotions were, and how he occupied that crazy sexual space and owned it, never allowing her certainty of who she was in the world, taking her a new existence. It was so hard for her to believe another man, any man, president or king or God, could ever do what Glen had done to her.

On the plane, Rebecca paid no mind to the presidential candidate each time she walked past him. She didn't have the capacity. She had no attention left in her reserves and it took all the strength she could muster to stop from swooning and losing track of her duties each time she caught Glen's grin in her periphery. She hated how he affected her, turning her into a jellied cliché of desire and supplication and ridiculous dreaming, but there was no denying his effect. Rebecca needed a glass of water and a good long sit.

But there was something different about him. She wondered why she'd stopped seeing him around at the airport, before vowing to forget him. After her fling with Dave ended, she'd gone hunting for him in the terminals, in vain. She finally forced herself to stop wondering. She dove so deep into the world of internet dating, into so many stupid adventures she regretted and cherished in equal measure, that she had no room left in her brain to think about someone who'd taken as much space as Glen. How had he become a bodyguard to the governor? Or was he secret service?

He emanated professionalism as he watched over the famous man in his protection. She saw in him a calm and—in spite of his shitty, self-pleased grin—something like maturity. This was all conjecture of heart and instinct, Rebecca reminded herself. She had no idea what she'd find Glen to be like, now, if she actually spoke to him. She wasn't sure if she wanted to, if she could even handle interacting with him again.

The flight to Atlanta passed too quickly, and as they landed, Rebecca was terrified that she'd never see Glen again. There was nothing she could say or he could say, not now, not without risk of professional loss. They were both in a situation that required them to be statues, utter props and decorations for the people they served around them. Seen, but not heard. As she stood stiff at the plane's doors and Glen passed her by and she felt her whole self falling into a hole with no bottom, he handed her note.

For the next hour, as her boss congratulated her crew and held them at attention to review their flight with the governor, Rebecca could focus on nothing but Glen's note burning through to her skin, touching and staining the bone of her hip. As soon as they were released, she ran to the nearest terminal bench to read it. It was brief.

"Rebecca," it read. "I made myself not think about you for a while, but it didn't work. I've been celibate for some time. I think I've been waiting for you."

Rebecca held her phone, shaking with anticipation as her finger hovered over his number.

THE END

KEY MAKER

The rituals we perform in the dark are such a miracle

With lightning dancing in our eyes

The calm of night between our shoulder blades

Peaks, valleys, forests, seas waiting to be explored

The only earth that could make a God see Olympus as paling in comparison

Zeus fell in love with a mountain range named glory

Deemed dawn a lesser shining

Proclaimed that night was the only fitting backdrop

Commanded Apollo to choreograph a fitting applause in the midst of thunder and rain

Our indulgence is mythology

A thing of art and literature

We paint ourselves across each other and write our intentions with fingers and tongues

What a glorious celebration it is

- DASAN AHANU

CPSIA information can be obtained
at www.ICGtesting.com
Printed in the USA
BVHW081748140121
597740BV00004B/291